BRUISED

Also by Tanya Boteju

Kings, Queens, and In-Betweens

BRUISED

TANYA BOTEJU

SIMON & SCHUSTER BFYR

NEW YORK   LONDON   TORONTO   SYDNEY   NEW DELHI

SIMON & SCHUSTER BFYR

An imprint of Simon & Schuster Children's Publishing Division
1230 Avenue of the Americas, New York, New York 10020

SIMON & SCHUSTER BOOKS FOR YOUNG READERS
and related marks are trademarks of Simon & Schuster, Inc.
For information about special discounts for bulk purchases, please contact
Simon & Schuster Special Sales at 1-866-506-1949 or business@simonandschuster.com.
The Simon & Schuster Speakers Bureau can bring authors to your live event.
For more information or to book an event contact the Simon & Schuster Speakers Bureau
at 1-866-248-3049 or visit our website at www.simonspeakers.com.
Jacket designed by Sarah Creech
Interior designed by Tom Daly
The text of this book was set in Adobe Caslon Pro.
Manufactured in the United States of America
First Edition
2 4 6 8 10 9 7 5 3 1
Library of Congress Cataloging-in-Publication Data
Names: Boteju, Tanya, author.
Title: Bruised / by Tanya Boteju.
Description: First Simon & Schuster Books for Young Readers hardcover edition. |
New York : Simon & Schuster Books for Young Readers, 2021. | Audience: Ages 14 up. |
Audience: Grades 10-12. | Summary: Daya Wijesinghe sees a bruise as a mixture of comfort and control,
but joining a roller derby team pushes her toward big truths about love, loss, strength, and healing.
Identifiers: LCCN 2020022701 | ISBN 9781534455023 (hardcover) | ISBN 9781534455047 (ebook)
Subjects: LCSH: Sri Lankan Americans—Fiction. | CYAC: Interpersonal relations—Fiction. |
Self-mutilation—Fiction. | Roller derby—Fiction. | Roller skating—Fiction. | Orphans—Fiction.
Classification: LCC PZ7.1.B6755 Bru 2021 | DDC [Fic]—dc23
LC record available at https://lccn.loc.gov/2020022701.

If you can agree that strength is in the soft parts, this book is for you.

If you can't agree, I understand. This book is still for you.

AUTHOR'S NOTE

If you're new to roller derby and want a little background context about this amazing sport before or after reading this book, head to page 321 to find out more. Enjoy!

Prologue

The seat belt had left a perfect diagonal stripe across my chest. Blistering red and purple from shoulder to hip like a grim pageant ribbon lifting from my skin.

When my aunt and uncle finally arrived to tell me that both my parents were gone, my aunt hugged me close and I let her, too exhausted to resist. A sharp ache seared me from the outside in and somehow, the pain felt right. Deserved. I let it settle deep inside my chest, hoping it would remain there for as long as possible. That no one else would be able to get at it but me.

Chapter One

Endless stippling spread across my bedroom ceiling, tiny bumps of white pushing back at me like thousands of stubby, pointing fingers.

Fuck you, stubby bumps.

Lying faceup on my bed, I glared hard at the ceiling for a few moments before extending my left arm above me and bringing my hand down—hard—against my headboard. The ritual, started a year and a half ago, sent a familiar sting through my palm, a kind of shield against the day ahead. I'd feel the bruising every time I held a mug or grabbed my backpack strap, whenever I pushed open a door, clutched an apple. The pain was something to focus on—like a messed-up stress ball to squeeze whenever I needed it.

I wasn't proud of this thing I'd come to depend on—far from it—but the need to do it was so overwhelming sometimes that knowing I'd feel shitty about it afterward wasn't enough to stop me from doing it. It was protection against other people discovering all the rot in my gut. It was punishment. It was proof I could handle everything on my own.

I forced myself out from the covers and placed my feet on the carpet. Fall air slipped through my open window, crisp and biting.

For a moment, I let the chill lift my skin into goose bumps and stared at my bare thighs spreading across the edge of the mattress. Two quarter-size bruises decorated the middle of my left thigh, and a larger one curved around the outside of my right. I lifted my feet into the air and admired a shin bruise from a week ago. The bruise was barely visible now, its darkness lightening and almost hidden against my brown skin. But I knew it was still there from the painful tenderness when I pressed my fingers into it, which I did now, closing my eyes to let the pain sink in.

"Daya Doo Wop! It's almost eight and you can't be late again! It's still September and you've been in detention once already . . . remember?"

Jesus.

My uncle's singsongy voice surged through both my bedroom door and my quiet moment, each sentence rising into a high note. He knew better than to come in, but he still thought these cheerful reminders would help get me going faster.

"I'm up!" I called back, swallowing back the other words constantly threatening to escape from my mouth: *Leave. Me. Alone.*

Handling my uncle and aunt demanded a balancing act: Keep our interactions light and consistent so they didn't worry about me, but discourage excessive interaction in case they mistook it for intimacy. Keep my head above water at school, but not so far above that they got excited about my prospects. Date boys like a "normal teenage girl," but not for too long and not the type my aunt and uncle would approve of. Go to counseling, but only to make them feel better. Get involved, but not too involved.

I listened as Uncle Priam's footsteps receded down the hallway, practically skipping across the hardwood. He and Aunt Vicki were now my official guardians. The paperwork had been finalized recently, after a painful, slow process following my parents' deaths. Priam was my dad's brother, but I'm sure when my parents named him and my aunt my godparents, Priam and Vicki never thought they'd actually have to take me into their home and look after me.

That's just what they've been doing these past many months, though. And they must have learned their version of parenting in theater school, where they met, because I felt like I was in an epic musical most of the time.

P.S. I hate musicals.

If my uncle and aunt weren't singing duets at the dinner table, they were playing dress-up. They were forever trying to get me to watch all these old-timey musicals on TV with them, and a while ago they'd tried to give me singing lessons for my birthday. I pretended to go for six weeks, but in reality I was at the skateboard park.

It was clear we didn't get each other. So my balancing act was as much for them as it was for me—aim for coexistence and not much more. Don't waste their time or mine.

I stood up and stretched, my body aching from an extra-long skateboarding session the day before. Skateboarding kept me muscular, and having more muscle meant experiencing more soreness, which was perfect for me. I lived for that ache. And I liked seeing my body stay thick and strong too. My muscles made me feel like I could defend myself—but also invite pain when I needed to. I pulled on my jeans and hoodie, both protecting and preparing myself for the day ahead.

Chapter Two

"Butterfly, you *must* understand!" Vicki implored.

"But honey, it's *Pinter*." Priam was sitting beside me at the kitchen table, hands out in a plea, face in an impressive sulk.

If it were up to me, mealtimes would look like me eating on the way to somewhere else. But good old Priam and Vicki insisted we eat as many meals together as possible. As part of my balancing act, I relented. But I paid for it.

At breakfast, I usually had to sit through a truncated version of some kind of drama. Sometimes it was real-life drama, sometimes it was an elaborate, fictional kind. Today I was treated to the real-life sort, although it was still hard to believe. Priam had, apparently, booked tickets to see a play that, apparently, was on the same night as Vicki's Glee Girls' Night—a monthly excuse for her and her friends to sit around singing show tunes while drinking wine and cognac.

Currently, Vicki was flapping around the kitchen, banging

cupboards, moving food around for no particular reason, sighing with the weight of a thousand grievances. "That is not the capital *P Point*, Priam! You *know* how deeply I feel about my Glee Girls. How *full* they fill my spirits. You *know*."

"Of course I know, darling." Priam collapsed against the back of his chair, arms falling to his sides. "But it was the only night with tickets still available. What was I to do?" he questioned, his voice gliding upward to its maximal plaintive whine.

Now Vicki swept to the chair beside him, yanking it out and sitting on its edge with a small bounce. She took his hand and held it in both of hers, peering into his face. "Sweetheart. You do what is *right*. What is *needed*. For *you*. For *me*. You buy *one* ticket. You go experience *Pinter*. You share him with me *afterward*. *That* is what you *do*." She punctuated these rousing words with a desperate kiss to Priam's hand.

Leaning my cheek in my palm and working a piece of apple with my jaw, I stared blankly at the scene unfolding in front of me. I wish I could say this was an atypical morning at the Wijesinghe household, but . . . it wasn't.

As the denouement of this particular episode came to a close, they kissed and made up—also typical (and gross)—and once again remembered I was sitting at the same table. I didn't mind their episodes entirely—it limited the amount of time they were focused on me, at least.

Unfortunately, Vicki focused on me now and her face ballooned in excitement. My jaw halted mid-chew, my defensive shield rising. "Daya! Are you free? Next Thursday? *You* could have my ticket!" She turned back to Priam, his hand still in hers. "Wouldn't that be a capital *S* Solution, darling?"

Priam didn't look quite as certain. "Well . . . it's *Pinter*, Vicki. He might be a little . . . highbrow for someone so young, don't you think?"

Priam wasn't really worried about my capacity to understand Pinter. He and Vicki loved forcing me to experience arts and culture. He was freaking out at the thought of being alone with me for three hours. And I got it. I didn't really want to sit around watching some boring play with him for three hours either.

Both Vicki and Priam preferred dealing with me as a tag team. The few occasions I'd had to spend time alone with either of them, we'd filled it awkwardly—trying to find some common ground.

But we'd failed. Every. Time.

I took another bite of my apple and sputtered my reply through a mess of pulp, because I knew it drove them nuts. "I'm busy that night. Sorry." A piece of apple flopped to the table.

Priam's chest rose and fell in relief while Vicki stared at the fallen apple, a hint of repulsion skimming her mouth.

When I made to leave the table, taking the rest of my apple and a piece of toast to go, Vicki shook the mild disgust from her face and thrust out her hand in my direction without actually touching me (she knew better). "Daya, maybe we could spend some time together"—she glanced reassuringly at Priam—"the *three* of us, this weekend? I feel like we never see you!"

Precisely. "Uh, maybe. I have lots of homework and some

other stuff, though, so I'll have to see. Can I let you know later?"

They shared a quick look—always a tag team—and Priam said, "Of course, Daya. Of course. We'll just be waiting in the wings for your grand entrance!" He let out a fluttering laugh at his own joke, and Vicki chimed in with her own tinkling chuckle.

I had to will the judgment off my face. "Cool," I replied, and escaped stage left like a pro.

Even before I had to live with them, I'd grown weary of Priam and Vicki. My dad was weary of them, and I took that as a sign that I should be too.

Priam and Dad immigrated here with my mum from Sri Lanka before I was born, and Priam met Vicki shortly after, when he abandoned the path set out for him in engineering to pursue musical theater. Thatha was pissed about Priam's choice, but because they were brothers, my mum had explained, Thatha had helped support Priam through theater school nonetheless. Thatha worked extra-long hours at his engineering job to make sure Priam could live out *his* dream.

Lucky you, Priam.

Before the accident, we mostly saw Priam and Vicki for Sunday night dinners, special occasions, and the odd performance one of them found themselves in. And when I say "odd," I don't mean "occasional." I mean rolling-around-on-the-stage-in-spandex-between-inflatable-palm-trees odd. I remember my dad shifting in his seat during the first half of these performances, then dozing off during the second half. He and I would make fun of these ridiculous shows afterward in the car ride home, while Amma sat quietly in the front seat.

Amma had thought more highly of Priam and Vicki than we did, and I remember overhearing one conversation where she tried to convince my dad that Priam did the right thing by following his passion. It was rare for her to speak up like that, and I'd been surprised. Not that she'd convinced my dad or me, though.

I guess Priam and Vicki had seen how much Dad pushed me toward engineering and science, because they constantly sent Amma websites for fine arts classes and kept inviting us out to various performances. Thatha hated that. And I did too, even though part of me was intrigued by the blurbs Amma read out to me—photography workshops, pottery making, taiko drumming. But my contact with Priam and Vicki was limited because my dad made it so.

Once I asked Thatha if he'd be closer to Uncle Priam if Priam was an engineer too, like my dad was. Thatha had laughed. "Priam doesn't have what it takes to be an engineer. Don't talk nonsense." So whenever my mum asked if I was interested in one of the activities Priam and Vicki had suggested for me, I responded with some version of, "Sounds like nonsense to me."

Sitting through Vicki and Priam's morning soap operas—while truly absurd and awkward—could at least be entertaining once in

a while. But sitting through classes was just plain excruciating—
the kind of pain I *didn't* invite. I had to remind myself, though, to
keep my eyes on the prize: graduate and get the hell out of here.
I had my sights on a college in Southern California, where it was
warm, skateboarding was still rad, and I could figure out what
I wanted to do with my life away from here. Away from anyone
who knew my "tragic past." Somewhere no one knew me enough
to constantly ask how I was feeling.

So though it was painful, I kept my head down and
jumped through enough hoops to get where I needed to go.
My reward at the end of each day was an afternoon of hurling
myself across the skate park. Something to leave me aching,
tired, and bruised.

But I had to get through this afternoon English class first.
Fucking English. And poetry today to boot.

"Daya, which line did you like the best?" Ms. Leung asked.

Hmm . . . the last one? 'Cause it was the end? "I thought 'following the darkness' was interesting."

"What did you find interesting about it?"

The words. They were made up of letters. "The word 'darkness' stuck out to me. Like the speaker was really frustrated or
something. Like she just wanted to leave."

"Hmm . . . good observation, Daya. Class, where does the
speaker want to go, you think?"

Anywhere but here, I thought, slumping back in my seat and
squeezing my pencil into the palm of my hand as tightly as I
could.

Chapter Three

"Your arms are spaghetti, Daya!" Dad's lips made that smacking sound they always made when he was irritated with something. "Is spaghetti strong?" he asked as he grabbed my boxing gloves and jiggled my arms around.

"Are we talking cooked or raw?"

He didn't smile. Sometimes he did. Not today. Today I'd made too many mistakes. "Don't be a joker, okay? It won't be funny when your opponent thumps you."

He held up his punch mitts in front of me. "Tummy tight, gloves up. Firm, quick jabs. Intensity, Daya!"

We worked like that for hours—Thatha coaching me, building me up so no one could take me down. Boxing had been his "thing" in Sri Lanka when he was younger. An interest passed on by his father. He'd been competitive, too—winning small titles here and there. But when he came here, boxing just became another thing he'd had to give up. When

I'd asked him why he'd quit, he'd made that lip-smacking sound and responded, "What? You think we had all the time in the world when we moved here? When would I box? Before work? After night classes? Don't talk nonsense."

Now that he did have time for a few side interests, he spent that time coaching me. I think it was his way of protecting me. Of making sure I knew how to protect myself.

"Mental toughness," he would tell me, "is vital for physical toughness. You can't play sports without both, and you can't succeed here without both either. If you show them weakness, Daya, they win. You *must* be better. Stronger."

I kept his words in mind each boxing session, each match, every obstacle I faced, trying to show him I could be tough enough for whatever life brought me. And he kept pushing me to be stronger. So a layer of toughness had begun to grow along my skin even before my parents died, although I hadn't been sure if I'd ever been strong enough for my dad. And now I knew I hadn't been. I'd failed both of them, eventually.

But I was tough enough now. That layer along my skin had thickened, a full suit of scarred armor that could withstand anything. And I'd keep testing it to make sure it always would.

Chapter Four

My front wheels dropped in over the edge of the bowl and I leaned my body weight forward, sending myself careening downward and across to the other side. I almost made it up the vertical before toppling backward, my skateboard banging into my knees and my ass banging into the concrete. After another annoying, long day at school, this particular tumble at the skate park was just what I needed.

"Ooh, nice!" Fee called from where they were sitting on a picnic table nearby.

Fee and I met about nine months ago at this park. Skateboarding was a relatively new pastime for me. Shortly after the accident, I'd taken to wandering the neighborhood, mainly to escape Priam and Vicki's excessive attempts to "connect" and get me talking. I was already being forced to see a counselor. The last thing I'd wanted was to talk about more shit at home.

I'd also quit boxing soon after the accident, and I guess

I'd been craving something physical—some kind of contact that didn't involve sharing my damn feelings . . . an activity that didn't remind me of my parents. I'd found myself at this park, watching the skateboarders whipping in and out of the bowl, performing tricks, stumbling or crashing to the ground. Something about their plunging motions, the way they just gave themselves over to this deep dive into a concrete basin, seemed so appealing to me. So uncomplicated and gutsy. Throw yourself into a free fall and come up the other side. Or not. And each "not"—each time someone bailed—it was like I could feel the hit against my own arm, or ass cheek, or shoulder, jolting me out of my thoughts and into my body.

After I'd spent a few consecutive days watching from beneath a nearby tree like a creep, Fee had been walking by on their way to skate. I'd noticed them before—they seemed so calm and focused. They didn't interact too much with the other skaters—just came, did their thing, and left. But as they walked by me that day, they'd paused and asked, "Where's your board?"

After a lot of mumbling and awkwardness on my part, Fee had finally convinced me to get a skateboard and come back when I did. They promised me they'd show me some basics, and they'd done that and more. I'd spent so much time skateboarding with Fee these past few months, you couldn't even tell I was a newbie.

Since then, Fee and I'd become something like friends, I guess. A first real friend, kind of, since I'd always been a bit of a loner. Fee would often drive me home, and sometimes we'd even grab a bite to eat or hang out. I hadn't shared much with them—they knew my parents had died in a car accident and that I lived with my aunt and uncle—but I liked that we mostly talked about skateboarding or that Fee would ramble on about their own life without expecting me to reveal too much about mine. They seemed to get that I just wanted to be at the park, skating and crashing.

I went over to the picnic table now and sat beside them. Fee was huge—like, over six feet—and *broad*. They used to play ice hockey, until they couldn't play anymore in the league they wanted to, since they didn't fit the "gender requirements" or whatever. Stupid shit. They said they'd taken up ball hockey and skateboarding shortly after as a way to get out some of their excess energy.

"Hey, Hulk, you're extra savage today. Something in particular crawl up your big green butt?" they asked, leaning into me and crossing their eyes. Fee was brown like me but had these wicked gray eyes—"Colonial vestiges, no doubt," had been their explanation.

I leaned back. "Nah, I'm fine. I mean, besides the usual bullshit."

"Yeah. All that bullshitty bullshit." They contemplated me for a moment, like they were waiting for me to say something else. When I didn't (because what else was there to say?), they tapped my knee and pointed out to the bowl. "I know I've said it before, but I wish you'd come play on my ball hockey team—we could use someone who dives into things like you do. Someone fearless."

Fearless my ass. But this felt like a compliment from someone I saw as truly fearless. I elbowed them and let their comment just hang in the air. Fee had been trying to get me to play on their queer ball hockey team for the past year. I'd turned eighteen in the summer (I'd missed some school after the accident, so I was a bit behind), which made me eligible to play, and I think Fee was convinced I was going to come out sooner or later. Like, "come out," come out. They weren't pushy about it or anything and had never actually said as much—they just kept hinting I'd fit right in due to my "grit and guts."

It didn't bother me that they thought I was queer somewhere deep down. It wasn't the first time someone had assumed I liked girls, even though I dated boys (well, "dated" might be a stretch). My skater uniform—baggy jeans, hoodies, ball caps, and skate shoes, plus my undercut and piercings—suggested I might not conform to all kinds of "gender norms." But every time Fee hinted, I just laughed it off.

It wasn't that I was a homophobe or anything—I mean, I could admit I'd even crushed on a few girls. But that didn't mean I could—or would—hook up with one. It just seemed too soft or squishy or something. Not my thing.

After we'd finished skating, I threw my stuff into the back of Fee's Subaru and climbed into the front seat, pulling the belt across my body and clicking it into place, taking deep, measured breaths as I did—one of the few things I learned from my counselor after the accident that actually helped. It had taken me weeks to get back into a car after the crash, and when I finally did, I'd panicked as soon as the car started, and stumbled out and onto the pavement, dry-heaving over the sidewalk.

Only three months later, once I'd done a shitload of CBT—cognitive behavioral therapy—that had me sitting in the car over and over until I didn't fall apart every time it started, was I able to finally make it through an entire ten-minute car ride to the grocery store with my aunt by deep-breathing my way into my seat belt. And then wrapping my left hand around the buckle and gripping the shit out of it for some added protection, the physical pain pressing down the moments and memories constantly trying to pry their way into my chest.

That last part had been my idea, not my counselor's.

Fee seemed to pick up on my car troubles without me having to say anything, so they always pretended to shuffle around in the back of their car, giving me time to deal with myself before they sat down in the driver's seat and started the engine. They thought they were being sneaky, but I knew what they were up to. I wanted to be bothered by the soft handling, but I knew I needed it if I wanted to get anywhere in a car. Not that I'd ever admit that out loud.

Belt properly buckled and palm bruise activated, I settled back into my seat feeling pleasurably sore and exhausted.

We didn't speak for a few minutes—me zoning out in my

post-skate stupor, Fee humming along to some Mika on the stereo.

After a while, Fee said, "You know why I loved playing ice hockey so much?"

"Yeah, 'cause you like bashing the shit out of stuff, like me," I replied, facing the window and smirking.

They laughed. "Yeah, that too. But also 'cause there was just something about the way I could use my body and strength— I didn't have to hide it. And other players would give whatever they had back to me. It was like there was an understood agreement that we were just going to trade hits. But not just like, hits and hurt, you know? More like *energy*. Man, I miss that."

I turned to look at them. They stared ahead, a slight curve to their lips. Fee had a tendency to get philosophical from time to time. But not in a pretentious way. I liked how thoughtful they could be without making me feel like a five-year-old. "Don't you get that feeling in ball hockey?"

Fee nodded slowly for a few seconds. "Yeah, sort of. I mean, I can be physical and stuff, I guess. But there's something about being on ice—skating is more fluid, you know? Ice hockey can be brutal, but also kind of smooth . . . elegant, even. Ball hockey's more lurchy and jarring. I love a good hit as much as the next person"—they glanced at me—"but there's gotta be more to the game than just that. For me, at least."

Fee continued to gaze straight out the windshield into the distance, but I sensed they were trying to hint at something.

Like I said, Fee had never pushed me to talk—about my parents or my proclivity for "hits and hurt"—but they'd listened without judgment to my minimal complaints about school, Priam and Vicki, the jerks I hung out with or hooked up with—and I knew I *could* share almost anything with them without having to worry about them trying to fix me or whatever.

But the few times my parents had come up, my chest seemed to catch on fire—like my insides were boiling up and threatening to spill out. It all felt too messy, too . . . hot. Hitting the ground was simpler.

When I didn't say anything, Fee flicked me in the arm and their smile broke out. "Hey—I just wanna move the way my body was meant to move, you know?" They cranked the hiphop song playing on the stereo and started gyrating in their seat, their front teeth biting over their lower lip. A few James Brown–style grunts punched out of their mouth. "I got so much groove to give, Daya—can't you just see it thumping out from all dis business?" They jabbed their right hip out toward me a couple of times to the beat of the song.

I shook my head. "Weirdo."

But when the song finished and we were almost at my house, Fee asked, panting a bit from their performance, "You cool? You know I got you, right?" They pushed their fingers through their tangle of hair.

I squeezed my knees. "Yeah, I know. And if I have anything to say, I promise you'll be the first person I bore to death." I forced myself to grin.

When we turned onto my street and drove up to the house, Fee parked and turned to me. "You bore me anytime you need to, got it?" They palmed my face like a basketball and gave my head a soft wiggle.

I kept the grin on my face and pushed open the car door, swallowing back the tiny bubble of ache in my throat. After I grabbed my skateboard, I leaned down and said, "See ya, weirdo."

Twisting toward me, their arm stretched across the back of the passenger seat, Fee winked at me. "Takes one to know one."

Chapter Five

Dr. Hoang held her hand out in front of her. I'd been using the little rake thing in her miniature Zen garden to whack around the rocks like hockey pucks. I don't think she appreciated it. I dropped the rake into her palm and slumped back in my chair, refusing to look her in the eye.

"Thank you," she said, and placed the rake well away from me.

This last visit to Dr. Hoang had been three weeks ago. I was still seeing her every month, even though she'd wanted to see me more often. But I'd thrown a fit and Priam and Vicki had caved. At first I'd had to go every week, even though I hated it. I mean, it'd helped a bit, I guess—the breathing thing and CBT. At least I could get into a car now.

But the hour sessions felt so damn *long*. It took me only seconds to cause a bruise. Talking took forever. It had never really been my thing. Not before the accident, and definitely not after. Self-expression hadn't exactly been a family trait, and now, I just felt like talking would make everything so much worse. So much harder.

"How's skateboarding going, Daya?"

She was trying to connect with me. *I know all your tricks, Doc.* "Fine." I zipped and unzipped my hoodie, appreciating the tiny vibrations it caused in my fingers. "Would love to be doing it right now."

"I know you would. And I know you don't love coming here. But I'm grateful you do."

Well, good for you.

"You must be getting pretty good now. You've been skating for quite a while, right?"

I sighed as heavily as I could. "Yup."

"What's the hardest thing you've learned so far?"

Everything's hard. Especially the concrete. That's why I like it. I shrugged.

I could see her uncross and recross her legs from where I stared at the floor. "Sorry if this is a silly question, but do you wear padding when you skateboard?"

I snorted. "No."

"Doesn't it hurt when you fall? Or don't you? Fall, I mean?"

"All the time. It hurts. But it's fine."

She paused for a moment, probably searching my face like she often did. I remained stone. "Well, you're definitely braver than I am. My sport of choice is checkers. Monopoly, maybe. But my husband cheats."

I glanced up at her. She was smiling.

This was another one of her tricks. Making fun of her husband to get me to lighten up. Like I cared what her dorky husband did or didn't do. "Those aren't sports," I said, knowing full well she knew that.

"You haven't seen me and my husband play Monopoly." She was still smiling. I was still not smiling. This never seemed to faze her, which was annoying.

"Daya, we're almost at the end of our time. Are you sure you don't want to revisit some of our earlier conversations?"

She was referring to the topic of my parents and my refusal to talk about them. Not so much "refusal," I guess. More like inability. And maybe refusal.

"I'm sure."

"You don't think it will help? Eventually? To talk about them?"

Her habit of speaking in broken, continuing questions irritated me to no end. I shrugged again.

"Most people do find it helpful. I know it might seem like it's too hard, and it *is* hard, but what's the alternative?"

I already had an alternative that suited me just fine. Well, not fine. But it worked to keep things level. To keep life manageable.

Dr. Hoang glanced at the clock strategically placed on the wall behind me. She leaned forward in her fancy chair. I stared at the sand pile I'd made in her Zen garden but could feel her eyes on me. "I hope we can talk more the next time I see you, Daya. In the meantime, we're going to try something different. Talking about this stuff is hard for you—I understand that. But I want you to get it out somehow."

I lifted my eyes as she pulled open a drawer in the table next to her and reached in. I knew what she was going to pull out before she actually did, and I had to quash my eye roll.

"I know, I know—you're not going to like this either. But just humor me a little. Just try it out. A line a day, a couple sentences. Whatever. When you feel overwhelmed or like you're having to force down your feelings, write what it is you want to say but don't feel you can. I won't read it. I won't even know if you've done it or not. I'm just going to trust you to do it anyway."

She pushed the small notebook across the table toward me.

The eye roll escaped anyway as I swept up the journal and shoved it in my bag.

Chapter Six

When I walked in the door after Fee dropped me off, Priam immediately swooped down on me, as if he'd been perched, lying in wait all day. Which might have been true. He was between shows at the moment and had way too much time on his hands.

"Daya! Come, come—I have a surprise for you!" He shuffled backward down the hallway toward the door to the garage, trying to entice me with his hands.

I clung to my skateboard, pressing the end of the deck into my palm. *What now?*

Priam flicked on the light switch in the garage, and the smells of rubber and fuel met me as I followed him in. I rarely came in here. It was a double garage, and Priam and Vicki's car took up one half. Boxes and racks of costumes took up the other. So, no good reason for me to enter, ever. Loads of reasons to avoid it, though.

This time, however, the car wasn't in the garage. Instead a punching bag hung from the ceiling.

My chest immediately tightened. Priam didn't seem to notice that I'd frozen. He was too busy bouncing over to something on the other side of the garage. I still hadn't left the doorway when he turned, his hands engulfed by brand-new boxing gloves. He danced around me, punching the air. My skateboard was still in my hand, and it took everything I had not to smack the gloves away from me with it.

"Look, Daya! Your very own little gym—Vicki and I thought you'd be wanting to get back to your favorite sport!"

The gas and rubber odors in the room turned my stomach. Every part of my body tensed against the bag, the gloves, Priam's voice, the smell. . . .

Daya, if you box soft, you lose, plain and simple.

My dad's voice like a sharp object dragging across my chest. Shoulder to hip. Like a belt of heat and sorrow and guilt.

I tried to press the pain into my hand, into my skateboard. It wouldn't go where I wanted it to. It just kept pushing through my chest, threatening to get out.

Priam stopped dancing. The gloves fell to his sides. His face fell too. "Daya? What's wrong?"

The pain started to seep out. "Are you fucking kidding me?" My voice tasted bitter, like bile, passing through my lips.

Priam's eyebrows dipped. His eyes glistened in disbelief. Everything about the look stirred up images of my dad's face. *What do you want to do?*

I couldn't break down. I couldn't be soft.

I pressed harder. Harder still. But the pain just kept rising.

I needed to get out of here. I needed to get this shit under control before it all came out.

Without saying anything, I turned and left.

I woke up the next morning feeling like garbage and stayed in bed extra long to avoid breakfast. I figured Priam wouldn't be brave enough to force me down there today.

I'd given my hand an especially good whack, but the pain barely registered.

After leaving Priam standing in the garage looking like the most beatable boxer in the world, I'd gone back to the skate park and thrown myself across every obstacle there, trying to beat back the shit boiling up inside of me. A few skate dudes had eyed me up, probably wondering if I was just a really shitty skater or high or something. I didn't care what they thought, though. The need to control what was coming out of me was too overwhelming.

What the hell were Priam and Vicki thinking? Their "gift" just proved how little they knew me. I'd given up boxing right after the accident and never shown any sign of wanting to go back to it. Even though boxing would've been the perfect way to collect bruises, there was just too much of the other kind of pain—the kind I didn't want to feel—wrapped up in it all.

No matter how hard I hit the ground, though, no fall seemed to distract me from the ache in my chest or the festering in my stomach. It wasn't enough. Skateboarding and my morning ritual had been my saving grace since my parents died. They'd shifted the garbage in my guts to my hand, to the flesh on my legs, hips, arms. They'd helped me prove I wasn't going soft. That I could be hard. Withstand anything bubbling up inside of me and anything coming at me from the outside.

If this stopped working, how would I cope?

Breathe my way through it?

Bullshit. That worked for car rides. Not this.

After Priam and Vicki left the house in the morning, I skipped school entirely, in no way capable of facing other people or sitting in a classroom all day. I didn't really know where to go or what to do instead, though. I tried skating again, but no piece of concrete seemed hard enough right now. I fell on my knees so many times they throbbed, and I knew they'd be black and blue tomorrow, but that ache still pulsed in my chest. I forced my body into tricks I knew I couldn't do and came crashing to the ground, reactivating old bruises and generating new ones. The ache just continued into my throat. When I bit hard on my fist to stifle the sound trying to escape, a muffled sob seeped out anyway.

Exhausted and feeling helpless to stop everything rising up inside of me, I ended up just sitting in the park, staring blankly at a little kid throwing sand around in the sandbox, their mom watching nearby with a smile on her face.

Somehow, seeing that hurt more than anything.

Chapter Seven

Around four, I was spread out across a picnic table and zoning out to music. I think I was so drained that I'd gone into some kind of stasis. Like rock.

My phone rang. It was Fee. The only person I thought might not annoy me right now. But I didn't feel like talking to anyone. I let it ring.

My phone pinged with a message thirty seconds later.

Two words: roller derby. More words: tough-ass folks on skates. What else were you doing tonight?

True. I sure as hell didn't want to go home and see Priam or Vicki. And skateboarding wasn't doing its usual job. Plus, the words "tough-ass" practically glowed. I needed a distraction. Maybe this was it. I called Fee back.

"Hey," I said. I hadn't spoken or eaten all day, and somehow my mouth felt both sticky and dry.

"Whatareyoudoingtonight?" they blurted, all in one breath.

"Whoa—not much. What's this roller derby thing?" I'd only vaguely heard about it before.

"It's everything you were made for, Daya!" They giggled like a little kid. "I just saw this flyer today for a bout and haven't been in ages. You should defs come—you'll love it."

Fee's giggling created a tiny crack in the heavy cement of my chest.

"That sounds cool." From the little I knew of roller derby, it involved a lot of serious contact. My tired brain slowly whirred to life and began to process the possibilities. Skateboarding had provided me with plenty of chances to bang myself around and toughen myself up, but the past twenty-four hours were making me think it wasn't enough anymore. I needed something else. Putting myself in the midst of a bunch of other people who maybe loved to smash themselves around as much as I did seemed full of potential, and I was desperate to find something that would keep all the memories, voices, feelings in check. "Yeah, sure, let's do—"

"Great! Pick you up in an hour."

The crack widened enough to let in a small pocket of excitement.

When Fee and Caihong (Fee's girlfriend) arrived at the park, I climbed into the back of the car and waved to Cai, who I'd met a number of times by now. I'd first seen her when she came by the skate park to meet up with Fee, and I'd been as intimidated as hell. She was only a couple of inches shorter than Fee, with loose, long black hair, a glinting nose piercing, and a curvy body that seemed to move in waves like water. Everything about her seemed so fluid and easy and peaceful. I could see why Fee had been drawn to her.

But that didn't mean I wasn't a shit show when Fee introduced us. Cai communicated using American Sign Language— but that wasn't the part that threw me for a loop. It was the fact that she was stunning and confident. I stumbled over my words as Fee translated for me and fumbled my skateboard so it almost fell across Cai's foot. My absurdity at the time may have also contributed to why Fee thought I liked girls—they'd watched the whole thing, amused—but I don't think it's so unusual to be nervous around someone like Cai. Since then, however, I'd figured out how to be a less ridiculous version of myself around her without hurting anyone.

After they'd both graciously accepted a rumpled and sweaty teenager into their back seat, Cai signed something to me. Fee translated, as they mostly did, though I'd picked up a few signs over the past months. "Cai says, 'Hey, girl—how're those kickflips and whatevers coming along?'" Both Cai and Fee were twenty-two but already seemed like an old married couple.

"You know—same, same," I replied as I buckled myself in behind the driver's seat and took my breaths. Fee relayed the message, then pretended to fiddle with the mirror, then their phone, then their hair, to let me get settled in. I wondered if they'd told Caihong about my car issues and hoped they hadn't.

On the drive to the arena, Fee explained that roller derby players all had these alter-ego names, and I listened as they and Cai tried to come up with names for themselves as we sat at a red light.

"Feisty Fury!"

"Cai-ZAM!"

"Fast and Fee-rocious?"

"Cai-OWN-You!"

Fee's voice got increasingly high-pitched the more ridiculous their ideas became. Cai's signs were as animated as Fee's voice. Then they just dissolved into a fit of giggles, which managed to make me half smile, despite everything else I was still feeling—sore, exhausted, frustrated—not to mention all the other stuff I was trying to ignore.

"Nerds," I said.

Fee stopped giggling for, like, two seconds, then burst into giggles again. Cai just kept on giggling, since she hadn't heard me.

I let out an exaggerated sigh, even though I kind of liked their nerdiness. They were easy to be around, at least. Never pushing too hard to get me to talk about anything hard. Like now, for instance.

"Oh, come on—you know you want a roller derby name too," Fee said, eyeing me up in the rearview mirror.

"My name would be Don't Mess With Me, Asshole."

They smirked and offered, "Catchy."

"Thanks. You inspired it."

"Sweet," they said, bobbing their head as they checked their side mirror.

The roller derby rink was housed in a gigantic warehouse next to a bunch of big-box stores off the highway, and about fifteen minutes later, Fee swung into the arena parking lot. I left my skateboard in Fee's car, and we all made our way inside with throngs of other folks in various forms and shapes and sizes—from parents with their little kids to teenagers to elderly folks to twentysomethings. Lots of punkish-looking people too—tattoos and dyed hair and piercings, leather, jean wear. And folks who looked like they'd just arrived from the rodeo. Yuppie types. Disco fashionistas.

So basically, everything under the sun.

I'd never seen such a collection of all sorts . . . except maybe at Priam and Vicki's weird performances. At least here, though, some of the people looked like *my* kind of people— rough around the edges, ready to watch some fierce action on the track.

When we got inside, a couple of girls were sitting at a folding table and selling tickets. We paid our ten dollars each and followed the pounding music.

Walking into the arena felt like entering a rock concert or something. Flashing lights, loud music, a cheering crowd. I hadn't expected everything to be so large-scale.

"Aw, man, this is gonna be sweet!" Fee signed and said as they swept the venue with their eyes.

Cai signed something with a cheeky look on her face.

"Not even your snide comments can dampen my spirits, ma'am."

More signing.

"Do your worst," Fee challenged.

Thumbs-up and a grin.

They were so disgusting. And kind of cute. And disgusting. "Are you two done? Can we find seats already?" I inquired. This had been the right decision. Being around these two and all this other excitement was keeping my mind distracted from the rest of my body and its rumblings.

After Fee interpreted, they both shrugged and continued walking. I started to follow them, but then noticed a sign for the snack bar. I hadn't eaten all day. My stomach had been too agitated, but now it was pissed at me. "Wait! I need food. Text me when you find seats. Want anything?" The atmosphere in here was starting to make me a little giddy, which wasn't generally a word I used to describe myself, especially after the crap Priam and Vicki pulled last night.

They passed on the food but agreed to text me. I followed a stream of people toward the snack bar in the outer concourse of the arena.

As I waited in line, I watched two little girls with their dad at the snack counter, ordering candy and drinks. Both wore neon tights, crinkly crinoline skirts, and bright purple T-shirts with ROLLER BABE written on the back. Even better, their dad *also* wore a crinoline skirt and a T-shirt with the same words on it.

"Order?"

"What?" I said.

The girl waiting for me to give her my order blinked at me emphatically. "Order?" she repeated.

"Oh. Uh, I'll have a lemonade. And a hot dog. Please." The two girls in their purple skirts pushed past me, one in front and one behind so I was pummeled from everywhere with crinoline. Their dad gave me a *Sorry* look as he tried to catch up with them. Roller derby warriors in the making, I guessed.

By the time I'd found Fee and Cai, the teams were warming up, circling the track and stretching. As I stood and watched for a moment, entranced, the guy behind me grunted and said, "Down in front."

I gave him a toned-down version of my best bitch face and then took an extra-long moment to stretch/annoy him. I was in no mood for anyone else's bullshit. Fee and Cai seemed to miss the whole thing, because when I sat back down, Fee just side-glanced at my hot dog—they and Cai were both vegetarian—and said, "Mm . . . pig butt."

I stared at them and took a big bite, then smiled through the processed meat and bun.

"Dang, you cold, girl," they said, then whistled and crossed their arms.

Before I could reply, Fee sat up, punched me in the arm—nailing a deep bruise I'd managed to cause this morning—and yelled, "Hey, check out forty-four. I used to play ball hockey against her!" They pointed down to the oval track the teams were skating around.

Number forty-four looked hard-core. Tattoo sleeves down both arms. Legs like thick tree trunks. She and some other girls were skating together and kind of pushing each other side to side, like they were warming up their arms for all the hits they were about to give and get. The thought sent a spark of anticipation through me.

"Oh yeah? What team did you play on?" the dude behind us asked, his voice barely masking a taunt. "Girls or guys?"

What the . . . ? Who the fuck are you, mother—

But Fee calmly offered, "Aw, this was in another city—you wouldn't know 'em, kid."

I stared at him. He didn't look like a fucking kid to me. Heat rose in my chest—this time from anger instead of pain.

"Try me," he said.

Dude actually leaned forward and put his chin on his fucking knuckles, like he was asking some kind of intelligent question. My heartbeat pounded. I lifted myself to twist my entire body in my seat and thumped back down to face him. "Hey, asshole, why don't you just keep your fucking questions to yourself?"

I felt a hand on my arm. "Daya," Fee said, "I need to pee. Come on."

I started to protest, but Fee pulled me up with them as they rose from their chair. "Be right back, babe—you cool?" Fee signed and said to Cai, who just nodded knowingly and blew

Fee a kiss. I had little doubt she'd have this jackass in his place in seconds if he tried anything else, but I wished I could get a crack at him first.

Fee and I pushed back past the other people in our row. When we hit the aisle, Fee put their arm across my shoulders and guided me back down to the arena concourse. I took a vicious bite of my hot dog because I didn't know what else to do. Once near the bathrooms, Fee stepped in front of me and put their hands on my shoulders. "Listen, I appreciate you getting pissed on my behalf—I really do—but I can handle myself in those kinds of situations pretty well. Been doing it for a while."

Their gaze flitted past me and to the outer corridor, where a line of merchandise tables had been set up by the various teams in the league. "Maybe check out the merch tables and find me something cool?"

What? Really? My entire body was vibrating. All I wanted to do was charge back to our seats and pound the shit out of that guy.

If you show them weakness, Daya, they win. You must be better. Stronger.

I could be better and stronger than this guy, all right. Maybe this was just what I needed—a chance to show I wasn't going soft.

"Daya?" Worry wrinkled Fee's brow. My body had tensed back into rock, but seeing Fee's concern, I instantly felt guilty. They were so excited about everything, and I was making them worry about me instead.

I cracked my neck back and forth, trying to work out some of my irritation. "Yeah, sure," I replied, and took another hostile bite of my hot dog.

"Great. Meet you back here in ten."

"What the eff? How long does it take you to pee?"

"Okay, maybe I need to take a dump, all right? Jesus. Can a kid just do their thing without everyone knowing about it?" They play-punched me in the stomach before turning toward the all-gender bathrooms.

As I turned to the merch tables, I thumped the heel of my hand against my thigh a couple of times, mostly out of habit, since it didn't seem to help much. I found myself wishing I could beeline straight for the roller derby track for a more intense pounding instead.

Chapter Eight

Squeezing through the still-busy crowd, I took in the team names—Hell Beasts, Hair Force Babes, Skintastics, Killa Honeys. They plastered everything from water bottles to wristbands to T-shirts to stickers. I stopped at one table—the Killa Honeys—and perused their collection of shirt buttons.

"Hey, don't get hot dog juice on the goods, you know?"

Still frustrated and needing an outlet, I whipped my head up, ready to take down whoever had spoken, but when I looked up at the person who'd said it, she was smiling. And so unassuming that my anger had the wind knocked out of it. She was wearing a Killa Honeys ball cap and bright aqua glasses. A near-black braid rested over her bare shoulder, which had light brown freckles across it. "Killa Honeys" was written across her tank top as well. She looked to be about my age or a little older.

Without thinking, I said, "What kind of person doesn't love a little hot dog juice?"

"Uh, every kind of person. Everywhere." The girl leaned back in her metal chair and folded her hands in her lap, amusement in her eyes. "Tell you what—I'll let you handle the merchandise if you can shove the rest of that hot dog in your mouth."

Say what? But I actually looked at my hot dog, and the competitive part of me kicked in. There were maybe two bites left. Easy.

I gave her an eye roll and crammed what was left into my mouth, but when her eyes grew big and she let out a massive bellow, I started to laugh too and had to cover my mouth before I spat everything all over the table. I turned away from her, chewed, and finally swallowed. When I turned back, she started a slow clap.

"Unreal, dude. You win the prize." She picked up a button that had a vicious-looking bee in roller skates on it and held it out to me.

"For me? I couldn't," I said as I swiped it out of her hand, which made her laugh again, which, for some reason, I liked. I didn't generally inspire laughter in people. I didn't usually inspire much of anything in people except frustration. I dug in my pocket for a couple of bucks and handed them to her anyway, though. "Here. I probably would have shoved the whole thing in my mouth even without the challenge."

She accepted the money and replied, "Yeah, I could tell you'd done it before, so I'll take your cash."

I looked at the button. "This is cool, thanks."

"No problem."

"'Kay, well—thanks," I said again, like a dumbass. I started to go before I said anything else pathetic.

"Enjoy the bout!" she called after me.

I looked behind me to give her a nod or something equally unnecessary, but she'd already turned her attention to a new customer.

Whatever.

I attached the pin to my jacket. Over the loudspeakers, I heard the announcement for the start of the bout and made my way back to meet Fee. Music blared and the announcer called out amazing-sounding names like Jiggy Bounce and Wanda Betta-Booty.

Fee came out of the bathroom practically skipping at being poop-free, and I had to laugh. Admittedly, I felt a little lighter now too. Noticing my pin, they asked, "Where'd you get that? I wanna get one for Cai!"

Something in my chest jumped at the chance to bring Fee back to the Killa Honeys table—I told myself it was just because Fee's enthusiasm was contagious, but I also found myself wondering what that girl's name was.

I led Fee against the crowd, which was mostly moving into the arena. We'd miss the start of the bout, but I was okay with that at the moment. There'd be plenty of time to see just how brutal this sport could be.

The girl at the Killa Honeys table was just pulling off the lid of a big rubber container to start packing up her merchandise. As we approached her table, she looked up and did a double take.

"Hey, Hot Dog Champ! Back so soon? The bout's just starting."

Fee looked at the girl and then back at me. "Hot Dog Champ, huh?" they said, their eyes gleaming.

"Uh, yeah . . . ," I mumble-laughed, suddenly regretting coming back to the table. *This is embarrassing. What am I doing?*

The girl grinned at Fee. "Yeah—serious hot-dog-eating prowess here," she added, indicating me with her thumb. "So what's up?"

"Uh." I wrestled with my tongue and muttered, "My friend—just wanted another pin. Like this." I pointed to the pin like a nerd.

"Oh! Cool, cool." She pried open a smaller box in front of her and rooted around for a pin. Finding one and handing it to Fee, she said, "Two bucks, please."

Fee paid, all the while eyeing up the girl, then me. I could tell what they were thinking and I was trying to give them as much side-eye as I could muster. My entire body was telling me to get the hell out of there.

Ignoring my attempts, they piped up with, "Hey—my friend here really wants to get a good look at the action—she's never been to a roller derby before. Think you'd be able to get her into the Crash Zone, by any chance?"

What the . . . ? My face must have broadcast my confusion-slash-irritation, because the girl asked, "You do?" and watched me carefully.

Did I? "What's the Crash Zone?" I asked. It sounded like it might involve some of the savage action I assumed was part of the package and my interest was piqued, even as I tried to keep that interest from showing too much.

She continued collecting items from the table. "It's where friends of the teams hang out. It's right on the floor next to the track, too. Pretty sweet view, if you're interested in being up close and personal with the players." She glanced up when she said this last part, and I wondered for the first time if I *was* actually getting hit on, like Fee probably assumed. She didn't look gay, but you never knew these days. I probably looked gayer than she did.

The Crash Zone did sound pretty sweet, though. It'd be cool to see the contact up close—to get a sense of how hard the hits really were. Because maybe if they were hard enough, I might have found a new way to collect bruises and manage my shit. To keep all this stuff rising to the surface deep down, where it belonged.

"That sounds all right, actually."

"It's better than all right, actually," she said, still focused on her task.

Okay, Schmarmy McSchmarmypants. Her brief hints of sass were both appealing and annoying. "You could get me in? You sure?"

At this point, Fee squeezed my shoulder and said they were going to get back to Cai. "Don't worry, I'll keep your seat warm. Unless you have somewhere else to go"—they winked at me—"in which case just text me to let me know."

"And I can definitely get you in—so don't worry about that, either," the girl added, looking up at me. She kind of beamed, and it took me back a little. She looked so eager to bring me along. It made me both uncomfortable and something like . . . grateful, which I didn't understand at all.

I was clearly outnumbered, so I gave in, hoping the payoff would be worth going this far out of my comfort zone. I wasn't exactly used to meeting new people and spending time with strangers. I definitely wasn't used to all this giddiness and excitement surrounding me and needling its way into my body.

The girl continued to look at me, her hands tinkering with a button pin. Something about the action made me shiver.

"Well, if it's cool with you, I'd be game, I guess."

"Yeah?"

"Sure."

Fee slapped me on the back and practically ran back to their seat.

I'd never been great at branching out, letting myself tiptoe outside the box. Or the boxing ring, I suppose. I'd been a good student—Thatha made sure of that—and spent most of my time outside of school training. I hadn't had a lot of opportunities for parties or hanging out or whatever. Seemed like a waste of time, anyway.

As with Priam and Vicki's not-so-subtle proddings toward artistic pursuits, Amma did, on occasion, try to get me to make friends and have some fun. My dad and I didn't see eye to eye with her on that, either.

But there were a few times, at least, when my mum and I managed to find the same page. When Dad was away on business, usually. Something about his absence opened up a small space for us to see each other more clearly. I got glimpses of her, not in reaction to my dad, or to my dad and me, but just her, acting on her own. And I felt at these times that she almost appreciated all the things that made me so different from her—my tomboyishness, my athleticism, the way I rarely hid my disdain for things that didn't sit well with me. I'd catch her gazing at me with an expression that looked like pride. It wasn't a look I was used to seeing on her face, so I couldn't be sure that was what it was, but something about it made me feel like I was doing something she appreciated.

One time we'd even found ourselves in the backyard together—a rarity. Usually it was my dad and me back there, doing some kind of strength training or cardio. But in his absence, I'd work out by myself, progressing through a routine he'd put together for me to help me build my upper-body strength.

Finishing a set of push-ups one late afternoon, I'd looked up to see my mum's bare feet stepping across the grass toward me. When I raised myself up to kneeling, I discovered she had boxing gloves in her hands and a shy smile on her face.

"Hi. What's up?" I'd asked, unsure what to make of my mother with sporting equipment in her hands.

She turned the gloves around, her eyes trained on them as though inspecting their composition. "I don't want to interrupt your working out, but I thought, maybe . . ."

I remember the twinge in my chest took me so by surprise that I thought I'd pushed myself too hard.

Maybe it was because I'd been caught off guard, or maybe it was something else, but it only took a moment for my open hand to extend toward her.

We hadn't spent much time boxing that afternoon. My mum had basically just danced around the yard, poking at me with her bare hands while I kept my gloves up, like Thatha had taught me to do. Seeing her timid jabs, the way her feet bounced in the grass—I hadn't even cared that I wasn't accomplishing anything useful. I saw a brief glimpse of my mother I hadn't realized existed—playful, giddy, free. And for that moment, I remember almost wanting to be that way too.

Chapter Nine

"So I guess I should tell you my name. It's Shanti. With an *i*."

Shanti sounded like a brown name, but this girl didn't look brown. She didn't look entirely white either, though. With my usual tact, I blurted, "That sounds brown."

We were in the parking lot, loading up a van that belonged to her and her sister. I'd offered to help, since she was getting me into the Crash Zone for no good reason (that I was aware of, anyway). But just before Shanti introduced herself, I'd been rethinking my decision to go along with all of this. Jumping into things wasn't exactly my style. What'd I know about this girl anyway? What was I walking into?

At least she didn't seem fazed by my inane comment. "Yeah. My Chinese dad wanted a 'Western' name, and my white mom wanted a Chinese name. They settled on a name that was neither. Now I get to explain it for the rest of my life." She laughed. "And your name is?"

"Daya. Not exactly a typical Sri Lankan name either. I guess we're kind of in the same boat," I said, attempting to converse like a normal human being despite my second guesses. I handed her the box I'd carried.

"You're from Sri Lanka?"

"My parents—" I stopped myself from saying *were*. Past tense made things complicated. I didn't need to go there. I just let my sentence hang unfinished instead.

"Sweet." She shut the back of the van. "All right. You ready for some serious action?" she asked, slapping her palms against her thighs. Beneath her thick glasses, Shanti's eyes seemed gigantic, which made it easier to see the cool, green tinge in them.

"Yeah, sure." I hoped we'd get to that action soon. As we walked back to the arena, I asked, "So you're not part of the derby?"

"The what?"

"The . . . derby." As I said it, I realized it sounded not quite right.

She laughed. "We don't say 'the derby'—makes it sound like horse racing or something," she said, amusement continuing beneath her words.

Whatever.

When I didn't say anything back, her face grew serious and she added, "Sorry—it was just cute, that's all. I forgot your friend said you'd never seen roller derby, right?"

"Nope." I was irritated. "Cute" wasn't really my thing.

She must have noticed my face turn hard, because she briefly touched my back and said, "Hey. I wasn't trying to be a jerk. Don't be mad."

I just shrugged, despite the weird warm feeling caused by her hand on my back. That feeling just irritated me more. I wasn't here to make friends or have cutesy conversations. I wanted to know more about roller derby and if it might be what I needed right now. "So what am I supposed to say, then?"

"Just, 'Do you play?' or 'Do you skate?'"

"Okay . . . do you skate, then?" I mumbled.

"No—well, not really. I dabble. But I'm just the team's manager mostly. Once in a while I'll throw on some skates, but I'm not very good at the aggressive part. It's not really my thing." She stared at her shoes as she said this, and I guessed she was a bit embarrassed by this admission of weakness. I would be.

"What does a manager do? Besides sell merchandise?"

"Whatever they need, really. I help tape them up, get their water, cheer, create pamphlets for the league, make those pins." She pointed to my new savage bee pin. "Stuff like that. Roller derby's pretty DIY."

"How'd you get into this, if you're not really into roller derby?" I held back the real question, which was *How did someone as tame as you get involved in something so hard-core?*

"My sister's on the team. And the rest of the team is like my family too. Plus, I like roller skating, even if I'm not into all the pushing and hits." She prodded her glasses up her nose.

Meanwhile, I couldn't stop thinking about all the pushing and hits.

Shanti led me around the arena to an entryway near the concession stand. A guy was leaning against the wall, scrolling away on his phone. He didn't look up as we approached. Shanti stopped abruptly and whispered, "Pretend you're my girlfriend? Just for a second?" She held her hand out in front of her, her face somewhere between friendly and questioning.

Hmm. Fighting my instinctual response to scoff and turn away, I kept my face neutral and lifted my hand. She smiled and took it. I made sure to keep my hand as limp as possible, in case she got the wrong idea.

The guy finally dragged his head away from his phone and stared at Shanti, then looked at our hands, then pushed open the door to his left. Shanti gave him a head nod and my hand a squeeze as we passed by. A sting surged through my palm just as something twinged in my stomach.

We walked up a concrete corridor, and with all the cheering and lights, I felt like a boxer entering the ring. My breathing increased a little as I remembered the punching bag in the garage. I automatically clenched my hand and regretted it when Shanti looked back at me, her hand still in mine and a searching look on her face. She didn't show any sign of letting go, though, so I went to take off my jacket and shook my hand free of hers to do so. Holding hands wasn't really my thing either.

As we made our way through a crowd of people, a single, sharp whistle blew across the arena.

Shanti shouted, "A jam's just starting. Come on!" I followed her through to the front of a cordoned-off area at one side of the track. Shanti waved me forward to an open spot just behind a rope separating the track from the Crash Zone. On the other side of the rope and farther down a bit was a set of folding chairs, and on a bunch of those chairs were team members wearing gold and black uniforms.

I squished in next to Shanti and she explained, "That's our bench. My sister's the jammer—do you know what that is?"

My head turned sharply toward her to see if she was patronizing me. But her face held what looked like genuine curiosity.

Chill out, Daya. "No—what is it?"

"It's the skater who scores the points—the fastest one, usually." She said this with a little pride, which made her eyes shiny beneath her glasses. "Number forty-four—see her? With the gold star on her helmet?"

She pointed to the girl that Fee used to play hockey with—the one who looked like she didn't take any bullshit from anyone.

At the moment, forty-four's sole purpose seemed to be to burn her way around the track. Her quads looked like they were made of concrete. She must have been about five-seven or five-eight—two or three inches taller than me—but she was crouched like an attack cat, sending herself forward with her powerful legs but keeping her center of gravity low, I guessed. Her hair was dyed a bright green and flowed freely from beneath her helmet. Up close like this, I could see her tattoos clearly—dragons and serpents. Maybe some flames, too. *Hot,* I thought.

"Wow. She looks hella strong," I said.

"Yeah. Her personality's strong too, but you have to be strong across the board to jam." She pushed her glasses up again.

"What's her name?" I asked, completely mesmerized as I watched her thrust her way through a group of skaters.

"Kat. But her roller name is Killa Skillz."

"Cool," I said, continuing to watch Kat. Instead of avoiding the other team's skaters, it seemed like she aimed straight for them, inviting every hit she could as she plowed past them, her face steel and her eyes lasers. I couldn't take my own eyes off her. "Man, I need to meet *her*. She seems like my kind of person," I said, maybe a little breathily.

When Shanti didn't reply, I turned to her. She was staring out at the track, and her demeanor had changed—a small frown across her forehead, a slump in her shoulders.

Confused, but unwilling to dig into whatever her deal was, I asked, "So what else should I know about this stuff?"

She blinked a couple of times before speaking. "Um, well, there are five skaters in all: the jammer, three blockers, and a pivot." She paused and seemed to have deflated a bit.

I wasn't so good with other people's feelings (or my own, for that matter). They just seemed to get in the way and complicate everything. So instead, I just charged ahead. "Okay . . . and what do they do?"

"Uh—" She stuffed her hands in the pockets of her jeans. "The jammers score the points every time they skate through the pack of other skaters. The blockers are like, the ones who create holes for their jammers and keep back the other team's jammer. They're the muscle."

I tucked that bit of info away for later.

She continued, "The pivots have the stripe on their helmets. They're basically blockers but can also switch with the jammer if needed." She shrugged, as if giving up on something.

"Right . . ." Figuring that was enough info to work out the rest on my own and also not wanting to ask any more questions, given Shanti's weird turn of mood, I just watched the action in silence. Shanti didn't offer any more advice, either.

This is why I don't hang out with chicks. So damn sensitive.

I quickly lost focus on Shanti and got sucked into the track action, though. In all the sports and stuff I'd ever participated in, I'd never seen anything like it. Nothing so brutal but also full of finesse. Skateboarding could be quick and fluid, full of sweet bails. And I loved that it was just me and my board—I didn't have to depend on anyone else.

But this . . . watching all these people smash into each other and wipe out . . . I felt like I was watching a perfect opportunity to collect dark, deep bruises across my skin. For once, surrounding myself with other people might actually work in my favor. All that pain, aimed toward me. No time to think or feel or remember. Just jabs across my skin to keep my focus there and only there. As I watched the skaters elbow, coast, dig, jump, and thrust themselves around the track, my heart matched their pace.

I needed this.

"What do you have to do to get on a team?" I asked, without letting my eyes leave the bout, and as casually as possible, given my heart rate.

I could feel Shanti shift her gaze to me. "You want to try it?"

She sounded surprised, so I turned to her now. Something—maybe disappointment?—seemed to tug at her eyes.

"Yeah, it looks savage. I think I'd love it." *I know I would.*

She brought her hands out of her pockets and gripped the thick rope in front of her. Facing the looping skaters, she said, "This is just an exhibition match. So if you wanted to, you could still try out, I guess."

"Great. When? Where? What do I need?" My mind was already racing with all the possibilities—I'd need to be a blocker, obviously. And I'd be the baddest blocker out there. Ruthless. Fearless. I could show everyone that I was tough as hell *and* gather bruises by the dozens. My hips would be weapons. My arms and legs would be coated in purple.

"I can text you the info. But . . . are you sure? It can be pretty brutal. Fun—but brutal."

As if to demonstrate Shanti's point, two skaters flew off the track, tumbled over each other, and rolled to a stop near our feet. They pushed at each other on the ground, and everyone in our area cheered, including me.

After they'd untangled themselves and raced back to the track, I turned to Shanti. "I'm pretty used to brutal, don't worry. It's my specialty," I said, flushed with excitement.

She considered me for a moment. I guess she thought that was a weird thing to say, but I didn't care. "Okay . . . well, this jam just ended. I should get out to the bench. I'm supposed to be . . . keeping stats." She pulled out her phone.

Stats? Really? For roller derby?

"Oh, okay. Sure." She handed her phone to me. I added my number and gave it back. "Uh, thanks for bringing me down here." I found myself irritated by this inexplicable turn in her mood but also wondered if I'd done something to cause it. It wouldn't surprise me if I had. It wasn't like I was very good at any of this social stuff.

"Yeah, no worries," she murmured as she dipped beneath the rope without another look.

I watched her join the girls on the bench. I noticed she didn't take any stats, though—just sat there, watching the action and handing towels to team members as they came off the track.

I was right. She just wanted to ditch me.

I pulled my eyes away to set them on the other team instead, hoping the shift would stifle the confusing prick of disappointment in my chest.

Chapter Ten

It didn't take long for my brain to move from Shanti or however I'd screwed up to the frenzy on the track, however. The Killa Honeys were definitely the superior team. They not only had the stronger, quicker skaters, but each one of them probably had about ten pounds on the other team's players. They were simply bigger and better. But the opposing team tried to make up for their shortcomings by being particularly brutal. At least one of them was in the penalty box at all times. I couldn't quite figure out what some penalties were for, but one or two were pretty clear—no yanking on someone's ponytail or tripping, apparently. Still plenty of opportunity to clobber each other, though.

Unlike in ice hockey, the "box" was really just a few chairs, and the action from the track continued on into this area in an exaggerated manner. Before the skaters even got to the penalty box, though, they had to undergo some ridiculous "punishment," ranging from being spanked by the other team's subs with foam paddles to doing twenty push-ups in front of the fans. These exploits were decided by the "Penance Wheel" and closely watched by the "Mistress of Penalties," someone named the Shizz.

The announcer—a woman in a top hat, coattails, and a bright green spandex onesie—called out plays made and instructions to the audience with lots of enthusiasm. She explained at one point that most leagues had abandoned these added penalty embarrassments, but not this one. She seemed proud of the fact.

I, on the other hand, thought it was a shame they'd kept it up. Though I enjoyed watching the madness, I wasn't sold on any of it for myself. I wasn't so much interested in the absurdities of roller derby—I was drawn to the action, the competition, the open season mentality. All this extra foolishness seemed pointless to me.

But seeing the unapologetically brutish skaters in the box gave me tingles. Each had their own body shape, size, look, and demeanor, but all had one thing in common: they looked tough as hell. Even the smallest skaters, who were more finesse than muscle on the track, seemed to be made of steel. The skinniest arms were built of sinewy muscles, the thickest legs seemed to have no trouble crouching low or moving fast. The folks with heavy makeup on their faces sweat just as much as the rest and were equally as fierce.

The crowd's energy around me was almost as frenzied as

the action on the track—people rose and dropped doing the wave, kids bounced in their seats like Santa had arrived, folks lining the track reached out like they just wanted to touch some magic as skaters tore past them.

I tried my best to keep up with the rules, and I thought I was getting the gist of things. Each game consisted of a bunch of "jams" or rounds, which could last up to two minutes. It looked like the jammer had to break through the pack first to become the "lead jammer" before she could score any points. She could stop the jam whenever she wanted. I also gathered you couldn't use your elbows, but lots of hitting happened above the waist and at the hips, which I could easily make do with.

By halftime, the Honeys were up 27–19, and my skin was hot and sticky just from watching them. A bunch of people left the Crash Zone to grab drinks and snacks, and as I hovered around behind the rope, my phone pinged. I pulled it out of my back pocket and checked the message. Fee.

I see you down there. Having fun?

I looked up to where they and Cai were sitting, and they both waved. I waved back, noticing the asshole behind them wasn't in his seat anymore. I texted back: Where's Dickhead?

He went to get us snacks.

???!!!!

J/K. He started talking smack again and everyone around us basically told him to suck it before I even had a chance to myself. He huffed off. Poor pumpkin. ;)

Obviously these roller derby folks were my kind of people. I kind of wished I'd been there to join in and was a little frustrated at myself for making Fee have to basically escort me away, like some uncontrollable brat. But I was glad Dickface got ousted. I sent Fee a little brown thumbs-up emoji.

Back on the track, Shanti was busy filling water bottles and re-taping wrists. I noticed how most of the girls on the team gave her high fives or a pat on the butt or some equally affectionate gesture as they milled around and waited for halftime to finish. She'd respond with a grin or a smile and some words of encouragement. Seeing Shanti playful and at ease among the team, like she was everyone's little sister—something about their interactions pulled at me.

But then Shanti's *actual* sister, Kat, skated in to the bench and hollered for everyone to huddle up while shoving her water bottle at Shanti. No request for a fill-up or anything. Shanti's face displayed something between embarrassment and disappointment . . . until she glanced my way and then went to fill the bottle. Bit weird.

I was a little put off by Kat's actions but could also see that she was a big deal on this team. And the way she battled her way through the other skaters and whipped around the track in no time at all only to dig right back into the pack again convinced me she needed to feel that brutal contact as much as I did. I could wait for Shanti to help me get to her, but judging by this recent display, I wasn't sure that was my best bet. I decided I'd need to take matters into my own hands.

As I was contemplating my next move, though, something ran into the back of my leg, and before I could even bask in the glory of an unexpected bruise, a warbling voice shouted, "Dammit! This crap is shit!"

I turned to find a 150-year-old woman yanking around a walker. She must have been taller at some point but had hunched over with age to my height. Her meager head of hair was dyed blue-black, and neon-blue eye shadow painted her eyelids, made only brighter by the thick black eyeliner bordering her eyes. Her mouth was a twist of disgust as she banged her walker up and down, presumably teaching it a good lesson. I noticed, looking down at the metal victim of her fury, that the woman was wearing blue-and-black-checkered tights and red Doc Martens. I don't think I'd ever seen a woman like this, let alone a woman this old like this.

But then another one stepped into the picture.

"Bee, what're ya trying to do? Can'tcha see ya whacked this poor kid with ya death-mobile?" This equally ancient-looking being carried a cane instead of a walker. Her attire was a little more restrained—black pants, white silk shirt, bolo tie. A tight, perfectly round bun of utterly white hair sat on top of her head.

When the first awe-inspiring woman was finished brutalizing her walker, she finally noticed me and her mouth untwisted into an O shape. "Are you what I hit, doll? Did I hurt ya?"

"Of course ya hurt her, Bee! Don't be ridiculous," Bolo Tie

said, poking Bee's butt with the end of her cane. Bee batted the cane away and Bolo rolled her eyes, but I could tell there was fondness underlying the whole scene.

Bee turned back to me. "Sorry, girlie, this damn thing has a mind of its own!"

"Somebody's gotta have a mind around here," Bolo added, straightening her already straight tie.

"It's fine. No harm done," I uttered, a little stunned by these two characters.

Bolo gave me a once-over and said, "You don't look like a skata. What are ya? A fan?"

"Oh, I'm not—I mean, I'm not a skater. But I'm a new fan. Does that count?"

"Yeah, sure, honey—that counts," Bee cried out. She was shouting way louder than she needed to, even with the music blasting over the sound system.

"Uh . . . great," I responded.

"I'm Bee. I use-ta be a rolla girl. My rolla name was Ginga Vitas." She jabbed her thumb back at Bolo Tie. "That's Yolanda, aka That Damn Broad. She use-ta be the enemy." She made an exaggerated grimace.

"Oh yeah, yeah, keep it up, y'old ninny." Yolanda poked her again with her cane. "What she means is"—and here she straightened her back as much as she could and spoke with obvious pride—"I was the masta of ceremonies. The keepa of the game. The head zebra!"

My face must have registered my confusion, because

Yolanda's eyes rolled freely again and she added, "I was a referee! I put this one here in the box more than a few times, that's f'sure."

Bee cackled while a small smile cracked Yolanda's mostly rigid face.

"Wow—when was that?"

"Oh, just last year, hon," Bee offered, then nudged Yolanda while looking at me, as though I wouldn't notice she'd just nudged Yolanda.

"Right. You two must be in some shape, then." I smiled. Just a little.

"Oh, we are. We *are*," Bee exclaimed.

She giggled. Yolanda shook her head. I smiled a little more.

"So you're a new fan, are ya? How ya likin' it, sweetheart?" Bee asked.

I couldn't quite pick out her accent. Something East Coast, I thought. "I love it. I wanna do it."

Bee's eyes lit up. "Yeah ya do!" she called out. "Aw, hon, you gotta do it if you wanna do it. There ain't nothin' like it. You'll fall head over *wheels*!" Another cackle.

"Do ya know anyone on the teams?" Yolanda asked, her voice indicating that she was certain I didn't. "'Cause if ya don't, we know lotsa people—we're famous around here, ya know." She was a little pompous, but I kind of liked it on her.

"Oh yeah?" I wondered if these two were for real or if they were just two nutty superfans. "Do you know Kat? From the Killa Honeys?" I tried.

"Aw, shit! Yolanda, she wants to know if we know Kat!"

Bee pawed at Yolanda gleefully, and Yolanda let her.

"Sweetheart, do we *eva* know Kat!" Bee shouted. "Kat's my granddaughta! Killa instinct runs in the family, doll!"

Oh man, I couldn't believe this. "Really? She's amazing. I can't believe how tough she is," I said.

"Yeah, she gets that from me, honey. I use-ta be a real bruiser—"

"That's why she was always in the box!" Yolanda interrupted, thumping her cane once for emphasis.

"Yeah, well, sometimes ya gotta take one for the team, right?" Bee countered.

"Yeah, I get that," I offered. *Sometimes you gotta take one for yourself, too.* I decided to take one for myself now. "Could you introduce me?"

"Oh sure, sure, honey! Be happy to. Come on ova this way," Bee said, and started step-thumping her walker over to where Kat was standing and talking across the rope to some people who looked like fans, judging from their doe eyes. Yolanda nudged me forward, bossy as ever, and we followed Bee, who walloped her way through the group of fans to the rope, knocking a few more legs on the way.

"Hey, Kat!" she cried, startling Kat, who'd been signing some dude's chest with a Sharpie. When Kat saw who it was, however, she grinned and enveloped Bee in a huge hug, bending over to reach Bee's stooped frame.

"Nana! How's it going?" Kat yelled over the music as she pulled back.

"Oh, fine, fine, doll! You're really knockin' some girls

together out there, aren't ya?" Bee yelled back, sending some of the fans around us into titters.

Kat laughed. "Yeah—it's in my blood, right?"

"Damn right it is, kid!" Bee pronounced, jabbing Kat in the chest with a bony finger.

At this point Yolanda poked Bee in the butt again for the umpteenth time and shouted, "Hey, Bee! Enough preening already! We got guests—or didya f'get?"

Bee craned her neck back to see who the guest was, remembered it was me, and then cried, "Oh! Yeah, of course!" She let go of her walker to wave me forward with one hand. "C'mere, doll!"

I shuffled toward them, suddenly a little shy, and stood next to Bee. In front of Kat, I felt like a kid.

"Kat," Bee explained, "this he-ya is . . . uh . . . uh . . . oh shit. Honey, what's yer name?"

I realized that in my awe over these two, I'd never introduced myself. I looked from Bee to Kat and stuck out my hand. "Hey. I'm Daya."

"Daya! Kat, this is Daya! She wants to be a rolla girl like us! Ain't that perfect?" Bee hollered.

Kat took my hand in an extremely firm grip, her eyes meeting mine. She had her wrist guards on, and I felt like I was shaking hands with a cyborg. "Oh yeah? Hey, Daya. Kat Chen. But out here I'm Killa Skillz." Up close like this, I could see how flawless her makeup was, even under the shine of sweat. She had the same near-black hair as Shanti, judging by the roots showing beneath her green hair dye, but her skin was a bit lighter. Her tattoos were, in fact, dragons and fire and seemed to pulse among the many bruises scattered across her arms. The sight sent a shiver across the back of my neck.

It was like meeting an action-movie star, and I kind of wished I had something for Kat to sign, even though I never usually went in for that sort of thing. But something about her made me starstruck.

The beginnings of a smirk on her face suggested she could sense this. "So you skate?" she asked, after our hands parted and she'd placed them on her hips.

"Uh, yeah—well, I *can* skate. And I skate*board*," I offered. "But this"—I gestured to the track—"looks unreal."

"Oh, it's *very* real. Trust me. *This* real." Kat swung her hips around and pointed to a spot just below her right butt cheek, where a gigantic bruise splashed across her skin, almost engulfing her entire hamstring.

My brain swirled. *Whoa.* "That's a beauty," I said, my heart beating a little faster.

"Gotta be prepared for a little bruisin' if you're gonna skate, kid," Yolanda inserted, appearing suddenly at my side like some kind of sketchy butler.

"Oh, I have no issues with that. Don't worry." I said this directly to Kat to make sure she knew I meant it.

Just as I was going to ask about trying out, Dickface from before stumbled into me, plastered. He must've been drowning his pathetic sorrows in the beer garden after getting shunned from the stands.

"Heyyyyyy—you're that chick from before . . . ," he started.

My neck and shoulders instantly tensed. "And you're the asshole who was harassing my friend." My eyes iced over.

He got all up in my face, blowing his yeasty beer breath at me. "What'd you call me, bitch?"

I didn't move an inch, even though I could see every pore on his face. "You heard me. Why don't you—"

"Pal—I'm gonna sign your forehead and then you're gonna take off, all right?" Kat had stepped up beside us, Sharpie wielded like she was going to stab something.

Dude blinked a few times—processing Kat's size and hotness, no doubt—then laughed and leaned forward, presenting his big shiny forehead to her. She rolled her eyes at me and wrote *Buzzkill* on his skin. "'Kay, BYE," she said, and gave him a robust push toward the bar. When he was a couple of feet away, she aimed an air kick at his ass, which was extra impressive, given she was in skates.

She turned to me. "Hope you're not pissed I stepped in. You looked like you had it under control—I just got sick of listening to his dumb ass."

Normally I would be pissed, but Kat's actions just reinforced what I already thought—she and I seemed cut from the same cloth. "No, it's cool—I was sick of him too. Thanks."

"You don't back down, huh?"

"Not generally, no."

"Nice," she said, nodding.

"So, hon"—Bee's face poked in between us—"what's a girl gotta do to get on a team these days?" Then she elbowed me and continued without letting Kat respond, "In my day, we hadda go through all kinds of rigmarole to get on a team."

Kat smiled at her with admiration and amusement. "Yeah, Nana, those were the days, huh?" She winked at me. "Well, we're not half as tough as these two ladies," she said, "but there *is* a process." She looked me over like Yolanda had and seemed to appreciate my broad shoulders and wider hips, because she added, "You look like you could fit right in."

I actually blushed. I was starting to feel like a total fangirl, which I didn't love. But I also really needed to get in on this roller derby stuff. If I didn't, I wasn't sure whether I'd make it through the next few months—whether I could keep the shit in my chest at bay. Kat seemed like both someone who appreciated a good bruising and the right person to help me get what I needed. And I needed this—the contact, the competition, the chance to pull all the pain away from my chest and into my skin.

Chapter Eleven

The horn sounded to signal the second half, and Kat had to go. But before she did, she told me to stick around after the match and she'd give me some info.

I watched the rest of the match with Yolanda and Bee, listening to their play-by-play and watching the two teams battle it out just as hard as they had in the first half. Nestled in between Bee and Yolanda, I felt an unfamiliar mixture of both admiration and discomfort. With Priam and Vicki, I mainly felt discomfort alone, but with these two, their zest for this brutal sport sparked excitement and desire in me, even as their quirkiness reminded me of Priam and Vicki. By the end of the bout, the Honeys had won by an impressive lead and Bee pretty much lost her mind, while Yolanda thumped the crap out of her cane, which was both overwhelming and funny.

After the match, I texted Fee to let them know I'd find my

own way home and grab my skateboard from them later. They texted back with every happy face emoji available and firm instructions to fill them in later.

Yolanda and Bee shuffled me over to Kat and the rest of the Honeys to say congrats on the win. They gave Shanti a squeeze as well, and from the look on Shanti's face, I could tell she loved the hell out of both these women. The sight caused a tug in my chest, which I quickly countered with a squeeze to my left palm. *Eye on the prize, Daya.* And the prize here was finding another way—maybe a better way—to keep those tugs under control.

Kat pulled herself away from her adoring fans to address me. "So, Daya. Still wanna try out?"

"Hell yes."

"That's the spirit, dollface!" Bee cried. She placed a knobbly but strong hand on my shoulder. "Shuga, you give us a call if you need skating equipment or tips. We got the inside track on folks who are always ready ta help a new rolla kid." She looked at Kat. "Kat, make sure this babe gets our numbah so we can hook 'er up with Alma and Joe."

"Yes, ma'am, I'll do that right now," Kat assured them, and winked at me.

After Kat had added their number to my phone, the two older women waved goodbye to us and shuffle-stepped away with the exiting crowd, Yolanda patting Bee on the butt affectionately.

"Cute, huh?" Kat said.

I turned back to look at her and nodded. "And effing hilarious. Are they together?" I asked.

"Yup. Have been for years. Since their roller derby days," Kat answered.

"They call themselves the long-term lezzies," Shanti added, which should have been funny, but she said it so seriously I wasn't sure I should laugh. Thankfully, Kat snickered, so I did too. Shanti just stared at her feet, which were kicking aimlessly at the floor. I had an urge to tell her to look up, but shook it away. What did I care what she did or didn't do?

"Have you two met?" Kat then asked, pointing back and forth between me and Shanti.

Shanti eventually did look up at me but didn't say anything, so I offered, "Yeah—Shanti brought me over here after I got this sweet Honeys swag." I held up my jacket to show off the pin. I tried smiling at her to show her I really did appreciate it—because I did. How else would I have gotten this close to the action? My attempt brought out a hint of the warmth I'd seen in her at the merchandise booth—friendly eyes and a shy smile back.

Kat examined me, then Shanti, and raised a questioning eyebrow. Shanti looked away. The mood was getting weird again, so I blurted, "Roller derby looks amazing, and I want in. How do I do that?"

Before Kat could answer, we heard, "Hey! Forty-four! You bitch—you wrote this shit on my forehead?"

I couldn't believe this guy was back. Dickface must've kept

imbibing because he was senseless enough to step right up into Kat's face and point his big dumb finger at her, his beer sloshing over his other hand.

"Whoa, bro. You wanted me to sign it, remember?" She didn't look like she gave two shits about this guy.

"Oh yeah? Did I? I don't remember asking you to write 'Buzzkill' on it, you c—"

Nope.

My hands were suddenly ramming into his arm and he stumbled sideways, his beer sloshing all over his shirt. It felt gratifying to finally let out some of my rage at this guy. Adrenaline bolted through my body.

"What the . . . ?" Once he'd righted himself, he started coming back my way, but Kat stepped up beside me, hands on hips like fucking Wonder Woman. A few other fans and skaters had gathered around us too. I balled up my fists, ready for whatever was needed. *Give me one good reason, asshole.*

He hesitated and then threw his empty beer cup at our feet. I took a step toward him, crushing the cup as I did. Before I could take a second step, he mumbled, "Fuck you," thrust up both middle fingers, and stalked away.

As she watched him go, Kat held up her fist toward me. I bumped it with my own. This felt like a serious win on so many levels.

"Dude, that was awesome," Kat said, finally turning to me.

I couldn't wipe the satisfaction off my face. "Yeah. That felt good."

Out of the corner of my eye, I caught Shanti folding her arms and looking away. *What's her problem?*

Kat laughed. "Okay, back to business. You're keen to join, huh?"

I nodded.

"Well, roller derby's for anyone willing to put their body on the line. If you're ready to give and get the hits and bust your butt for the team like you seem to be, you've got a fair chance. You said you skate—how well?"

"Oh, I can skate." Okay, skate*board*, and I knew how to *ice* skate. But she didn't need to know all that. "And I can hit. And I'm not worried about taking hits either. Trust me."

"After that display, I believe you. We've got tryouts next week. Make sure Shanti's got your number, and she can text you the details."

I looked over at Shanti again, but she was busying herself with the team's equipment. "She's already got my number."

Kat's folded her arms and widened her stance. "Oh yeah? You hittin' on my sister now?"

"What? No, I just—"

Kat laughed again. "Chill, dude. I was kidding. She's not your type, trust me."

'Scuse me? How would you know my type? But I tamped down my instant resentment at Kat's assumption to avoid messing up my chances of getting on the team. "I already asked her to send me the tryout info."

"Perfect." She punched me not-so-gently on the arm.

"Come on, I'll introduce you to some of the Honeys."

Shanti glanced at me and turned to leave with a massive load of equipment swung over her shoulder. I was impressed to see her carrying that much. I also hoped she hadn't heard any of that—she seemed nice, after all, if a little moody. I caught myself wondering if she'd agree with Kat—if she thought she was my type or not. I made a weird face when I realized what I was thinking and hoped no one saw it.

I followed Kat to the Honeys' bench, where her teammates were removing their skates and gulping water. The whole space around us was still abuzz with all kinds of folks helping to clean up and take down equipment—officials, refs, teams, even little kids.

"Hey, gang—got some possible fresh meat!" Kat called out.

Good to know these folks could be as crass as some of the guys I skateboarded with.

The Honeys looked over at me and I held up a hand in greeting, my defenses rising. I wanted to believe I could fit in on a team—I had to believe it—but this was far from what I was used to, and my body wanted to retreat. The skateboard-ing crowd held a certain amount of comfort for me. Most people kept to themselves save for the odd head nod. Besides Fee, I'd been able to skateboard and bruise in a relatively soli-tary state, which was my preference.

But there just seemed to be so much indestructible energy in this arena—so much voluntary and deliberate exposure to pain—that I was convinced: if any people were my people, these were them. If I was going to join a team, it might as well be a team of people as dedicated to bruising as I was. And to my relief, this team greeted me back with friendly waves. I let my shoulders ease back down for now.

"Daya, the Honeys. Honey bitches, Daya." She turned to me and asked, "Pronouns?"

"Oh, uh—she/her."

To the group, Kat announced, "She's gonna try out!"

"Hey, Daya."

"Hey, girl."

"'Sup, Daya."

I gave them head nods and "heys" in return and forced myself to add, "You all looked effing awesome out there."

A few of them replied, "Thanks," and one girl—built like a Mack truck—asked, "So you wanna roll with us, hey?"

I glanced at Kat and replied, "Yeah. I do." Kat grinned and punched me in the other arm.

It hurt. I could tell that this girl was my kind of tough and I loved it.

Amma hadn't appreciated toughness the way Thatha and I did. I'd always held it against her, I guess. "Aren't you being a little too hard on her, Nihal? I don't like all this punching and hitting."

"What? You want her to be soft? Where will that get her here?"

I'd been standing by the front door when I heard this

argument between my parents—Amma's voice floating
wearily from the kitchen, while Thatha made no attempt
to keep his opinions quiet. It hadn't been the first time I'd
heard them clash over this particular topic.

"She doesn't have to do all this boxing to do well, Nihal."
My mother's words already sounded defeated, as usual. She
gave up so easily.

"She needs to learn to stand her ground. To not let anyone get to her, Sunita. Fighting in the ring will teach her that.
You know we have to work twice as hard. Be twice as strong.
What—you want her flouncing around like Priam and Vicki
instead?"

This was one of Thatha's tactics—bringing up Priam and
Vicki always shut Amma down. If it weren't for Thatha, Priam
wouldn't be where he is now, living his so-called "dream." Bringing them up was a reminder of this, of how Thatha's strength
and determination—his willingness to deal with bullshit—
made it possible for all of us to live here and do as we pleased.

Amma would generally concede at this point. And even
though I thought she was right to, part of me wished she was
tougher. That she'd stand her own ground for once.

Chapter Twelve

By the time I got home that night by way of two buses and a twenty-minute walk, it was almost ten thirty. I'd hung around with the team for a bit, listening to them go over the bout. It sounded like there were actual plays and stuff, and as I'd never competed in team sports, working with others wasn't something I was used to. I'd have to deal with that part later.

I hadn't managed to talk to Shanti again, though she was hovering nearby the whole time, helping the team with their gear and joking around with some of them. I'd kept glancing over to see if she'd show any sign she was happy that I'd been included by Kat and the team, to be let in on some of the jokes—she'd invited me into the scene, after all. But she pretty much ignored me, and instead of wasting any more energy on caring what she thought, I gripped the back of a metal chair and focused on trying to understand what the hell the team was talking about.

Though I'd texted Aunt Vicki to let her know I'd been studying and would be home a bit later than expected, I was still super pissed about the whole boxing thing. And though she hadn't mentioned it in her text, I also figured my school had probably called to let Priam and Vicky know I'd skipped. So I was ready for battle by the time I walked in the door.

As I hung up my jacket, Vicki and Priam appeared with a flourish from the kitchen, Vicki's red hair loose and swirling around her shoulders, Priam's hands twisting together in front of him. It was obvious that they were *perturbed*.

"Daya, the school called. You weren't there today? And it's a little *late* to be out on a school night, isn't it? Even if you *were* studying. Who were you studying with, anyway?"

I avoided eye contact by kneeling down to carefully unlace my Vans, which, obviously, I never usually bothered to do. "Anna," I replied, staring at the top of my foot. Anna was this friend I'd made up last year. As in "Anna-nymous."

"Oh, *Anna*! The darling. How *is* she?"

"Fine."

"And school today? Is everything all right?"

I clenched my jaw. "I just needed a day off." I glanced up at Priam, who, I noticed, hadn't said anything and looked uncomfortable. I rose and kicked off my shoes, then tried turning to head up the stairs, praying they'd just let this shit go. But of course, they didn't.

"Daya—" Priam began, but paused.

I stopped and turned, the look on my face and the tension

in my shoulders sending signals I hoped would dissuade them
from whatever it was they were about to launch into.

"We're sorry . . . ," Priam continued.

"So very sorry . . . ," Vicki added.

". . . for the boxing equipment . . ."

". . . and we hope you understand . . ."

". . . we were just trying to help."

"We returned everything."

They glanced at each other nervously, then back at me.

The panicky heat in my chest was back. If I opened my
mouth to speak, I wasn't sure what would come out. Probably
anger, but possibly some other stuff too. Stuff that was better
left unsaid. Stuff I didn't want to think about. I couldn't risk it.
I just barely managed a nod instead.

"Okay . . . well, then . . . good night, Daya," Vicki said.

Not giving them a chance to say anything else, I turned
and thumped up the stairs to my room.

As I undressed, I stared at the notebook sitting on my
desk. It'd been there since my last counseling session. I hadn't
even cracked it open. If I had to, what would I write now?

Nothing. I threw my shirt on top of it.

Sitting at the edge of my bed, I pressed my fingers into
the bruises on my legs, envisioning all the damage I'd do on
the roller derby track and across my body—each push a small
defense against everything that was trying to climb its way out
of my chest.

* * *

The very next morning I texted Shanti. I wanted the tryout info so I could figure out what I needed to do to make the team. Given the weirdness with her, though, I constructed my message carefully.

Hey, it's Daya. Thanks again for bringing me to the Crash Zone yesterday. I really appreciate it. Could you please send me the try-out info? Thanks! 😊

I never used happy face emojis.

Halfway through second period, she texted back.

Here's the link to the info. They're next week. You'll need gear. Call Bee. She'll set you up.

Okay, not the warmest response, but at least I got all the info I needed. During English, when I was supposed to be doing some nonsense grammar sheet, I checked out the link Shanti sent me. The first of two tryouts was on Monday, which meant I only had four days to find a bunch of equipment and start practicing. The info said the first tryout would focus on skating and there'd be no hitting. That sounded like some straight-up bullshit to me, not to mention it made me instantly more nervous. If I wanted to make the team and get to the hitting part, I'd need to impress them with my skating skills? I'd been betting on my brute strength to get me on the team. But while I was confident I could balance and move on four wheels, I just wasn't sure how well or how fast. I'd definitely need help. Something I wasn't great at asking for.

Feeling panicky, I told Ms. Leung I had to go to the bathroom. I checked the other stalls to make sure no one else was in any of them and locked myself in the least disgusting one. Leaning against the closed door, I pressed my thumb into the palm of my hand and closed my eyes. I did *not* want to look like an ass on skates, but I also hated that I'd need to ask for help. Letting Fee help me learn to skateboard had been hard enough, but their hands-off, chill way made it easier to let them in—and only partially in. Bee and Yolanda seemed like a whole other ball game. They didn't seem to have a lot of boundaries.

But as I pressed into my palm as hard as I could, feeling only the slightest relief from the tightness in my chest, I realized I didn't have a choice if I wanted to make this team.

I pulled out my cell phone and pressed Bee's number in to see if she and Yolanda would actually connect me with some equipment and maybe some skating help as soon as possible. Sure enough, Bee answered the phone, full of as much pep as she'd shown the previous day. My chest continued to tighten, but I managed to get my words out well enough.

"Of course, honey! Let's go tonight! You got a pen and pay-puh? Write this down."

After she gave me about a page's worth of directions to some place that seemed to be down a rabbit hole and somewhere in Wonderland, we agreed to meet there at five o'clock.

The equipment list included quad skates, helmet, wrist guards, elbow pads, kneepads, and a fitted mouth guard. The mouth guard concerned me a little, I'll admit—bruising fulfilled a need in me that burned high and hot, but losing my teeth was less tantalizing.

That was a lot of equipment, but I was all right for cash. I had a bank account with a bunch of money my parents left me, and Vicki and Priam let me use whatever I needed from there. Vicki had tried to keep close track of how much I was using at first, but she gave up after I had a fit over it and accused her of trying to keep my dead parents from me. Guilt could be a useful thing, when it wasn't a shitty thing. Now she just checked in once in a while to make sure I wasn't being completely reckless with the money.

When I got off the phone with Bee, I was glad to at least have a line on some equipment, but I still had no idea how I was going to up my skating game by Monday and panic continued to pulse through me. I remained in the stall for several minutes, waiting for my chest to loosen.

Chapter Thirteen

After school, I reviewed the directions Bee had given me. Apparently, the place she and Yolanda were taking me to didn't really have a name and the street numbers weren't easy to see. "You gotta look for the roller skates hanging from the telephone pole," Bee had said.

Really? Like for drug deals? I'd thought, but added this to the directions anyway, doing my best to trust these two feisty ladies and their superior wisdom even if my natural tendency was to close myself off to most other people's input. Besides, I needed these damn skates and I was determined to get them tonight so I could start practicing as soon as possible.

I hopped on a bus heading vaguely in the right direction. It took me close enough to where I thought I was going, and I walked the rest. Bee had told me to look for a skate park first, then the dubious hanging roller skates. The days were definitely getting shorter, and by the time I got to the park, the light had begun to dim.

A smattering of skaters glided and flipped across the curbs and ramps, looking indifferent. I wished I had my board with me. I could use a good bail right now. But then I remembered that even a good bail on my board wasn't doing it for me anymore.

Just as Bee had said, two white skates with neon-pink wheels dangled from a telephone pole next to the park. Just behind the skates was a property bordered by a picket fence on the edge of a cul-de-sac. From the lawn in front of the house grew an assortment of shrubs, all embellished with ornaments made of old roller-skate wheels. A two-car garage neighbored the house, its frame fringed with multicolored twinkle lights, its doors a flamboyant lime color. What the shit was this place and why hadn't Bee just told me to look for the weird bushes and lime doors? Maybe to her and Yolanda, this was normal.

I walked up to the gate entrance. On it, a sign said, ROLLING, DANCING, LOVING SINCE 1978. According to Bee's instructions, this was the place. She'd said that if she and Yolanda weren't outside waiting, I should just *march right on up to that door and ding that donger!* so that was what I did.

The doorbell had barely stopped chiming when the door swung open. The guy standing in front of me was maybe in his fifties or sixties. He was lean. And wiry. And bald. And wearing shorts—kind of short shorts—and a thin tank top with tiny roller skates all over it. His very tanned legs were taut with muscles. He kept shifting his weight back and forth from one leg to the next, like he was performing some kind of warm-up dance. In each hand, he squeezed those springy hand-grip exerciser things in and out. He stared at me for a moment, practically vibrating, and blinked. Then his eyes lit up. "Madam!" he said. "Might you be an associate of our long-term lesbian friends?" Squeeze, squeeze.

"Uh, yeah—Bee and Yolanda? They said to meet them here? That you might have some reasonably priced skates?"

"Yes! Yes! Yes!" He threw his hands up in the air, still squeezing in and out. "We have reasonably priced skates for the masses! Give me one hot second!"

He disappeared around the corner, hollering for Bee and Yolanda, and then came back with keys in his hand instead of the squeezy exercise things.

"Come, come! Follow me! Right this way! I'm Joe, my dear! Bee and Yolanda will be right out!" He leaped past me toward the garage.

Something about this guy reminded me of a circus ringleader. *Come in, come in, one and all. Follow me into the effing madhouse.* His steps were quick and light, like a skipping pony or something, and I had to jog to keep up with him.

He unlocked one of the wide garage doors. Yanking it upward with a flourish like it weighed nothing at all, he revealed a wonderland of skate stuff. He flipped a switch on the wall and a disco ball began to twirl, scattering little square patches of light around the space. In front of me, across the cement floor, rows and rows of roller skates spread out, with narrow pathways here and there for navigating the merchandise. Along the back wall, shelving held boxes of random bits and pieces, like spare wheels, toe stops, protective gear, etc.

"Here we go, here we go! What d'ya need, hon?" He clasped his hands together and waited, eyes bright and wide.

I still hadn't crossed the threshold of the garage. My brain had resumed its second thoughts. I was, after all, about to step inside a garage with some guy I didn't know. Skate fanatics could be psychopaths too. Had Bee and Yolanda sent me to my death? Where *were* they, anyway?

"Um. I need roller derby skates . . . and some gear."

"Well, well, then—let's find you a pair of skates that will make your feet sing!" He waved me in, and I couldn't help but think that this guy was way too excited to find me some skates to pause long enough for murder. I shuffled inside.

"What size, my dear?" he asked, looking at my feet. "Seven? And a half?"

Bingo. "Yeah, mostly seven and a half. But sometimes eight. But I dunno. How are skates supposed to fit?"

"Fit to your feet, of course!" He pulled a pair of skates from the row at his own feet and eyed them up, then eyed my feet up again, then back to the skates. "I'll bet I can find you the perfect pair in one try! It's my trick! I'm very good at it! One try!"

"Uh—cool," I said, and bit at my thumbnail. Was it possible he *always* spoke in exclamations? He handed the pale blue skates to me. They weren't as heavy as I thought they'd be. They looked like they'd rolled their way around the earth a couple of times, but what did I know? Low ankle cut, black laces, fat red wheels.

"Sit! Sit! Over here, my dear!" Joe pointed to a stool standing in the middle of the garage.

I sat down and pulled off my Vans.

Joe popped down onto one bony knee and placed the skates before me. He handled them like they were made of silk and gold, even though they were made of leather and hard plasticky stuff.

"Here you go, my dear! Let's see if we can get some magic happening, shall we?"

He rolled one boot next to my right foot and held it steady for me as I pushed my foot into it. It kind of felt like an ice skate—a tight fit, sturdy and hard. My toe reached the end of the skates, and I told Joe as much.

"Okay! Let's see what they're like when you get zippin'!"

Once we'd gotten both skates on and Joe insisted on tying my laces, even as I protested, he popped back up onto his feet and held out his arms like he was inviting me to dance. I pushed up on the stool and steadied myself. I could feel the tips of my toes at the end of both skates, but just barely. I rolled my feet back and forth a few times. Now, with these skates on, I was almost eye to eye with Joe. He viewed me, eyes shiny and expectant. He flung his wrists around a few times, his arms still raised.

"Well? And? Yes?" he asked, beginning his side-to-side dance again.

"They feel all right so far. Can I take a few strides outside, though?"

"Oh, of course, of course! I insist you do! How else will your skates choose you?" *Jesus. Please don't start rhyming, too, Joe.* He bounded across two mini pathways and out the open garage door. Like a frickin' gazelle.

I rolled myself along one pathway to follow him. I was pretty good on ice skates, and being on a skateboard felt like home some days more than my own two feet, but four wheels on boots like these was a mostly foreign feeling. Luckily, I wasn't really worried about falling, which helped me move more confidently.

By the time I made my way out of the garage, Joe was crouching next to one of the shrubs on the lawn. He'd produced some gigantic shears from somewhere and clipped with precision at the plant's leaves, his feet still dancing away in the grass. This guy.

I began pushing myself forward with longer strides, trying to envision Kat's posture and style as I did. I crouched low to keep myself sturdy and thrust my legs out to the side. I was used to pushing straight out backward from skateboarding, but I'd noticed when I was watching the skaters last night that the right motion seemed to be back and out—just like ice skating.

The driveway was on a bit of a slant, rising up toward the sidewalk. I propelled myself up the incline, really focusing on using the muscles in my thighs, which I had plenty of.

The skates hugged my feet. Nothing dug in too much— my arches felt supported, my heels flush against the back of the boot. The wheels seemed a bit worn, though, a *tick-tick-tick* sound coming from my left boot and the right wheels moving as though through thick honey.

"Um, Joe, these boots feel pretty good, but the wheels are a little slow. Would you be able to fix that?"

He stopped clipping leaves immediately and whirled around to face me. "Can I fix that, she asks! Can I fix it!" He dropped the shears onto the lawn and bounced back into the garage, yelling, "Let! Me! Have! Those! Skates! My dear!"

I rolled to the bottom of the driveway, trying to use a toe stop as I did. I realized quickly that toe stops weren't very helpful. I felt like I was going to tumble forward onto my face but caught myself with the garage wall. I made a mental note to figure out stops ASAP.

I rolled back to the stool and unlaced the boots. As soon as I'd yanked them off my feet, Joe swept them up and began to work on them.

"Bearings, my dear! Bearings! We'll have you moving smoothly in no time!"

"Um, cool, thanks." I didn't really care how he fixed them, so long as they'd hold up when I threw my full body weight at people and those people did the same to me.

As Joe worked on the skates, humming something that sounded like "Thunderstruck," I picked out some used protective gear and scanned the cork bulletin board hung on one of the walls. A bunch of photos and posters fanned out across its surface.

Skaters of all kinds appeared in the photos, which looked

like they were maybe from the eighties and nineties. Taking up a large portion of the board were roller derby skaters in packs moving around a banked track—unlike the flat track the teams had been on last night—and team photos of tough-as-hell-looking women with their tongues and middle fingers out. But an equal portion boasted people in old-school roller skates linking arms and skating in long lines, or frozen in agile dance moves.

I could make out from a few of the photos that Joe had been a hunk as a younger dude. Some of these photos showed him contorted in several positions on a roller rink. But he was also in a few of the team derby pics, wearing the same short shorts and tight tank tops, face eager as ever. His lean muscle mass hadn't changed, but he'd had hair once. A full head of wavy brown hair and a scruffy beard, it seemed. He was the only dude in the photos, and I wondered what his deal was. Coach? Husband? Father? Fan?

Like a pop-up character in a book, he appeared beside me, holding the newly refurbished skates as well as another set of eight wheels in a plastic bag. "Ta-da!"

I jumped a little at his sudden appearance and his burst of speech. "These skates might be previously adored, but they will serve you just as well as any of those fancy-fancy skates you get elsewhere, don't you worry! And here"—he held up the plastic bag—"are some outdoor wheels. A special bonus for a first-time customer!"

"Wow. Thanks." I went to take the skates and bag from

him, but he switched his attention to the wall before I could.

"You're perusing my history here, madam!" He leaned forward and peered into a photo of himself with a team of women dressed in faux police uniforms, except with low-cut tops and high-cut shorts.

"Check out these bruiser ladies! The Cop-a-Wheelies! They looked like cops, but acted like hoodlums!"

"Were you their . . . ?" I let the question hang in the air, hoping—knowing—he'd fill in the blank.

"Coach! Well . . . they didn't really need a coach, but they let me think they did, and I pretended to know enough to be one!" He chuckled.

Just as I was about to ask how he'd found himself coaching roller derby, a voice called out, "Joe?" from somewhere beyond the garage door.

Joe turned toward the open door and yelled back, "In here, darling! Come join the party!"

A surprising twinge of excitement twisted in my chest. Was I about to meet Joe's partner? I couldn't imagine what such a person might be like, and I guess my curiosity got the best of me.

Around the corner of the garage door appeared said person. She looked to be about Joe's age and wore a shiny teal tracksuit. Her graying hair was shaped into a short Afro close to her scalp. On her feet were plush pink slippers. She must have been only about five feet tall, but her perfect posture made her seem taller. My eyes darted from one feature to the next. Curves. Many curves. Skin darker than mine. Cat-eye glasses. Pastel-pink press-on nails.

Behind her, I heard the telltale thump-step of Bee and Yolanda and their walking aids. The two appeared alongside Joe's partner shortly after, gleaming in sequined bodysuits. My mouth fell open.

Bee's face expanded into a bright smile when she saw me, and she exclaimed, "Daya, dollface! Sorry to keep ya waitin'. It took Alma here a little longer than we thought to get us into these beauties. Nothin' like a little dress-up!" She indicated Yolanda's and her attire. Yolanda looked less thrilled about her attire than Bee did.

"Oh, that's okay. It was worth the wait," I said, meaning it. That sent Bee and Alma into a titter, which actually made me feel kind of awesome.

Joe piped up with, "Hello, my darling! Up to your usual antics, I see!"

"Hello, sweetheart," Alma said, gliding across the garage toward us. She extended her hand out in front of her. "A customer! How lovely." Her voice emerged deep and resonant from glossy pink lips.

I hesitated and then received her hand with my own. She held it carefully. Without letting go, she said, "As already mentioned, my name is Alma. Pardon my appearance. I've just showered and didn't have time to get into *my* jumpsuit. And you are Daya." She said this last part like she'd known it all along.

Nothing about her appearance suggested any special elegance, but the way she spoke reminded me of one of those actresses in black-and-white movies—all graceful and dignified.

"Yes. Daya." These two words were about all I could get out at the moment. All this felt like a lot of stimulation. Priam and Vicki would love these people, which made me a little wary of them. But like Bee and Yolanda, at least their enthusiasm was aimed at something amazing and fierce like roller derby.

"I hope Joe is treating you magnificently."

"He—he is. I think we found some skates for me." She still had my hand in hers and now added her other hand around mine. Usually this kind of contact would make me twitchy, but I found her steady hold somehow soothing in all the surrounding animation.

"Well, that's fine, then, isn't it!" She looked at Joe and he beamed back, his chest puffing out just a little more. To me, she leaned in and conspiratorially added, "He's a wonder, isn't he?"

I couldn't help but smile.

"We were just admiring all this history on the wall, darling! Our lovely friend here is a beginner derby skater! Isn't it grand?" Joe said.

Alma's eyes brightened. "My dear! That *is* exciting. There still aren't enough chocolate girls like us gracing the track."

Bee cut in, making her way over to the wall. "That's right! Alma was one of the first and finest cups o' hot chocolate you eva saw! Look, there she is, right there—look at all that chalky skin around 'er." She pointed to a photo on the wall of a team dressed in disco-inspired uniforms—miniskirts, glitter tops, bell-bottoms. Every single person in the photo was white, save Alma, who was as curvy as now, with tight braids beneath her helmet and a gleaming smile.

"Those are the Disco Cheat-as," Alma explained, letting loose my hand and gazing into the photo. "Joe and I started that team together in 1978, not too long after we met."

"Shortly after we met and fell head over wheels in love, that is!" Joe gushed. I noticed he used the same joke Bee had used and wondered if it'd been the running joke of yesteryear. All four of them certainly found it funny enough to giggle over. Well, Yolanda's lips just kind of twitched. So I didn't offend any of them, I let out a small laugh.

Alma threaded her arm through Joe's and leaned in so he could give her a quick peck on the cheek. "That's right. Joe and I met at a roller disco, you see—"

"Alma was a champ, Daya! A real champ! You've never seen anything like it—Alma gliding across the roller rink, smooth as butter, quick like lightning, feet skipping, whirling, jiving, jumping! Nothing like it! I fell in love with the way she moved before anything else! And then I discovered every other miraculous thing about her and fell in love with those, too!"

Patting him on the arm—I wasn't sure if it was a thankful pat or a *Now, now, dear. That's enough* pat—Alma continued, "I have really loved my roller life, that's for sure." Her eyes focused on me. "Disco and roller derby—both have made me feel so . . . *full*. Like I'm part of the crowd, my teammates, the music and lights. It's pure joy. You understand?"

The way she looked directly into my eyes when she spoke felt too intimate—like she was sharing something she'd only share with friends. Her comments reminded me of what Fee had said about the energy they felt while playing hockey, too. It all seemed so different from what I felt when I was skate-boarding. Maybe you just had to be a certain kind of person to experience it. But something about what Alma was saying felt appealing, even as it felt impossible.

I ignored her question (because I didn't at all understand) and broke our eye contact to search the photos. "Are there any other photos of you from those days?" I asked.

Joe, Alma, Bee, and Yolanda all leaned into the bulletin board at the same time, then pointed at the same photo.

"There she is!" Yolanda declared, pressing her index and middle finger against a gorgeous photo of Alma dressed in a sparkling gold bodysuit with bell-bottoms and gleaming white roller skates. Her hands rested on her hips, her stance firm, but her head was thrown back in laughter. It seemed the camera had caught her in a moment of that pure joy she'd mentioned.

I guess I'd been staring for a while, because everyone giggled again and Alma placed a hand on my shoulder and squeezed. "Not too shabby, hmm? I'll bet you'll find great delight in your new roller skates too, Daya."

I folded my arms across my chest. "Yeah." Staring at Alma's

photo, though, I doubted a camera would ever capture in me what I was seeing. Something in the way she carried herself— even now, standing next to me—seemed so distant.

Joe broke into my self-consciousness. "Well! Daya! Want to give your new wheels a whirl?" He'd been holding the pair of skates this whole time and held them out to me now. He and Alma grinned at me like proud parents. Or what I imagined proud parents looked like.

I took the skates and sat back down on the stool. As I laced up, I snuck glances up at the two couples, who still stood in front of the bulletin board, arms around each other's backs. They pointed and giggled and hooted like kids. The sight opened up a small black hole in my stomach. I'd never see my parents like that. I wasn't sure I ever had. I yanked hard at my laces and pressed my hands into the stool before getting up.

It had grown darker outside, but with the Christmas lights across the edges of the garage and strewn along the shrubs on the lawn, enough light peered over the driveway. I rolled around the pavement. The new bearings spun smoothly, and I felt sturdy and strong in these skates.

While Joe resumed his horticultural endeavors, Alma gave me a few tips and Bee and Yolanda wrapped themselves in a blanket and watched, calling out the odd direction here and there. Normally, I'd be annoyed if strangers tried to give me unsolicited advice, but I'd take anything these women were willing to offer me. My earlier apprehension about asking for help had withered away under the force of these four individuals. They all seemed to know what they were talking about, and I needed all the help I could get.

Each adjustment Alma suggested resulted in a little more balance, a bit more thrust, a lot more confidence. I must've rolled around for about forty minutes until I remembered that I didn't know these people that well and they probably hadn't planned on handing out free roller-skating lessons all night.

I turned my skates outward to stop near Alma, like she'd shown me. "This was really helpful. But you must be getting cold."

"Oh, Daya, I'm a tough old gal. Don't worry about me," she said, and tittered again.

"Darn right ya are, my darling!" Joe piped up from across the lawn.

"Well, thanks so much for all your advice," I said to Alma. "And for the great tip about this place," I aimed toward Bee and Yolanda. "And for all your help too, Joe. You found the right skates in one try!"

"Told you, my dear! Utter pleasure!" he called back, still clipping.

"Daya, you let us know if we can be of any more assistance in your roller derby adventure, all right?" Alma said.

Bee added, "Oh, it'll be an advencha all right! She'll be on Kat's team, Alma! A Killa Honey! Won't that be somethin'?" Yolanda gave a stiff nod beside her.

"Oh, uh—I'm actually not on a team yet. I'm trying out next week. I might not even make it."

Alma tugged on one of my hoodie strings. "Not with that attitude you won't." She smiled, which took the edge off the defensiveness rising inside of me at her minor chastisement. "I'll bet you not only make the team, but that you show those girls a thing or two about skating with style and flair!"

Style and flair. Not really what I was going for, but I couldn't tell this graceful woman that I was more interested in smashing the shit out of myself and others. I mean, she looked like she could've done some damage in her day, but from what she'd taught me tonight and the way she spoke about roller skating, the brute strength and pain of derby didn't seem to be her focus. I let her think what she wanted, though.

"Uh, yeah—maybe. But thanks for the offer—I'm sure I'll need more help." I wasn't used to wanting to be around too many people, but I found myself not completely opposed to it right now.

Alma called out over her shoulder to Joe, "Darling, would you run inside and get one of our cards, please?"

"Nothing I'd love to do more, sweetheart!" Joe called back, tearing across the yard and into the house. He returned in less than thirty seconds, leaped toward us, and held out a "card" that looked more like photocopy paper cut into a wonky circle—meant to be wheel-shaped, I supposed. The paper read ALMA & JOE: ROLLIN' SINCE THE '70S. WELL-LOVED ROLLER SKATES AT AFFORDABLE PRICES—

WHEEL THIS WAY! Their phone number was at the bottom.

"Cool. Thanks," I said, and tucked the card into my hoodie pocket.

After I'd removed the skates and paid for all my equipment, the four of them waved goodbye to me as I walked off. I flung the bag with my new skates over my shoulder, the weight of them sending a satisfying thump against my back.

Chapter Fourteen

The next day, Friday, I switched to my outdoor wheels and brought my skates to the park to show Fee.

"Whoa, these are sweet, Daya!"

I didn't know if it was adrenaline or nerves or both, but my words flew out. "Right? You should've seen the dude who sold them to me. He was a work of art. Pop art. Or some kind of weird art that moves when you move. Like in a fun house." Fee stared at me. "Whatever. The point is, this shit's happening, Fee, and I'm stoked. And nervous. Tryouts are next week and I need to learn how to skate like a pro, ASAP." Alma and the others had helped a lot, but I wasn't going to just count on that to get me on this team.

"Well, shit, what're we waiting for, then?"

"You'll help?"

"Sure—I mean, I've spent way more time on ice skates than roller skates, but I think I can still help you out. Show me what you got!"

We spent the next hour practicing crossovers, stops, and strides.

As we paused to catch our breath, Fee asked, "So there's no hitting on Monday?"

"Yeah, it sucks."

They shrugged. "Makes sense, though. Roller derby involves more than just hitting, Bruiser."

The look on their face—serious, questioning—made my stomach sink. Fee had all kinds of nicknames for me, but the way they said "Bruiser" now made me feel like they knew more than I wanted them to. I tried to hide my unease beneath sarcasm.

I held my chin with my thumb and forefinger and cocked an eyebrow. "Does it, though? Really?"

Fee tipped their head to the side, their face remaining earnest. "Yes, really." After an uncomfortable beat, the seriousness fell away and their eyes thinned into a squint. "Listen, sister, if you want on this team, you're gonna need a lot more than brute strength. I mean, I know you're hella tough, and that'll be an asset as well, but you've got more to offer, ya know?"

Relieved that the weird moment had passed, I let my face convey my skepticism. Fee noticed and continued, "*For instance*, your balance is excellent, you've got great endurance, and I have no doubt your teammates will be able to trust you to give it your all."

I rolled my eyes. "'Kay, yeah, whatever, but my *real* strength is strength, and I can't wait to show Kat and the

Honeys that. So now help me work on skating with contact."

"You mean you want me to smash you around for a bit while you skate?"

"Yup."

"Okay." They paused. "But only if you wear your gear."

"What gear?"

"You got elbow pads and stuff, right?"

"Yeah, but they're at home."

"Why?"

"'Cause I never skate with padding. I'll wear it when I need to."

"You *need* to *now*, Daya. Roller derby's a whole new bag of bruises . . . and more. There's being tough and then there's being foolish. You're not foolish." That steady, somber look was back. "Go get your stuff." They crossed their arms.

I crossed my arms too and held Fee's eyes, ready to win a staring match. But what I saw in their eyes was concern and a plea, and the look put me off-balance. I wasn't used to Fee getting serious with me.

"Daya, roller derby could be really awesome for you, but maybe not just because of the hits, you know? Now go."

Jesus. So pushy. Fee was lucky I needed their help on this so badly. "Okay, *fine*," I said. "Gimme twenty minutes."

By the end of the weekend, I was starting to feel a bit better about my skating skills, but I still wasn't sure how I'd measure up against the other people trying out. Fee had shown me lots of basics and helped me practice staying strong against contact, but I needed to be extra good if I couldn't depend entirely on my hitting skills.

All weekend, I spent hours watching skating videos on YouTube instead of doing my homework, paying close attention to how the skaters moved side to side and almost step-shuffled across the track instead of just skating, or how they transitioned from one direction to another.

I also went to the skate park in the morning when no one was there, so I could practice everything I'd seen. On Sunday I went for a superlong skate—up some hills for endurance, along the Seawall to dodge Rollerbladers and dog walkers, and backward around and around the cement track at my high school.

By the time I got home around dinnertime, my legs were jelly. I'd taken more than a few nosedives and tumbles, and after my shower, I took stock of the day's war wounds.

Standing mostly naked in front of the mirror in my bedroom, I started counting. Tallying my bruises had become a daily habit by now. Immediately after I bruised myself, I could barely look at my body. I knew what I was doing had weakness in it, and that just boiled up a different kind of guilt and discomfort in my chest.

But later, like now, something about assessing each bruise calmed me, gave me focus. I'd press into each one to judge its tenderness, measure some of the larger ones to see if they matched or beat out my biggest bruise of seven inches—the result of a brutal and beautiful plunge off my board a few months ago.

That bruise had bloomed across my hip bone, the deep purple in the center reaching outward into a greenish yellow. I'd pressed the tips of my fingers into the middle—the darkest spot—wincing at the pain and then pressing harder.

Hip bruises could last for days, if you did it right. And no one could see them, so I could avoid the concerned looks and assumptions and questions. They had the added bonus of being felt as I walked, a soreness reaching across my hip bone each time my leg hinged forward and back. A constant reminder that the bruise was there, blood spreading into the muscle like paint across tissue paper. A reminder that my pain was mine only and I could control it.

None of my current bruises matched that one, but the soreness in my legs from all the skating I'd done in the past three days gave me some satisfaction as well. I didn't know how ready I was for these tryouts, but I knew I'd done all I could to prepare. I was surprised to find that that felt like an accomplishment too.

Chapter Fifteen

The next day I woke up with some intense shit stirring in my stomach, and my morning headboard bruising had little effect over the sensation.

Getting through the school day was more painful than ever, my nerves and excitement making it impossible to focus on whatever we were doing in class. When the final bell rang, I was relieved to escape and I headed home to grab my equipment, which I'd snuck into the house and kept hidden in my room. Priam and Vicki never stepped foot in there. I wasn't completely sure why I didn't want to tell them about roller derby. Partly, I knew they wouldn't approve: skateboarding was incomprehensible enough to them, and I could just imagine their response to roller derby.

"They do *what*? On *skates*?"

"How *beastly*!"

But also, I guess I was maintaining my balancing act with

them. That attempt to reintroduce me to boxing had skirted dangerously close to breaking a pact I thought we'd all silently agreed on: to avoid the past, my parents, and anything to do with them. I needed to reestablish our boundaries, and avoiding sharing of any kind seemed like the best option right now.

Once I'd grabbed my equipment and thrown it all into an old duffel bag, I waited outside for Fee. The rink was far by bus, and I'd begged them for a ride to the tryouts. They'd agreed, but I needed to help them and Caihong with some errands beforehand. I suspected it was their way of distracting me from my nerves too.

The "errands" consisted of helping paint Fee's mother's shed. Which was less of a shed and more of a small house with gardening stuff in it. And by gardening stuff, I mean a sit-down lawn mower and enough equipment to supply a small landscaping business. Which was what Fee's mum ran.

I didn't know any of this until Fee told me while handing me a can of paint and a paint roller.

The three of us painted for a while, listening to Fee sing along to their ridiculous eighties playlist as we did. I hadn't spent a ton of time with Fee and Cai together, and I snuck glances at them now, as they traded kisses between brushstrokes and such. Even though I had no interest in being in a serious relationship, I liked seeing the two of them together. They made everything look so natural and simple. No overdone antics like Priam and Vicki, no fighting—just a chill vibe and easy laughter.

"Hey, how're you feeling about the tryouts, Killa?" Fee asked.

I stooped to roll paint over my brush. "Fine, I guess. I mean, besides wanting to throw up."

Fee laughed and translated for Cai. "You'll be great, Daya," Fee repeated for Cai as she signed her response. "Fee said you're a good skater."

I gave Fee a questioning look.

They shrugged. "Like I said, you're more than all those rippling muscles, kid."

"Yeah, yeah," I scoffed, laying on a coat of paint.

"Marvelous!" A small brown woman appeared on the pathway from the house. Some—not all—of her straight black hair toppled around her head in a loose bun, while the rest flung about her face. She signed *Hello* to Cai and then said, "This looks professional!"

"Hey, Ma—this is Daya. Daya, this hooligan is my mum, Dotty."

Something in Fee's casual closeness with their mum caused my chest to tighten. I couldn't imagine ever calling Amma a hooligan. I wouldn't be able to call her anything now. I shook these thoughts away to focus on the smiling being in front of me. "Hi"—I wiped my hand on my sweats and stuck it out—"nice to meet you."

Dotty slapped my hand away and wrapped her arms around my waist. Her floppy bun barely reached my nose. How was this tiny woman Fee's mother? I let my arms fall loosely over her shoulders in my best impression of a hug and watched Fee and Caihong exchange an amused look. "Ma! Boundaries, woman!" Fee called out.

Dotty scoffed and finally pulled away after much more time than I was comfortable with, then grabbed me by both hands and said, "Many thanks for helping to paint my shed, Daya. For your trouble, how about I make you the best Gujarati meal you've ever had!" Each syllable and consonant rang out like its own little entity.

"Oh, no—it's okay. Fee's already paying me back by being my personal chauffeur." I smiled before I knew what I was doing.

Dotty sucked her teeth in scorn, and the sound tweaked something in my brain. My first instinct was to squeeze my palms, but Dotty's hands were in the way. I cracked my neck instead. "Are you trying to tell me you don't want my home-cooked food?"

I glanced at Fee, who was giving me an *Are you?* face.

"No, no—I'd love to join you," I said, my words tumbling out.

She made that upside-down smile brown mothers do best. "That's what I thought. And you better bring your parents, too, okay?"

Without thinking, I yanked my hands away and squeezed them tight.

Fee came forward. "Oh, Ma, Daya lives with her aunt and uncle." They looked at me. "And they're a bit of a handful, aren't they, Daya?"

My words weren't coming and I didn't want to talk about

this shit anyway, so I just nodded and kept squeezing, trying to gather the pain rising in my chest into my hands.

Fee glanced at my fists, then added, "Ma, we've gotta run—we'll finish the job in the next couple of days, okay?"

Dotty was giving me a once-over, her eyebrows knit together. "Of course—no rush." To me, she said, "Daya, I hope I haven't said anything wrong. I'm sorry if I did. Please come for a meal sometime anyway. Bring anyone you like!"

I forced a nod, then barely got out a "Thank you."

In the car, Fee eyed me up in the rearview mirror. "Sorry about that, Daya. You okay?"

"Yup. Fine," I said, pressing the belt buckle into the palm of my hand.

Chapter Sixteen

Fee drove me to the arena where the tryouts were being held. They said they'd be back in a couple of hours to get me.

But before I got out of the car, they said, "Hey—you're gonna blow them away, all right? Just skate as hard as you can, focus on the basics, and show 'em you'll be someone they can depend on. You got this, kid."

I nodded and said, "Right, thanks." But as I walked toward the entrance, Fee's words shook out a new fear in me. Skating hard and doing the basics was one thing—both had improved over the past few days—but being a dependable teammate was a whole other thing. Trying to be dependable sounded like a really great way to disappoint people. And if I screwed up and let everyone down, no one was going to want me on their team. And if I didn't make this team, how the hell else would I hold down all this stuff trying to push its way out?

When I entered the arena, I was greeted by a woman from

the team named Charlotte, with cropped hair and a shirt that said INDIGENOUS AF on it. She looked to be maybe the same age as my mum had been—in her forties—and the same height, too. Lighter brown skin, though, and definitely a lot butchier. She had me fill out some forms and grab a sticky name tag, which I was asked to add my pronouns to as well. I heard Fee in my head saying, *Damn right.*

Once I'd finished with the forms, Charlotte took a quick look at them and said, "Daya?" I nodded. "Cool. Welcome, Daya. You can head over there and get your gear on." My face must have shown my uncertainty, because she added, "Don't worry, girl. We want you newbies to leave loving roller derby. All you gotta do is work your butt off." A friendly wink followed, which actually helped a bit.

But as I checked out the competition while I suited up, I noticed there were a lot of tough-as-mofo-looking people here. Folks who looked like they knew what they were doing. Who looked like they might have bought their skates new and understood the rules better than I did. I hitched my gym bag higher up on my shoulder and gripped the hell out of the strap, trying again to force some feeling into my left palm, but only getting a dull satisfaction out of it. I reminded myself why I was here, how much I needed this, and tried to psych myself back up.

As I strapped on my gear, I heard, "Hey." Shanti appeared in front of me, wearing a sweet ball cap with COOLEST GRANDPA EVER across the front and carrying a case of water bottles in one hand.

"Hey." I looked at her, remembering her lukewarm text. She remained standing in front of me.

She was hesitant. I was distracted. And guarded. Now what?

She adjusted her glasses. Without warning, my heart softened a little. Against my will, I blurted, "I like your hat."

She tipped it with her free hand. "Thanks." Pause. "I like your . . . elbow pads?" Her nose scrunched up as she said this, pushing her glasses even farther up her face—what should have looked nerdy seemed really damn cute.

No, Daya.

"So, you ready for this?" she asked, stepping a little closer.

"For what?" *Ugh.* "Yes, I mean, yeah. I think so? I don't know. I mean, what do you think?" *Fer fuck's sake. Get it together.*

A slight frown creased her brow. "You'll be fine, Daya. Just do what you're good at." She pressed her fingers around my forearm and let them slide away as she walked by me, sending goose bumps across my skin. I tried to shake away the feeling.

Right. What I'm good at.

At seven o'clock, Kat and two other girls from the Killa Honeys—their name tags said *Lena/Mz. Biz (she/her)* and *Dominique/Fury (she/her/they/them)*—started calling people over to the center of the track. Looking around, it seemed like there were a lot of girls trying out. I counted at least twenty-five. *Shit.*

I wished I could have at least said hi to Kat before the tryout began—just to get myself on her radar again—but I never got a chance. I'd spotted her, but she'd been surrounded by a group of googly-eyed fans.

"All right, wannabes! Listen up. Get over here and sit your asses down," Dominique yelled to the rest of us. She was muscled, like Kat, but about six inches shorter. Her confidence made her seem ten feet tall, though. Once we'd done as we were ordered, Kat, Lena, and Dominique folded their arms and scrutinized us, their lips everything from pursed to smirking.

"Fresh meat!" Kat shouted. A ripple of laughter moved through the crowd seated on the floor. "That's you, by the way. And I wouldn't laugh. This shit's gonna be hard as hell, and we're not here to babysit you."

So much for just wanting us to "leave loving roller derby."

"We need folks who know how to rock and roll on the track," she continued. "So you better leave your blood, sweat, and tears out here!" Next thing I knew, Kat called out, "Catch me, bitches!" and we were on our skates and racing around the track after her.

I already knew that speed wasn't going to be my selling point, but it was clear within the first thirty seconds that about half the people trying out were way faster than me. A handful seemed to have no trouble gaining on Kat and then keeping pace with her. This small group of speedsters lapped another small group of super-slow folks. Luckily I wasn't in that last group, but I wasn't too far ahead of them either. With Kat's posse only a few feet behind me, I pushed every bit of strength I had into my quads, down my knees and calves, and out through my skates. I may not have been the fastest, but I knew how to push through pain.

After several laps, Dominique finally let loose a whistle and we all slowed to a stop in front of her. As I huffed and puffed into my knees, Kat whooped, and I looked up to see her high-fiving the six girls in her group of show-offs. I wiped the sweat off my forehead and straightened up. This wasn't the strongest start, and I felt frustrated with myself already.

I was further irritated by the fact that Kat still hadn't even made eye contact with me, and I wasn't sure what that meant. Did she not want to be associated with me? In case I was shit on the track? Or maybe she'd just forgotten about me.

"How many of you shaggy Muppets think you wanna be jammer?" Lena shouted, hands on her hips, skates slipping forward and back like she was revving up her engine. Two long black braids stuck out from her helmet and swung back and forth as she swiveled her head around at us. Alma'd be glad to see another "chocolate" girl on the track.

A few girls looked confused, like they didn't even know what a jammer was. *Jesus. At least do your homework,* I thought, with a little smugness. Several girls did raise their hands, though. Lena took a long look at all of them and snickered. "Can't wait to see you try, tater tots. Everyone always wants to score points. You're gonna have to be as good as Kat here before we let you anywhere near jammer. For now, don't worry about positions—just focus on the drills and skills, baby bees!"

For the next hour, we progressed through several skating

drills—most of which I'd seen during my YouTube marathon. I definitely wasn't the strongest skater in the pack, but Fee was right—my balance was far superior to most (thank you, skateboarding), and my lack of fear over getting hurt allowed me to try everything they threw at us without hesitation. By the end of the hour, I was starting to feel a bit better about my performance, despite the persistent niggling in my brain telling me I didn't have everything it would take to make this team.

At one point, Dominique randomly paired us up and demonstrated with Lena that we were going to practice holding our ground on skates while pushing up against someone. *Finally*, I thought, *some damn contact!*

My partner was roughly my height but nowhere near as thick. She seemed to be all elbows and legs. Her name tag said *Gwen (she/her)*. When we got paired up, she gave me a head nod, but not much else. *Friendly.*

"Hey," I said. Another head nod from her. *Okay, that's all you're getting from me, then.*

We were meant to push up against each other—not hard enough to force one another to the track, just with enough pressure to test out our stance and see if we could maintain our ground. When Dominique blew her whistle, all of us began pushing on one another, adjusting our skates as we needed to, giving and taking ground as we leaned into each other.

Gwen was stronger than she looked and started out pushing me harder than necessary. So naturally, I reciprocated. I could respect a good, all-out effort. But then she let up and stepped a couple of inches backward, which made me lose my balance and topple over sideways. Landing on my hands and knees, I quickly looked up to see if Kat and the others were watching—they weren't. I was thankful they hadn't seen me on the ground, but I also realized if they hadn't seen the stunt Gwen had just pulled, I'd have to deal with it myself—which was fine by me.

I got up, fists curled and face hot. Gwen was just standing there, hands on her hips like nothing had happened. Like she was impatiently waiting for me to get my shit together. *That's how you want to play it, huh? Game on, asshole.*

Without making eye contact or acknowledging her little trick, I skated back beside her and got low into my stance. She did the same and started pushing into me right away. I was ready for her, though, and didn't hold back. When she tried to swerve away again, I kept low enough to maintain my balance and managed to keep my shoulder against hers, moving with her and shoving harder. Before she could try and shift away again, I generated all the force I could and sent it up through my shoulder to send her flying sideways. She hit the deck like a sack of bones (which she kind of was), her helmet knocking the ground and her face twisted in pain.

Everyone around us stopped the drill. Kat, Lena, and Dominique skated over.

"What's happening over here, kids?" Lena said, mainly addressing me.

I couldn't say anything—my head and chest were boiling with anger. I just shrugged.

Kat rolled over to me while Dominique went to help Gwen up. "Daya, what's the deal?"

I figured if anyone would understand what the "deal" was, it would be Kat. I forced myself to speak. "You know how it is when someone's pissing you off. You take care of it."

She folded her arms in front of her. "That's how you deal with drunk assholes, maybe, but not folks who might end up being your teammates."

Seriously? What about sober assholes who play shitty tricks during a drill? I wanted to say, but I wasn't a snitch and didn't want to sound like I couldn't handle my own shit.

"Fine. Whatever." I looked away, trying to avoid eye contact with anyone, but ended up making eye contact with Shanti, who was watching from the stands, feet perched on the railing in front of her and a book in her hands. A *book*. At a roller derby tryout. But she was looking up at the moment, like everyone else, and when our eyes met, she blinked and frowned. I directed my eyes to the ground in front of me.

Lena broke the awkwardness, shouting, "All right, my feisty little chunks of cheese, break time! Grab a sip of water and get your sweet asses back here in five minutes. No sitting, though—keep those muscles moving!"

Dominique skated Gwen over to a bench—to look her over, I guess. I hoped Kat would just let it go, but she remained in front of me, hands moving to her hips. I still avoided eye contact.

"You think you can cool off enough to keep going?"

I just shrugged again. I definitely did not feel cool enough to respond in words. This was some full-on bullshit and I was extra angry that Kat didn't seem to get it.

"Okay, guess not. Why don't you head outside and do whatever you need to do to get your head on right."

What? No way! I didn't want to miss any of the tryout. "I'm fine," I ground out between my teeth.

"It wasn't really a suggestion, Daya. Just go take a few minutes. There'll still be plenty of chances for you to prove yourself." I needed to prove myself *now.* When I just stood there, staring at my skates and shifting them forward and back, she added, "Go."

I finally turned and skated toward the exit, ignoring the looks I knew I was getting from the others. Not bothering to take off my skates, which I realized was terrible for them but was too pissed to care about at the moment, I banged my way out the entrance doors and looked around for something metal and hard.

Spotting some bike racks shaped like rounded triangles a few feet away, I skated to them and looked around to make sure no one else was nearby. I placed my right hand on one section of the rack for stability, and then slammed my left hand down on the cold metal four or five times. But each time I did, instead of relief, my eyes just became wetter and wetter. If this stopped working *and* I'd just screwed up my chances of making this team, what was I supposed to do?

"Daya?"

I released the metal and stood up. My chest shuddered. I

wiped my eyes and turned around. Shanti was standing by the
doors, her hands gripping her book in front of her, her face
somewhere between concern and shock.

"Are you . . . okay?"

I didn't want her here. I cleared my throat. "Yeah—just
needed to blow off some steam is all. I'm fine. I'll be back
inside in a minute. Just . . . need to be alone." The words felt
like marbles tumbling out of my mouth.

"Oh . . . okay." She hesitated. "I saw, by the way—that
other girl. I know you were just frustrated. I'll make sure Kat
knows."

"Whatever. Doesn't matter to me what you do."

Her head tilted a little. I expected her to turn and leave—
like I wanted her to—but she didn't. Instead her hands dropped
to her sides and she walked right up to me, taking me by surprise. I could feel my left palm pulsing.

She looked me so squarely in the eyes I leaned back a little,
trying to maintain some kind of barrier between us. "I think it
does matter to you." She glanced down at my hand and added,
"Be careful with your body in there. You'll need it to make the
team, you know?" She blinked and swallowed. I did the same.
The barrier between us remained, but barely.

She turned and left me to try and reassemble the shield I'd
worked so hard to build.

When I was little, I would sit mesmerized as my mum dressed
herself in a sari. I remember her wearing them almost every

day back then. As I grew older, she began to wear them less and less. Eventually, she wore them only for special occasions. I remember wondering why she stopped—she'd always looked like some kind of precious stone or something when she had one on. Like an emerald or a ruby with glimmering hints of silver and gold.

Watching her as a kid, I'd try to follow the wraps and folds, tucks and pleats—not because I'd wanted to wear one, mind you, but because I always thought it was some kind of magic trick. Like one of those cup games where you had to follow the magician's hands closely to see where they moved the cup with the stone beneath it. My mother was the magician and her hands wove around her body, hiding bits and pieces of herself with every twist and turn. By the time she pinned the last fold, I'd always be lost, several steps behind but still completely spellbound. She'd enfolded herself into a magical shield, and I wished I could do the same.

Chapter Seventeen

I had a hard time getting my wheels to carry me back into the rink. They seemed to take me around the outer corridor instead, wheeling me in a giant circle while I tried to gather enough of myself together to take me back inside. It'd be so easy to grab my stuff and get the hell out of here. But the stubborn part of me didn't want to let some annoying girl push me out of this tryout. To let the others think I was weak. And some other part of me—one that I didn't want to admit was there—knew Shanti was right. I cared about this. Mainly because it might help me to cope. But I also couldn't help thinking about Alma and Joe, Bee, Yolanda, Kat, the rest of the Honeys . . . Shanti. I guess I didn't want to walk away from all that, either. The thought surprised and scared the hell out of me.

The rest of the tryout finished without incident. Gwen the jerk was completely fine and avoided me, the remaining drills focused mainly on more individual skating skills, and most people seemed to forget or not really care about the scene I'd caused. A few kept their distance, which didn't bother me that much. I managed to get through to the end by channeling the rest of my frustration into my skates—pushing the anger through my legs, into my wheels.

It was the confusion I'd felt after the exchange with Shanti that I had trouble pushing down and away, however. I was pissed she'd seen me dealing with my shit, and that she hadn't been scared away by it. I avoided looking her way for the rest of the tryout but found myself constantly aware of where she was and wondering if she was looking at me. Both hoping she was and wasn't. Hating every minute of it.

At the end of practice, Lena, Dominique, and Kat gathered us all up.

"Okay, fresh meat—not bad today," Kat started. "Some of you even looked like you knew what you were doing. Your skating skills are going to play a massive role in whether you make the team or not. The other piece that's going to matter a whole shitload is your team play. We're gonna focus on that next time, so come ready to show us you know how to kick ass *while* working together."

Kat definitely ended her sentence with a glance my way, which just brought my frustration and trepidation back up into my chest.

How the hell was I supposed to impress them with my team play when I'd never played on a team? Who was going to believe I knew how to play well with others at this point?

* * *

I'd wanted to play softball when I was eleven or twelve. I remember asking Thatha if I could join the Little League team near us because three girls in my class played on it and always messed around at lunch together. One would pitch, another would hit, and the third would catch and pass back to the pitcher. It was kind of like watching a sporty circus act—a fluid motion of passing, hitting, catching, with each girl's athletic body reacting to the other's actions. I remember thinking it looked so cool.

But when I'd asked my dad about it at the dinner table, he'd replied, "When will you box if you're playing softball? Besides, softball is for wimps, Daya"—except it sounded like "vimps" when he said it. "It won't teach you how to be strong, to stand on your own. You better just forget about it."

Amma had listened quietly. I wondered if she would have preferred that I choose softball over boxing, though. If she would rather I play a sport for "vimps" instead of one that involved punching and being punched. But she never said anything, never came to my aid—and I remember being mad at her for that. Being angrier at her than at my dad. I was definitely learning to stand on my own by then, but I guess I wished I could choose when I wanted to or not.

A possible cure for my teamwork deficiencies fell out of my pocket while I was throwing my dirty clothes into the washer Monday night after the tryout and Alma and Joe's card fluttered to the floor. I needed help again, and this time, no amount of equipment or skating practice or hitting was going to do it. I needed someone to show me how to play on a roller derby team.

The next day after school, I found myself at their open garage door.

"Beautiful!" I heard from inside the garage. "Stupendous!"

When I peeked around the corner, I saw Joe kneeling in front of a hulking dude with bright purple roller skates strapped to his feet. The guy was giggling, and the two of them high-fived with passion.

"Daya, what a delight!" I turned to find Alma walking toward me from the house.

"Hi, Alma." I'd called them in the morning to see if they were open that day and had time to chat. I hadn't told them that what I really needed was some kind of magical way onto the Killa Honeys. Joe, of course, had replied with several exclamatory statements.

"How are you doing, sweetheart?" Alma asked. She still wore a tracksuit, except this time it was a vibrant green. The same glossy pink shone across her lips and fingernails.

"I'm well, thank you. How are you?" Something about Alma made me want to speak in grammatically correct English.

"Oh, I'm plump and perfect, as always." She chuckled. "So when are the big tryouts?"

Just the word "tryouts" sent my stomach plunging. "They're happening. Now. The second one is tomorrow."

"Wonderful!"

Yeah. Super.

She tucked her hand into the crook of my elbow and guided me inside the garage. "Look who it is, Joe!"

Joe looked up from his debit machine, where he was processing the gigantic dude's purchases. "Daya! Welcome back, superstar!"

After Joe had taken care of his customer and it was just the three of us, Alma asked, "So, Daya, how can we help?"

I need to know how to impress the hell out of Kat. I need to bash the hell out of a bunch of tough-ass chicks. I need to prove I'm hard as hell and indispensable. Oh, and I also need to convince everyone that I'm not a hopeless teammate.

"Uh—I—"

I had no idea how to do this. Asking for skates and padding was one thing. Asking for a way to play well with others was something else. An admission. A confession that I had no idea how to be with other people. I had to swallow back a pang in my chest to speak.

"I'm . . . new to team sports."

"Oh, you've never played on a team, dear?" Alma asked.

"No. And roller derby looks so different from anything I've played before."

"That's true, madam!" Joe exclaimed. "It surely is a special sport!"

"Hmm, okay, let's see what we can do," Alma said, tapping one pink nail against her nose. "It's a bit tricky without an actual team, but we'll manage."

The next thing I knew, all three of us were geared up in skates, helmets, and padding (they insisted, I relented), and I was in the middle of the cul-de-sac with them.

"All right, Daya. You're hoping to be a blocker, correct?" Alma asked.

"Yeah." *Is it that obvious?*

"And why is that?"

I pulled my skates back and forth along the pavement. "I think I'll be good at it—I like bumping around and stuff. I guess I'm pretty tough." *I know I am.*

"Well, that will certainly help. Another important aspect of being a good blocker is working with your fellow blockers. I'm going to show you a few things about using each other to contain the jammer. It might require that you and I get a little cozy—are you all right with that?"

Staring at five-foot-nothing Alma in her roller skates, hands on hips, it was impossible *not* to be all right with that. I nodded. "Yes."

For the next hour, Alma showed me how to control a very enthusiastic Joe, who was acting as jammer. She taught me how to support her in staying sturdy by pressing my thigh against her butt cheek and sliding back and forth while staying tight with her as Joe tried to get past us. When we switched roles and she was behind me, I admired how solid she felt, despite her age and short stature.

Then she, Joe, and I practiced a triangle formation, linking up with one another and turning this way and that to keep a jammer at bay. They taught me how to brace them, to fill in any gaps a jammer might try to sneak through, and to flip places with the other blockers if needed. At one point, Joe brought out some chairs, which he placed on the outer edge of the cul-de-sac—to represent my other blockers—and they showed me how to lead the jammer (Joe again) into the cluster as a trap.

All these maneuvers took strength, for sure, but they also demanded a certain intricacy, a flexibility and quickness I hadn't realized would be involved. Alma was solid and powerful, but also hella nimble.

At the end of the hour, I said, between seriously huffy breaths, "How are you two this strong and fit at your age?" They barely seemed to be breathing hard.

"Love does all manner of magic to your body, Daya!" Joe called out to the entire neighborhood.

"That's true," Alma added. "Strength comes from all kinds of places." She accepted a peck on the cheek from Joe.

That sounded nice and all, but something told me these two regularly skated as well. I could tell I had my work cut out for me if I wanted to be an effective blocker. Not only would I have to support my fellow blockers, but I'd need to be able to adapt quickly and keep my eyes open for gaps and opportunities.

"Well, thanks for showing me all this stuff. It might actually help me to look like I know what I'm doing tomorrow," I said.

"If you can show you've got your teammates' backs and

work as hard as you did today, I think you'll be just fine, Daya," Alma said, giving my shoulder a squeeze.

I guess. I wasn't sold, but there was no way I was going to tell Alma that. "Thanks for making time for me, Alma, Joe. Can I give you some money for the lesson? Please?"

"Oh, Daya, don't be silly. It was our pleasure. Like I said, we need more chocolate on the track." She winked at me. "And I have no doubt we'll be seeing you on the track very soon."

She seemed so sure I would make the team, and while I still had my doubts, it did feel good to have this woman's confidence.

Chapter Eighteen

Now what I needed was the confidence of Kat and the others. Proving myself became the name of the game during the second tryout.

We'd started with some laps, warm-up drills, and stretching, at the end of which Lena yelled, "Baby pork chops! Hustle up!"

Dominique was standing next to Lena and without warning, she shoved Lena hard with her hip. Lena probably had about thirty pounds on Dominique, but she fell—also hard—onto the track. We all gasped, my eyes growing wide.

But Lena popped back up on her skates within seconds and flung her own hip back at Dominique, who toppled over sideways into the ground. The rest of us stared, silent and confused.

Dominique seemed to fall into a roll and continue right back up onto her skates. Then the two of them fist-bumped.

Hmm. A demonstration of sorts. And though I'd be happy to focus on knocking each other to the ground, I wondered what this had to do with team play.

Dominique and Lena looked out at us and laughed. "Don't worry," Lena reassured us, "we're not going to ask you to hit each other that hard—just a light shove will do. But before we get into any blocking drills and team stuff, you need to know how to fall. If you don't know how to get your butt back up, you may as well leave. In roller derby, hitting the floor isn't about 'if.' It's about 'when.' And that when is now, hunky monkeys. Find a partner."

Ugh. I hated being left to make our own pairings, even if being placed in pairs sometimes resulted in being matched with a jerk like Gwen.

A few girls seemed to know one another, so they instantly drifted together. The rest of us became ten years old again—the new kids at school walking into the cafeteria and searching for a place to sit.

After a few hesitant head nods and shrugs, more pairs formed. I was having a hard time making eye contact with anyone, worrying no one would want to pair up with me after last time, but in a matter of moments, I realized I was the only one without a partner. One second I was horrified. The next, Kat skated over and hip-checked me, and then I was doubly horrified. "Guess we're partners, bitch."

As we all found a space to practice knocking each other over, I quickly assessed the situation. I wasn't sure how Kat saw me after the last tryout—whether she was still disappointed in me. This was either an excellent opportunity to prove myself to her if I could fall like a champ and recover quickly, or it could be the beginning of the end if I wasn't able to handle her "light shoves"—which would, without a doubt, be harder than an average light shove.

Dominique piped up, "Keep low at all times. The minute you stand up is the minute you put yourself in some serious shit. If you know you're going down, try to go down on something padded—elbows, knees . . . a soft teammate." A few more titters. "The best fall is a small fall. Tuck your limbs in, roll with it, and get your legs up as soon as you can."

"All right, chicken nuggets, let's do this! Go easy on each other. We don't have insurance!" Lena bellowed.

"Lucky you," Kat said. "You get double practice today, since I obviously don't need it." She winked at me. A relatively friendly wink, I thought.

"Lucky me," I said, and tried a corresponding smirk to cover up my nervousness.

"All right, bend your knees. I'm coming at you from the side, so when you go down, try and go down into a roll and come back up again all in one motion."

Encouraged by what seemed to be actual coaching, I crouched low and braced myself. Kat crouched as well and came at me low and slow. When her hip made contact with mine, I could tell she was only hurling maybe 50 percent of her full force at me. Even half-assed, though, her hit was enough to throw me off-balance, and I had to cross my left foot over my right and take a couple of strides on my skates to stay standing.

I came back and lowered myself again. Kat came at me a little harder this time and I could feel myself going over, so I leaned into my right arm and aimed my kneepads at the ground. I tried using the momentum of the fall to keep rolling and then push myself back up onto my skates, but I could only get into a push-up position before resting on my knees and getting back up one skate at a time.

"Not bad, rook," Kat said. "If I'd hit you a bit harder and you'd actually been skating, you probably would've been able to get back up in one go."

Determined to show her I could take anything she threw my way, I replied, "So hit me harder, then," I said. *Give me all you got.*

Her eyebrow peaked. "You sure?"

"Perfectly sure." *This is what I'm here for.*

"Okay, you asked for it. . . ."

Her next hip check came in at about 120 percent, give or take. I flew so far across the track the others stopped to look.

Stunned at first, I took a second to sit up. My hip seared where Kat had hit me, and I had to blink to feel upright again. I got up as quickly as I could to show I was fine and sent Kat a thumbs-up. I could already anticipate how deep that hit would sink into my muscle, and the thought brought a kind of relief—relief that I'd been right about all this, that roller derby *could* bring back the release I needed.

She laughed as I skated over and gave me a fist bump. "Nice, rook. Way to play through the pain."

More like play *for* the pain.

Several hits and falls later, I was getting the hang of absorbing Kat's monumental sideswipes and rolling into my fall, then back up to standing position. Even when I didn't manage a successful "drop and roll," I still got some satisfying hip tenderness out of it. Some of the others had continued to watch us. Even better, at the end of the drill, Kat said, "You did good, rook. You're even tougher than I thought."

This acknowledgment felt like a golden light from heaven beaming down on me. I tried not to let my pleasure show, though, making sure that my toughness extended to my face.

But then she added, "Just remember *when* to be tough. You bring it when you need to protect your team."

This was obviously a reference to Gwen and dimmed the glow of her previous compliment. Clearly I'd fucked up, and though I realized I still needed to learn a lot about being on a team, I didn't get how putting up with some girl's bullshit helped the team. But knowing I needed Kat's approval, I kept my mouth shut for now.

Dominique called out, "All right, now that you know how to fall, we can get into some proper team play and blocking practice." They took us through some drills that had us skating together in threes to keep the jammers contained and showed us a few simple steps to bracing like the ones Alma had shown me—hands on hips, shoulders to shoulders. I realized quickly that you could get plenty of bruises from your very own team-mates as we pulled and pushed each other into place.

After that, the next thirty minutes involved many, many more opportunities for bruising. It was *precisely* what I'd been craving. They had half of us travel in a big pack around the track while the other half tried to bump and clobber our way through—no hands or arms, just hips and shoulders. Not only did I prove I could keep girls behind me, I also made it clear I could bash my way through the pack. Some girls were way more tentative than I thought they'd be, considering they were trying out for roller derby, while a few of the hardier chicks were stronger and more daring, but not necessarily great at keeping their balance after giving or getting hits. I kept myself low and sturdy, standing my ground and moving other bodies with my own, completely unafraid of the consequences—in fact, *inviting* the consequences.

But despite my own tendencies, I also heard Alma's voice in my head, guiding me into a supportive role. I tried a few of her moves, pushing fellow blockers into the way of oncoming skaters, holding them fast against the bodies coming our way. A couple of folks even caught on and started banding together with me to stop folks from coming through. The actions strained against my instincts, which were pressing me to take care of myself and not worry about anyone else. A few people definitely pissed me off when they didn't move the way I wanted them to or when they didn't seem to get what I was trying to do. I probably confused a few people too. I wasn't perfect, but Alma's pointers actually helped keep some skaters at bay—even without much contact. Sometimes all it took was an agile move or two to usher people one way or another.

During a short water break, Charlotte, who I'd noticed had been especially kind to the newbies during both tryouts—high-fiving us and sharing pointers here and there—skated over to me. "Hey, girl—some nice bracing out there. You played before?"

I tried to keep my pride under control. "No—just been practicing."

She nodded and eyed me up and down. "Sweet. Keep it up, awesome sauce." She held up her hand for a high five.

"I will," I said, slapping her palm with mine and feeling the sweet sting of success.

The rest of the tryout consisted of some easy maneuvering drills and a few attempts to show us some plays—likely to weed out those of us who couldn't follow simple directions.

After two hours, aches formed in places I didn't know I had, and my shirt was dark with sweat.

"Good team play out there. It's gonna be super important when they make their decisions." Shanti appeared while I was loosening the laces on my skates. She knelt down next to me. "How'd it feel?"

I still felt weird about our last interaction by the bike racks but tried not to let it show. If I ignored it, hopefully she wouldn't bring it up again. And I *did* feel good about my showing—I hadn't backed down from any of the brutal stuff, nor had I made any big mistakes that I could tell. And I think I even showed I could be a decent teammate. I definitely felt I was in the top third of this group overall. But I didn't want to sound like a dick, so all I said was, "Not bad," and kept focusing on my laces.

"You seemed to match up well with Kat out there. Not many people can withstand her hits like that." The words sounded like a compliment, but her voice seemed almost disappointed.

"You think?" I needed Kat to be impressed with me, but I was confused by the tone of Shanti's voice. I looked at her. She was studying my face, which made me distinctly uncomfortable.

"Yeah. You two seem to have a lot in common."

Again, this should have felt like a compliment, but didn't. What was up with this girl?

I pulled off my skates and tried to ignore the terrifying sensation settling into my stomach—the one that wanted to understand her and know what she really thought of me. To know whether I'd impressed her. But I had to remind myself that I'd proven myself to Kat, which mattered the most right now, and that was enough. It had to be.

"Daya, your swing is too low. Straighten out, like this," my dad said, taking the bat from me and nudging me aside. He took his stance and sliced the air in a deliberate, slow movement. "See? But you're doing this." He brought the bat back behind him and then swung it forward, dipping it at a ridiculous angle as though he were taking a golf swing.

I rolled my eyes. "Hardly, Thatha."

He gave me a serious look and handed me the bat. "You get my point, though, huh?"

I sighed. "Yes."

Thatha hadn't agreed to let me play softball on a team, but he'd bought a bat and balls so I could just play around and see if I liked it. He rarely shifted his stance on something, so I'd been surprised when he gave me the bat and said, "Let's go see if we can turn this 'soft' ball into something a little harder!" and then laughed at his own dad joke.

But if it was anyone's fault I'd been swinging low, it was his. He'd only ever bowled a cricket ball. And in cricket, the bowler aims lower than in softball. The batter also aims lower. So my very valid theory had been that his softball pitches were generally lower than the average pitch, and hence, so were my swings.

When I'd shared my theory with him, he'd rejected the idea with his typical, "Don't try to bullshit a bullshitter, will you?"

We worked well into the evening, me trying to show him I could hit anything he threw my way.

Eventually, once he was relatively satisfied with my swing (for the time being, anyway), we'd come inside, late for dinner, as usual.

Mum hadn't complained, also as usual. She didn't argue with us anymore about boxing time cutting into mealtime or chore time or even homework time. She'd been outnumbered too many of those times, I guess. Even if she didn't approve, she kept her feelings to herself.

It wasn't my mum's approval I was seeking by then anyway. Thatha was the one showing me what I needed to succeed, and I spent my energy trying to show him I had what it took.

That night, though, she'd asked, "How was this softball?"

"We worked on turning Daya's golf swing into a softball swing," Dad replied before I had a chance to.

"Ha-ha," I said, shaking my head.

My mum paused in the middle of ripping off a piece of pol roti. "Golf swing?" She looked from me to Dad, confused.

Dad started to chuckle.

"Ignore him, Amma—he thinks he's very funny."

"I am hee-LAR-ious!" Dad added, pointing a finger at me.

The expression on my mum's face should have told me everything I needed to know—about how she felt when my dad and I shared these inside jokes, about how much she wished she were included, how she'd do anything to be part of the joke. But I guess I didn't look hard enough. I was too busy trying to prove myself to my father.

Chapter Nineteen

We'd been told at the end of the second tryout that we'd receive a text by Thursday letting us know if we'd made the team. Based on my performance, I thought I had a decent chance. But I couldn't be sure. A lot of those other people were faster than me, some more experienced, and I still wasn't convinced that being a supportive teammate was as impressive as crushing the competition. On top of that, I could only guess at how Kat might rank me, despite what Shanti had said, and I was fairly sure her vote would count the most.

I hated that I wanted this so badly but had no idea how it would go. It all felt a little too pathetic, and needing a distraction, I'd texted Fee to see if they would hang out with me Thursday after school. They'd enthusiastically agreed to meet up once they were done work and then take me to their queer ball hockey game. Likely part of their enthusiasm was linked to their attempts to make me join the team as well, but I didn't care as long as I had something to do that night.

By the end of the school day, I hadn't received any messages from the Honeys, and all I wanted to do was take my mind completely off my phone. When Fee picked me up from my place, I explained that I wanted to throw my phone out the car window.

Fee just smiled and said, "Give it to me."

"What?"

"Gimme your phone. Now."

I handed it over.

They pulled to the side of the road and turned the sound off on my cell. Then they tucked it into their back jeans pocket. "There. Now if you want to look at it, you'll have to touch my ass. I know that just makes it extra enticing, but try touching my butt and see what happens." They fake-glared at me and drove away from the curb.

I smiled and shook my head.

When we arrived at the gym, Fee shoved my phone into their bag and said I could only look at it after the game. This would be painful, but I appreciated it.

A row of metal chairs lined one wall of the gym, and I made my way over to sit in one of them and watch the game. Fee waved at me from their team bench and did a little dance, pointing to their helmet, elbow and kneepads, and mouth guard. I pretended to scratch my forehead with my middle finger.

I'd seen Fee play hockey only once before, but watching

them play now, it was clear to me how much they loved it. They weren't particularly fast or nimble, but they weren't as brutal as I thought they'd be either. They were bigger than most players on the court, but mostly used their size to defend the ball or their goalie—like a fortress—instead of throwing their body around like I tended to do (like a cannonball).

And they were *smart*. You could just see their brain calculating each pass and play—waiting patiently for the right time, the most efficient maneuver.

If they were this skillful and smooth on the ball hockey court, I wished I'd been able to see them play ice hockey and watch them trade that energy with the other players like they'd talked about.

After the game, Fee brought over a couple of people from their team and introduced me. "Daya, this is Bo and Simi. Daya's the one who skates at the park with me."

I shook their sweaty hands and said hi.

"Fee said you'd be a wicked ball hockey player, Daya. We got some spots to fill," Simi said in a singsongy voice that reminded me too much of Uncle Priam.

I shook my head at Fee, immediately seeing through their attempts to recruit me. "Ha-ha . . . yeah . . . Fee's been trying to get me to play on this team for a while."

"Why don't you?" Bo asked.

"I—well, I don't really identify as—"

"Queer?" Simi said, and gave me a not-so-subtle up-down. "You don't really need to. I mean, it's not like we need to see some kind of queer ID or something."

They all laughed and so did I, partly to conceal my grow-ing discomfort and the sudden image of a cute trucker hat that popped into my mind. Fee must have picked up on my awk-wardness, because they said, "It's cool. Daya's probably going to be too busy with roller derby to play on our hockey team anyway." They winked at me and handed me my phone, which I hadn't noticed they'd had in their hand this entire time. "Sorry, it buzzed just as I was taking it out of my bag and I couldn't help but see." They grinned enormously at me.

I quickly unlocked my phone and stared at the screen.

Congrats! Ur a Killa Honey! Fresh meat report to the butcher's (Undesirables on E. Broadway) Saturday night at 7. Bring skates. Don't come on an empty stomach. But do come with ur roller derby name and polish up those dance moves ;)

My elation at the first few words quickly turned into anxi-ety by the last sentence. But I read the first five words again to remind myself of the most important thing—I'd made the team. I was a Honey.

Chapter Twenty

By Saturday, the initial excitement of making the team had fizzled as I'd gradually become more and more apprehensive about the approaching evening events. Now I didn't just have to worry about my derby skills not being good enough, but presumably from the text, the other new recruits and I would be expected to participate in some kind of ridiculous antics as well. As explained earlier—not my forte.

I'd also need to get creative and come up with some kind of funny or clever or cool derby name. Also not my forte. Sounded like a bunch of unnecessary nonsense that was just going to make me look like a fool. I'd already worked so hard to prove I was tough and capable—now this? And where before I could at least depend on my athleticism and strength, now I wouldn't be able to depend on any of that. What was left when my muscles and skills were stripped away? I worried the answer was . . . not enough.

I'd spent most of the day in my room doing a half-assed job on my homework so that over dinner with Priam and Vicki, I could carefully explain all the items I'd checked off my school to-do list before telling them I was going out and would be home late. It worked. They seemed pleased I was sharing anything with them—even if it was just the difference between alpha decay and beta decay—and were especially happy I was heading out for a "night on the town."

"Look at our Daya Doo Wop! Socializing!" Priam exclaimed, beaming.

As they moved on to gasp in whispers about some Broadway star who'd been caught lip-synching—"Can you *imagine?* The *nerve!*"—I let my mind wander to contemplate derby names. Staring at objects on the kitchen table, I tried, *Stick a Fork in It Daya. Spicy Daya. Daya and Spice? Daya-licious. Daya . . . Dip?*

Daya Jesus Fucking Christ.

Hoping something would just come to me on the way to the bar, I left Vicki and Priam to slowly pick apart the offending Broadway fraud.

I dressed in my usual protective hoodie and jeans, adding a ball cap in case I needed to shield my eyes from any particularly shiny lights or amused stares. Before pulling on my jeans, I sat on my bed and methodically pressed into each new bruise on my thighs and arms with my fingers, to see if the *aftermath* of roller derby could help keep my unwanted emotions at bay in the same way that smashing into Kat and the others had during tryouts. I tried to draw all my focus into each layer of damage—the skin, the blood, the muscle. Get out of my head and into the parts of my body I knew I put there myself.

The release lasted only a few moments, though. By the time I arrived at Undesirables, I was right back up in my head again with all the things that could go wrong.

When I entered the bar, the entire Killa Honeys team was already there with several jugs of frothy, bright beer adorning their tables. I was grateful for the fake ID I'd bought last year off a skater guy I knew. I'd already used it as proof of age for the tryouts and hoped to hell I didn't get caught out.

Calls of "Fresh meat!" greeted me as I shuffled over. Kat was sitting at one end of a table, and the four seats next to her had a shot of something beige and creamy in front of each. Three of those seats were filled by people I recognized from tryouts. Two looked almost as anxious as I felt. The other was happily pouring beer down their throat. The last seat, I assumed, was for me.

"We got a spot—and a shot—for you right here, sister!" Kat called out, and hammered the table with her open hand, sending beer slopping over the edge of several glasses.

As I sat down, I noticed Shanti standing near the bar. She gave me a tentative wave and a smile. I still wasn't sure what was up with her, but she'd sent me a text after I'd made the team, saying Congrats :), so I gave her a head nod back, trying to ignore the twisting in my stomach that felt like more than just nervousness.

Kat addressed the whole team. "All righty, Honeys. As you know, proving yourself on the track is only half the battle. You four"—she turned to us—"have made the team *bench*. But if you want to become a full-fledged Killa, you gotta show you're part of this team *off* the track too—and that means lots of hijinks, sweet things!"

The team started hooting and clapping at this. My stomach dropped.

Kat continued, "So, we have a special challenge for you, which we'll tell you about later. You don't have to drink tonight if you don't want to, but if you can't complete the challenge—sober or not—don't be surprised if you ride the bench all season." The rest of the team laughed.

I hoped their laughter meant this wasn't for real—playing time depended on making a fool of myself tonight? Kat couldn't be serious. I wanted to take Shanti aside to ask her, but the team had already started chanting, "Shots! Shots! Shots!" and beerguzzler champ beside me had already gulped back the shot in front of them. One by one, so did the rest of us. There was no way I was getting through this night without at least a couple drinks in me. The liquid was sweet. Too sweet for my taste.

"What is this?" I asked, my lips contorting with disgust.

Kat leaned over the table. "A Blow Job. We can get you a Muff Diver if you prefer that, though. Would you?" She winked.

Huh? Now I was getting weirdness from both sisters. But seeing Kat's cocky expression and absorbing the energy from around me, I felt a surge of resolve. I tried to refocus my own energy. I needed to be steel tonight. I'd made this team—so far—and I could deal with whatever tonight was going to bring if I had to, even if it meant this foolishness. At least that was what I told myself. I responded, "I prefer whiskey, actually."

She let loose a raspy laugh. "Well, shit, let's get this tough bitch a shot of whiskey!"

The team cheered. Someone got the whiskey. I drank the whiskey. More whiskey was ordered. More whiskey was consumed.

About an hour later, I felt well lubricated. I'd been smart enough to drink plenty of water along the way too, so I had my wits about me—but the liquor had increased my resolve. I decided I wasn't fucking around tonight. I was going to show these people exactly what I was made of—muscles, steel, concrete—no matter what they threw at me. No cracks tonight. No soft edges.

The three other rookies seemed to be in various stages of drunkenness. We'd introduced ourselves at some point. The gold-medal drinker to my left was Potts—wiry, pale, and baby-faced. Grace was the next over and was the quietest of the group. She'd pulled back her curly red hair into a ponytail and looked very serious about all of this. And then there was Sage, who had that "Asian blush" Amma used to get after one glass of sherry.

Potts had drunk the most out of the four of us but was clearly well seasoned in the art of consuming vast amounts of liquor, because they didn't seem that drunk at all. Grace, I quickly realized, was one of those drinkers who gradually became more and more intense as she drank. She'd already tried to get me to talk about what it was like to be a "young person of color," to which I responded with a look that clearly conveyed how annoying that question was. Sage was just plain happy and hilarious. Thankfully, she kept interrupting Grace's attempts at serious talk with squealing appeals for high fives.

At one point, Lena placed her fingers in her mouth and released a piercing whistle that stopped everyone mid-mayhem. "Hey! Anyone wanna hear these little bitty bee-bees' derby names?"

A calamity of "Fuck yeahs" and "Damn straights" followed.

Shit.

Lena made out like she was carrying a mic and held it to Potts's chin. "Introducing . . ."

"Potty Mouth!"

Giggles and a few whoops.

Fuuuuuuck.

Lena moved the "mic" to Grace.

"Grace Under Fire!"

Clapping and cheering.

Crap crap crap.

Sage was next.

"Guru Sage!" She looked around. "Get it? Sage? Like,

wise? Like a guru? Come on, high five!" A couple of girls slapped her roaming hand.

Mother—

Lena's hand was at my chin.

I panicked and said the first thing that came to mind.

"Daya Doo Wop?"

Oh my fucking God.

There was a moment of silence. Probably for my dignity.

Then laughter. Loads and loads of laughter.

"That's real cute, Daya. But we'll work on it," Lena said, pinching my cheek.

I laughed to cover up my mortification, but my face burned. *This is what happens when you try to fit in, dummy.*

Sensing a crack in my shield, I needed to go gather myself, but as I got up to escape to the bathroom, Lena placed a pointed finger in my face.

"Not so fast, sweet cherry pie. Sit yer bumblebee butt back down." She stepped next to Kat, who'd been imbibing more than we had this whole time. "Fresh meat! It's time for the Honey Hijinks!"

At this, the rest of the team started making buzzing sounds—like bees. Another girl from the team—I think her derby name was something like Hello Titty—brought over a lumpy duffel bag and dropped it by Lena's feet. Lena unzipped the bag and began pulling out various items of costumery and clothing: feather boas, crowns and tiaras, a clown nose, fake teeth and eyelashes, something fluffy, something else fluffy, wigs, and more.

These she laid in front of us among the empty shot glasses and beer mugs. I squeezed my hands into fists and got my game face on. *No cracks, Daya. You can do this.*

"Fresh meat!" she barked again, like a drill sergeant. "You have one minute to put on at least six of these items each! If you fail in this first task, Kat will provide special assistance!"

Kat raised her glass in affirmation, swaying a little as she did.

"Honeys! Count down from sixty starting . . . NOW!"

I think all four of us took at least numbers sixty through fifty-six to shake out of our confused, tipsy stupor and start picking up the items. Not one for dressing up—despite Priam and Vicki's repeated attempts to make me do so—I eyed up the various pieces, searching for the most mundane possible. Choices were slim. As Sage ripped into the package of fake eyelashes, Potts went straight for a boa and crown. Grace seemed almost as lost as I was but managed to start pulling on a rainbow-striped vest.

I yanked off my ball cap and fitted my head with a gray wig, then placed my cap back on top of that. No way was I going to put anything in my mouth, so I skipped the fake teeth and grabbed a pink lei instead.

A pair of sparkly suspenders caught my eye and I picked them up. The team was on number thirty-four of the count-down. I managed to clip the suspenders to the back of my pants without too much trouble, but when I tried to pull the front pieces over my shoulders, I accidentally let go of one and it flung backward into Charlotte, who yelped and smacked me on my ass. As I struggled with the suspenders, the team counted out thirty to eighteen.

At seventeen I finally got them on, but that didn't leave me much time to get another three items on my body. I shoved the clown nose onto my face and frantically searched the table for two more pieces. Sage and Grace had used up the eyelashes, and Potts was wearing all the boas by this point. The only remaining items were a pair of chaps and a headband with alien antennas on it.

Willing my brain to suddenly become drunker than it was, I planted the headband on over my hat and wig, then picked up the chaps. As I did, the team counted out one and then started buzzing like bees again to signal that we were out of time.

Everyone else had managed to get their six items on.

"Looks like you need some help, rook!" Lena called out over the hooting and clapping. "Kat, what d'ya have for our little piece of popcorn chicken here?"

Kat stood up woozily and dug into the duffel bag, which apparently had more items in it in case some inept rookie couldn't dress herself in time.

From the bag, she pulled out a pair of lacy panties that looked like they belonged in a porn mag and a bra that may have been Madonna's—at least from what I'd seen from photos of her back in the day—pointy cups extending far enough to jab your eyes out.

"Come 'ere, rook," Kat said. Her eyes had a bright glaze over them. She was well and truly sauced.

In response, I finished the third of a beer in front of me in three gulps, which earned a few hoots. Shuffling over to Kat, I tried to psych myself up. *Suck it up, Daya. If it means being part of the team. Suck. It. Up.*

When I stood in front of her, she indicated with her finger to step closer.

Once I did, she glanced around at the others and bounced her eyebrows up and down a few times, causing some titters and catcalls.

Christ, this was so effing unnecessary.

Staring at me the whole time, she lowered herself into a squat and held the panties out in front of me to step into. I did, almost losing my balance but refusing to use her for stability, and she slid them up my legs, which took forever because she was hammered and barely able to balance herself. When she got to my knees, I let my irritation get the best of me and reached down to yank them up the rest of the way. In doing so, I accidentally (maybe) knocked Kat's knees on the way back up and she toppled backward onto her ass. A few people laughed, but mostly, a simultaneous and emphatic "Ohhhhhh" spread across the bar, followed by silence except for the music and a few clinking glasses.

Kat propped herself up on her elbows and looked at me from the floor, her face a mixture of disbelief and maybe even a little respect? I knew I should say sorry, even if I wasn't, but the word parked itself at the back of my throat. Kat glanced sideways at the rest of the team and grinned. Her next words were, "Whoa, rook—if you wanted to get me on my back, all you had to do was wear those panties and ask."

Everyone else roared with approval, and Kat laughed.

Looking down at the porn panties snug around my crotch, I felt ridiculous. The laughter didn't help. But I had to play along—make sure they all knew I could handle myself. I forced my lips into a smirk.

Kat got up and said, "Turn around, rook."

I turned, barely masking an eye roll.

"Arms out in front!" she barked.

I brought my arms up with as much enthusiasm as I could muster, egged on by the hoots and hollers. Still behind me, Kat edged close enough that I could feel her chin over my right shoulder and her breath at my cheek—a little too close for my comfort. A vein in my neck pulsed. I shifted a bit to the left and stared straight ahead.

Steel.

One of the other Honeys yelled, "Wait! That's my bra!" and I was surprised to turn and see that the voice belonged to Shanti. "So I should get to do the honors, shouldn't I?" She'd made her way from the bar to Kat and me. I wasn't sure if she was drunk too or what, because this seemed like a bold move for her. And also, there was no way this was her bra. Or anyone's bra. Except maybe Madonna's.

Kat looked a little irritated, but the rest of the team loved this development, so she surrendered the bra to Shanti.

I was now standing in frilly panties over my jeans, a pink lei, gray wig, alien headband, and clown nose with Shanti in front of me. I could feel sweat dripping down my back and down my ass crack. *Super.*

The entire team shouted wild encouragements like "Boob it up, booby!" and "Double Ds for free!"

Among the clamor, Shanti leaned in a little as she fiddled with the straps and asked as casually as possible, "You okay?"

The way she said it—earnestly, honestly, and clearly not drunk at all—melted away some of the steel. I wondered if she'd taken over from Kat because she could see how drunk Kat was. Or maybe . . . she was just trying to help me out. Any which way, I was kind of glad it was Shanti doing it and not Kat, even though this was all still way outside my comfort zone.

"Go for it." I tried to lift the corner of my mouth a bit to show her I meant it, but wasn't sure if I succeeded, since my face was starting to feel numb—from the drinks, but also from sustained tension.

As Shanti draped the straps over my arms and pulled them up toward my shoulders, I could feel her hands shaking. Once she'd gotten the cups against my chest, she made her way behind me and fastened the clasps against my back. She must have felt me strain a bit against the tightness of the bra, because she began loosening it, her fingers gliding between the straps and my shoulders.

Something about the movement made the tension in my face release. And standing there, even with these ridiculous, pointy things extending from my chest, I started to feel a little loosened as well.

Shanti stood in front of me, hands by her sides, inspecting the situation. We looked at the pointy things. We looked at each other. She burst out laughing. I couldn't help but let out a laugh too. Everyone cheered because everyone was drunk.

Everyone except Kat, who, by the time I glanced over to her, was yelling at the bartender for another drink. She still looked irritated for some reason.

I didn't have much time to wonder about Kat's behavior, because Lena was back in my face, shouting.

"WOOOO! The baby bees are ready to roll! Finish your drinks and pay up, honey lovers—we're leaving in fifteen!"

In the flurry of gulping drinks and negotiating bills that followed, I felt Shanti's hand on my elbow.

"Hey—sorry about all that."

I looked at her. Her hand remained on my elbow. I had the urge to move closer to her but fought it. She'd somehow managed to slip into the cracks and that felt dangerous, like I might lose control. "It's cool. I mean . . . it's not," I muttered. "But it's fine." And then: "Is this really a thing?"

"Yeah. Mostly. It seems a little ramped up this year, though." I noticed she avoided eye contact when she said this, and I wondered if she meant the dressing-up part, the drunk Kat part, or the part where she'd dressed me in a pointy bra.

I couldn't ask, though, because she was thrust out of the way by a pile of people sliding out of booths and chairs and gathering their belongings.

"Fresh meat! Follow me! Everyone to the rink!" Lena called out.

The rink?

Chapter Twenty-One

In the ensuing mayhem, the four rookies were herded toward Kat's van, which thankfully was piloted by Charlotte, who was sober. Kat was riding shotgun, though, and on the ride to wherever it was we were going—I assumed the same rink the tryouts had been held—she wouldn't answer any of our questions. She just blasted Guns N' Roses and sang sloppily along with the music the entire ride until we got to our destination.

Which wasn't the rink I'd assumed.

This was an arena all right. But the main entrance of this arena was enhanced with wandering neon lights and had a long line of people snaking away from it. People who looked like they'd time-warped here from 1972. People who reminded me of the photos I'd seen in Joe and Alma's garage.

We parked, and when we all toppled from the van, I noticed a few other cars emptying of Honeys as well. As a swarm, we joined the end of the curving line of people dressed in bell-bottoms and bodysuits and beads.

Potts started to ask what the hell was going on but only got to "hell" before they staggered over to some bushes and dumped out their gut. They returned a minute later shouting, "Shots, shots, shots, shots, shots!" much to everyone's amusement.

On the ride over, I'd tried to steer my focus toward the goal. I'd listened to the music, to Kat singing off-key, to Sage giggling uncontrollably, and just taken it all in stride. No way was I gonna sit on the bench. I was made for this sport and determined to prove it tonight. If that meant playing along with all this ridiculousness, then so be it.

Once outside the arena, though, I found my focus drawn to Shanti and saw her standing with Grace, who seemed to be close-talking her about something especially intense. The alcohol in my system convinced me she needed rescuing, and I strode over.

"The only thing stopping you is you, you know? You just gotta see what you want in your mind, and then reach out and just, like, take it in your hands, and then like, pull it toward you," I heard Grace declaring as I approached, and I tried to stifle an eye roll. But then she laid her hand flat against Shanti's chest and started to pull Shanti toward her by her shirt. Shanti didn't look like she was about to resist—*Why doesn't she ever stand up for herself?*—so I moved faster, pulling off the sweaty clown nose and wig and stuffing them into my skate bag as I did. Somebody needed to cut this shit off, and that was definitely one thing I was good at.

"Heeeyyyy, Grace. Shanti doesn't want you all up on her, okay?" I wrapped my hand around Grace's grasping fist and pulled it—not so gently—away from Shanti's shirt. Grace wobbled a little and just gazed at me like she was trying to remember who I was. Then she slipped into a meandering grin and wandered away.

Feeling like something had finally made me look good instead of ridiculous tonight, I turned to Shanti, expecting—hoping for—that warm smile I'd seen on her face when I'd entered the bar earlier. Hating that I wanted it but wanting it anyway. But it wasn't there.

"You didn't need to do that," was all she said.

"Really? It seemed like you needed some help."

She stared at me for a moment. "Daya . . ." Then looking away, she said, "I'm not like you."

"Like me?"

Her eyes met mine again. They were full of disappointment. "I'm not tough like you. But that doesn't mean I'm a pushover, either. I deal with things in my own way."

"I never said you were a pushover." *But aren't you?* I glanced away so she couldn't tell what I was really thinking, but she managed to see it anyway.

"No. You haven't *said* it."

She started to turn away, but I didn't want her to go like this—I didn't want to be the one to make her look this way, feel this way. My free hand impulsively reached out and caught hers. She stopped and looked back at my hand around hers. She frowned a little as she lifted her eyes to mine, expectant. Again, I knew I should say something—probably "sorry"—but all I could do was hang on to her hand. She came as close to me as she could, considering the damn cone bra was in the way. I stiffened but stayed still despite the urge to let go and leave now that she was so near.

Leaning over my pointy chest so her mouth was only inches from my ear, she said, "I'm not interested in your hard side, Daya." She gave my hand a squeeze and released it.

Still finding it impossible to form words, I missed my chance as the line started moving and all the Honeys began bunching together and pushing forward, the energy truly like a hive. I tried to stay close to Shanti but got bundled up and away by Charlotte and Lena. I found myself wishing my hand wasn't empty, then curled it into a fist to distract myself from the void.

As we surged forward, I still had no idea what this event was or why we were here, and now I was even more disoriented by this exchange with Shanti. But things became abundantly clear as we approached the entrance. Disco music emanated from inside, and the entryway became engulfed in the kind of roaming, fractured light that could only be caused by a disco ball.

Disco. Roller skates. Dance moves.

I'd heard of this before. It was a thing. A thing made for other people. Not for me.

Roller disco dance-offs.

Dear God.

I struggled to reconstruct the steel and rock inside my body, but it felt like I was trying to build walls out of straw and dust.

Once we were inside, Lena, Kat, and the other established Honeys ushered us toward a section of benches to get our skates on. As I laced up, feeling more and more restricted by the lacy panties and cone bra I was wearing, I snuck a few peeks around me.

Tinsel and twinkle lights dangled from the walls, and an enormous disco ball whirled slowly from the middle of the ceiling above the rink. A long bar lined one side of the seating area, skate rentals at one end and food counter at the other. The place was packed. Lycra and velour and fake furs everywhere. And a lot of spandex. Like, so much. At the moment, a vaguely familiar disco song was playing over the speakers. Ketchup and boiled hot-dog odors seemed to rise up out of the worn carpet beneath our skates.

I couldn't quite see the rink itself yet—the barrier around it blocked my view from where I was sitting. But a blur of movement whipping along above the barrier suggested the rink was just as teeming as the seating area.

Lena, Dominique, and Kat had already laced up and stood before the four of us "baby bees" now. Yelling above the music, Lena announced, "Phase Two of the Honey Hijinks will commence! Honey drops, you have thirty minutes to choose a song—it's gotta be disco, obviously—and figure out a routine, 'cause shit's about to get *real*."

At this, Lena yanked me up onto my feet, while Dominique and Kat pulled the others with them, and we were unceremoniously hauled toward the barrier. Once there, Lena pointed to the floor, where, to my increasing horror, I noticed that among the general, seventies-inspired crowd, a few groups of people in matching costumes (*matching*, not random like ours) were rounding the rink, practicing well-executed dance moves on some seriously stylish skates.

"Thanks to Kat, who's got connections with the MCs, we got you the opening spot for tonight's dance-off! Sweet, huh?" Lena declared, hands in the air as though she really believed we'd be happy to hear this.

The four of us stared at her for a second, then glanced at each other.

"Better get crackin'!" Kat added, and annoyingly clapped twice for emphasis.

After a confusing moment where we didn't really know where to go to begin our practice session, Lena gave us a shove toward an area near the bathrooms that wasn't too crowded and yelled, "Have fun!" over the music.

We weaved through the crowd toward the spot. Drunk and dazed, I tried to tap back into the motivation and resolve I'd formed earlier—when I was determined to show everyone I could be part of the team off the track come hell or high water. But fire and flooding seemed like a delight compared to whatever catastrophe was surely about to take place in a few minutes.

Thankfully (maybe) and surprisingly, Sage took control of the current situation. She'd been mostly giggles and high fives tonight, but apparently, song and dance were her things, because she announced that we could do no other song than "I Feel Love" by Donna Summer and then quickly maneuvered us into a line, with her in the lead. No one was about to argue—our options and time were limited. I'd slipped into autopilot, going through the motions just to have it be done.

"Okay, no matter what, watch the person in front of you and just do whatever they're doing!"

Thirty minutes later, we had . . . something. I had to give Sage props—organizing three drunken, clearly incompetent dancers had to be a nearly impossible task. Grace appeared to be more interested in flipping her flouncy, curly hair from one shoulder to the next than she was in the moves. Potts seemed to be in a different time zone altogether—each move we completed, they completed about five seconds later. I, of course, was just as bad. I stood immediately behind Sage and kept accidentally hitting her because I couldn't get the timing right. I'm also sure my face was a combination of pure disdain and utter bewilderment.

But, whether we liked it or not, and I was certain only Sage liked it, we soon found ourselves in the middle of the rink, about to do whatever it was we were about to do. The other teams—four of them—had gathered in the center as well, and the rest of the crowd kind of did this slow skate around the circumference of the floor, eyeing us up as they did. It felt a little weird and ritualistic. And I guess we were the sacrificial lambs to the slaughter.

"Brick House" started playing, and to my surprise, out onto the rink rolled two familiar figures—Alma and Joe—both with gigantic smiles on their faces. As they skated around us and greeted the folks along the edge of the rink, everyone seemed to go nuts. Joe's wiry, lean body was fitted with his requisite short shorts and a mesh tank top that showed off a pretty damn tight chest for an older guy. A shimmering purple dress shifted around Alma's body, fluttering up to reveal bright red underpants over silver tights. Her head was wrapped in a glittery scarf.

Once the two of them had made one round to greet the crowd, they began to skate in earnest, holding hands and gaining speed. The crowd's volume rose the faster Alma and Joe skated. I couldn't believe how fluid and fast they were, and then my astonishment grew when they started to bounce and shake and hop and groove to the music. Joe's hamstrings were a wonder. Alma's hips were a miracle.

We had to follow this?

As the music faded, Alma skated over to the DJ, who passed her a mic.

"Disco lovers! Welcome to the Stardust Roller Rink and our weekly Roll-and-Bounce Dance-Off! I'm Alma Gonna-Get-You and this is my love, Jumpin' Joe. And if you're here, it's 'cause you love bumpin' and grindin' as you're rollin'! Tonight we have special guests, and I know you'll make them feel adored. Let's hear it for one of our local roller derby teams, the Killa Honeys, and their newly anointed little honeybees!" She winked at me and Joe waved in a practical frenzy. I was surprised they could recognize me in this getup. I half-heartedly waved back. I guessed they were the "connections" Kat had.

At Alma's announcement, the crowd skating around us clapped and hooted, which somewhat lessened the eeriness of their circular, down-tempo rotation. But not by much.

The other teams drifted away from the center of the rink and Alma came over to whisper to us, "When the music starts, so do you—just roll with it!" Then she gave my earlobe a squeeze and glided off to the side of the rink, Joe following her, with more grace in her left knee than I had in my entire body, which became evident in the next few seconds.

Our song choice must have been passed on to the DJ, because "I Feel Love" surged out of the speakers and we took the first eight beats just to get into our line. Sage pushed off and dove right into the first moves and we did our best to follow her, the crowd immediately responding with laughter and whoops. It didn't feel like cruel laughter, though—more like the genuinely entertained kind. Not that that made me feel any better. As Sage started to thrust herself forward, making up the voguing moves we'd all agreed to mimic no matter what form they came in, I could hear the individual voices of Honeys through the music and cheers, encouraging us to "Boog-ayyyyy!"

I focused on Sage's legs ahead of me and the sensations of my muscles tensing and releasing with each stride. Anything to avoid thinking about the bigger picture—the reality that I was making a fool of myself and didn't fit here. *Just get through this,* I kept telling myself.

But the faster Sage skated, the less in sync my arms were with hers. And I'd bet Grace and Potts weren't much better. The crowd still seemed to be enjoying it, though, and the other teams were clapping for us too. I had to repeatedly disregard the burning sensations in my stomach and face and just keep going.

Just. Keep. Going.

I guessed Sage felt more comforted and encouraged by the crowd's response than I did, because as we made our third lap of the rink, she decided to get really low and increase her momentum. She'd clearly been chosen by the Honeys for her speed, because it didn't take long for her to pull away from us. As the three of us busted our butts to try and catch up, Sage attempted a spin move. I'm not sure whether she was selected for her agility, too, but I doubted it. She lost her balance and ended up skate-running a few steps and then tumbling over. Predictably, the rest of us skipped the skate-run and proceeded straight to the falling-over part.

Skidding to a stop at the feet of some folks dressed in leopard print, we ended as a tangled mess of legs, arms, skates, and haphazard costumes. Somehow I'd managed to avoid piercing anyone with my cone boobs, though, so that was a plus. After a moment where all four of us blinked repeatedly in a daze, Potts let out a "Yee-haw!" that sent the others into giggles and cackles. I was pissed that we'd messed up, but it was hard to maintain my frustration with Potts whipping their boa over the top of our heads like a lasso.

Joe's voice boomed over the faded music. We had only gotten about a third of the way through our song, which I'm sure was fine with everyone involved. "Let's hear it for our rookie roller dancers, everybody! Aren't they spectacular!"

More cheers from the crowd, and then the leopard-skinned skaters pounced on our jumbled pile to help us up, shouting encouragements the entire time. A bunch of the Honeys skated over to gather us up as well. I noticed Kat wasn't one of them. Shanti was, though, and she reached for me and yanked me up with an ease that surprised me. I was also impressed to see she'd done it in roller skates.

"Well, that was something," she said, a gleam in her eye.

I could tell she was searching my face and I tried to keep it neutral, but I found myself relieved that she seemed to have moved past our earlier, awkward conversation and I felt the tension in my jaw ease a little. "Yeah, yeah," I replied, avoiding eye contact. I was all for ignoring awkwardness and just pushing through.

Once we were standing and stable, she said, "C'mon" and took my hand, lessening that earlier empty feeling. "Let me buy you a beer. You deserve it." We skated off the rink and I noticed she seemed really comfortable on skates—easy and fluid like Alma.

As we sipped our beers at the edge of the rink, the *real* dancing teams began the *actual* dance-off, which I couldn't help but be impressed by despite our debacle. In fact, I found the debacle bothered me less and less as we stood watching. No one else seemed to care that we'd messed up so bad. I also realized I hadn't even considered the bruising I must have gained from our mash-up at the end. The thought didn't occur to me until a drunken Potts toppled into me and I felt a tenderness on my left arm.

The sensation should have reminded me of my main goal— to make this team and collect more bruises—but instead, it made me glance over at Shanti, who was gazing out at the action on the rink. She must have felt my eyes on her, because she turned toward me and flicked my alien antennas. I would have turned toward her, too, but the cone bra was still in the way. I'd kept the clown nose off because it was making it hard to breathe, but Lena had told us we'd need to wear the costumes all night, so all the other nonsense remained on my body.

She leaned in so I could hear her over the music. "It was cool to see you out there tonight, being a little silly." Her eyes dipped for a moment, then found mine again, which made me look away. "I thought maybe Kat made you a bit uncomfortable back at the bar. She's a bit drunker than usual tonight."

I took a sip of my beer, hyperaware now that Shanti had shifted so that her body was tucked in against mine. Responding to both her comment and her closeness, a small spike of steel rose in my chest. "I can handle myself."

I could feel her lean in even more, and I willed the steel to grow higher, sharper. "I'm sure you can. It doesn't mean you have to."

What do you know? "Sometimes you do—have to," I said, an edge beneath my voice.

"Like when?"

I knew she was looking at me, that unassuming expression on her face, but this conversation felt too close, too dangerous. My brain could tell she wasn't messing with me, but that spike loomed near my throat.

I turned my eyes toward her, hard. "Like when people try and fuck with you."

Her eyebrows rose ever so slightly and her body shifted away from mine a little.

There you go. Now you're getting the hint. Keep moving.

But then: "That's one way to do it, I guess."

"Is there another way?"

She smiled a little. Actually smiled. I couldn't believe it. "There're lots of different ways." She shrugged like this was obvious and adjusted her glasses.

To combat the confusion and affection pulling at me, I responded with defensiveness. "Are you laughing at me?"

She surprised me again. "You know I'm not."

Fuck. Okay. None of my usual stuff was getting in the way here. My next move would usually be to leave, but my feet remained still in their skates. I found myself terrified but wanting to stay. My throat tightened around my words and I couldn't get any more out.

We were silent for a few seconds. Then Shanti touched my arm and pointed out at the rink. "Check out Alma and Joe—they're on fire!"

I could tell she was changing the subject, probably for my benefit, and I let her. I followed her finger to see Alma and Joe twirling and dipping around the rink like they were twenty years old—Alma laughing while Joe beamed at her.

As I watched them, some of the terror fell away and my throat opened enough to utter, "Those two are amazing." Suddenly wanting to make up for my sharpness, I added, "They helped me practice for the tryouts."

"They did? You asked them to?"

She looked genuinely surprised, and instead of bugging me, it felt like a win. "Yeah—I needed a bit of help around the whole team thing."

"Really?"

The look on her face *almost* amused me. "You don't need to look *that* surprised."

"No—I mean, you know—you just seemed more intent on getting out there and bashing the crap out of people."

True. I shrugged. "I still am. But like you said, team stuff seems important too."

She nodded slowly. "That's really cool, Daya. Yolanda and Nana have been friends with those two for a while. You chose your mentors well, Grasshopper." She nudged me with her arm.

We were quiet again after that, just taking in the rest of the groups wielding their skills on the rink. Potts kept swaying into me from my left side, banging away at that bruise, which made me lean more and more into Shanti on my right—no bruises to feel, just warm skin and muscle. I didn't mind it.

After the dance-off, regular skating ensued, although this wasn't like any roller rink I'd ever heard of. It was like the dance-off hadn't even ended—groups of people formed into trains and glided around the rink, switching feet and directions perfectly in sync, with the kind of fluidity Alma had tried to show me in her driveway and that she herself had clearly mastered. Some skaters were doing things with their bodies I didn't even know were possible on skates—splits, jumping, break dancing. It felt like a whole rink filled with professional roller skaters. I was surprised they'd let us on at all, even if for some brief moments of entertainment.

It was hard not to be caught up in the energy and looseness around me, so when Shanti grabbed my hand and led me back out onto the rink, I didn't resist, even though my heart started beating faster. We circled with the crowd but kept ourselves out of the way of the folks who really knew what they were doing. We didn't talk, just flowed around and around, listening to the music and taking in the buzz of everyone around us. I thought—maybe—I was starting to understand a little bit of what Fee meant when they talked about being part of some kind of synergy. It felt like we were part of one cosmic energy loop.

As soon as I caught myself thinking *cosmic energy loop*, I rolled my eyes. But the cheesiness didn't make it any less true.

After a while, Lena shepherded me and the other rookies into a huddle in the waiting area. "Honey babies, you were a miracle of nature tonight," she said, like she meant it. "Sometimes nature's miracles are messy and maybe even a little hideous—like birth—but they're still miracles. And so are you. All those things. Messy, hideous miracles. And now you're *our* hideous miracles! Welcome to the Honeys, bumble-heads!"

Chapter Twenty-Two

"Dare I ask how the journaling is going?" Dr. Hoang was leaning on one hand, her face soft and relaxed. I appreciated that there didn't seem to be any judgment in her expression.

I stared at my fingers as they scratched at the leather armrest of my chair. "It's not. Going." *Scratch, scratch.* "Sorry."

"You don't need to apologize. It was just a suggestion. I do still think it would help if you gave it a chance, though. I'll just keep checking in with you and hoping for the best—how's that?"

Shrug.

"So? What's new?"

So much. It'd only been two days since the Honey Hijinks, and I found myself actually wanting to talk about that and the tryouts and roller derby, but I'd remained silent for so long here that it was hard to know how to begin. And if I started sharing stuff like this, what else might come out? There was so much that needed to stay where it was.

When I didn't say anything, Dr. Hoang offered, "I watched some skateboarding videos."

I looked up from my scratching fingers. Dr. Hoang's face was serious, but her eyes smiled the tiniest bit.

"I don't know what kind of tricks you do, but that shit is *unbelievable.*"

My lips parted ever so slightly. She'd never sworn before. Was this some adult trickery to make me open up? My curiosity got the better of me. "Who'd you watch?"

"Oh, I can't remember, but it was older footage of a young woman. Peggy something? She was incredible. I can't believe you do all that."

"I probably don't. I'm not that good."

"Okay . . . I can't believe you do even *some* of that."

Before I could even think about it, I said, "I'm not really skateboarding anymore."

"Oh?"

"Yeah. You know much about roller derby?" *I bet you don't.*

"Roller derby? I mean, I've seen the movie *Whip It*, but that's about it. Roller skating, right?"

"Yeah."

Her face became incredulous. "Daya, that looks even *more* unbelievable. How in the world did you get yourself into roller derby?"

I paused, my guard rising. I'd never talked about bruising here and I didn't plan to now. But I didn't have to share *why* I was doing roller derby. Selective sharing worked best in these situations. "A friend introduced me."

"How do you like it?"

"It's good."

"How does it compare to skateboarding?"

The bruises are bigger, was my immediate thought. But then other stuff from this past week came to mind—skating in Alma and Joe's cul-de-sac, Charlotte's encouragements, Shanti's hand around mine. *Keep it simple.* "It's different. I have to think about more. Like, what other people are doing."

"Right. Because it's a team sport."

"Yeah."

"Is it helping at all?"

"Helping with what?"

"With anything. With feeling connected. With being happy."

Christ. Why does everything have to come back to my damn feelings? I shrugged again and frowned.

"Daya, don't retreat. You just seem a bit more open today, and I'm wondering if it has to do with roller derby, is all. It's okay to be excited about something and want to share that excitement."

I continued scratching at the armrest. *Except that sharing makes things real. Except that anything good can disappear in a second.*

Chapter Twenty-Three

Our first bout wasn't for another couple of weeks, but we had a few practices before that. Sage asked me if I wanted to get together and do some extra practice with her, Grace, and Potts, and even though it made sense to work on our skills together—we'd be in the same boat as rookies when it came to game time, after all—the idea of exposing myself to Grace's nosy questions, Sage's overzealous high fives, and Potts's hectic energy still sent anxiety through me.

I knew I needed to practice my skills both on the track *and* off it. To figure out how to maneuver around all these teammates and relationships. I'd started to enjoy myself at the roller disco, to feel something like contentment with Shanti—for a few moments at least. That didn't mean it'd been easy or that I'd suddenly fooled myself into thinking I didn't need to bruise anymore.

I said yes to Sage, telling myself, *Anything to get on that track. Anything to prove I can handle myself out there.* I reasoned that if bruising on the track helped keep my shit off the track under control, I might actually be *able* to navigate the social stuff I wasn't so great at. Maybe even enjoy it.

The four of us met up on non-practice days at a tennis court near Sage's house and worked at everything we could—skating, stopping, jumping, bracing, blocking, and more.

Sage was an incredible skater—so quick and light on her feet. Potts was a beast—completely undisciplined but somehow able to make their haphazard style work. Grace had pretty much memorized every basic roller derby play and was able to break them down into manageable parts for those of us with less organized brains (i.e., Potts). I assumed I was the brute strength in the bunch until Grace asked me to show her how to brace like I had at the tryouts. I guess Fee hadn't been too far off about me having other assets.

At the end of our first team practice, Dominique had gathered everyone together and handed out rule books. "Study up, folks . . . School's in sesh and you need to learn this shit by next week. We'll know if you haven't done your homework."

"Homewooooorrrrk!" Potts whined, and collapsed onto their back. "Whyyyyyyy!" The team collectively tittered and threw sweaty towels and clothing at them.

"Don't fret, snickerdoodles!" Lena piped up. "The Honeys aren't just all business, as our fresh meat knows all too well"— she paused so the team could give the four of us a round of applause, presumably for our disco performance the other night—"and there's plenty more party in the plan!"

"That's right," Kat continued. "We're mixing business and pleasure again this weekend for the first of our regular season fundraisers. If you're not free Saturday night, get free fast— you won't wanna miss this. Bring some friends, too."

I hadn't really seen Kat the rest of the night at the roller disco. She'd basically disappeared after our rookie debut. Someone said she'd left with some dude. Today at practice, though, she'd been all business, and a complete hard-ass. She, Dom, and Lena acted as dual skaters and coaches, but she was definitely the one in charge.

I could've just been making it up, but it felt like she was being especially hard on me. Even though I was already working my ass off, her only words to me the entire practice were some version of "You can do better than that, Daya!"

Shanti, on the other hand, had surprised the hell out of me by giving me a hug when we saw each other in the parking lot before practice. I wasn't sure what to make of it, but she seemed pretty casual about the whole thing, so I tried to just take it in stride, despite the fact that Kat was giving us the stink-eye the entire time.

As I was putting away my gear, Shanti came up to give me a stack of flyers. "Here—spread these around so we make lots of money this weekend. You're coming, right?"

I looked at the papers she'd handed me, a part of me exasperated by the prospect of yet another off-track social gathering. HONEYBEE HIVE. SWEETEN UP YOUR NIGHT AND

SUPPORT THE KILLA HONEYS ROLLER DERBY TEAM.
In the middle of the page was the fierce bee in roller skates
that was on the pin Shanti had sold me. Below that was the
address and time.

"Did you make these?" I remembered her saying it was one
of her jobs as manager.

"Yeah. Like 'em?"

"Yeah—this bee is so aggressive. My kind of insect." I
glanced up at her to see if I'd made her smile. I had. *Don't get
carried away, weirdo.* "Where's this address?"

"It's actually our place. It's too expensive to rent a venue, so
we just hold our fundraisers there. It's a big-ass house and four
of the Honeys live there, including me. So it makes sense."

The thought of seeing where Shanti lived sparked an interest in me. "Who else lives there?"

"Kat, Lena, and Chantel."

Chantel, also known as Hello Titty. I couldn't really picture Shanti living with that crew. Sounded like a lot of big
personalities in one house. And then Shanti.

"How's that?" I asked.

"What? Living with those three?"

"Yeah. Seems . . . crowded."

"It is, I guess. Kat and Lena can be a bit bossy, but Chantel
isn't as out there as her roller name suggests."

"Who you callin' bossy, sis?" Kat's arm was suddenly
around Shanti's shoulders. I couldn't read her expression—if
she was mad or amused or something else.

Shanti hesitated, but only for a moment. "You, obviously."

"Girl, if I didn't boss you around, where would you be?" She pulled Shanti in closer to her and gave her a noogie, which would have driven me up the wall. I hated shit like that. Shanti didn't look like she loved it either. But after what she'd said about not needing help, I tried to restrain myself. My hands definitely got twitchy watching, though.

"Kat, stop—" Shanti pushed Kat's torso, and her sister relented. I was relieved to see this, but still irritated.

"So sensitive, Shanti. Daya, did I mention how delicate my sister is? Like a soft, soft flower, right, sis?"

She must've hit one of those soft spots, because Shanti looked a little flustered for a second.

Ugh. I couldn't keep my mouth shut any longer, despite what Shanti had said. "She seems pretty tough to me."

Kat cocked an eyebrow my way. Shanti glanced at me and I was relieved to see a tiny hint of appreciation, I thought. She shook off Kat's words and straightened her spine. To Kat, she said, "Flowers are fucking stronger than you think," and walked away. My eyes widened in amazement.

Kat forced a laugh, but not before I caught a moment of surprise in her face as well. The laughter faded quickly as she turned to me. "Don't let her fool you. She's not that strong. I wish she was." She looked away for a moment and wiped the sweat off her forehead. I thought I saw a hint of something sad on her face. When her eyes came back to mine, though, it was gone, replaced by a hard look that I knew I'd mastered too.

She took a step closer. "You don't seem great at the soft stuff anyway. Here's some advice, whether you want it or not: stick to the Daya who knows how to hit hard and protect her team. Don't fuck things up by trying to be someone you're not."

Her words sliced the air between us, the truth of what she'd said cutting deep. But I was also pissed that she was trying to tell me what to do. And that she thought she could control whatever was happening with me and Shanti. Never great with words and knowing my fists would get me nowhere here, I just tried to hold Kat's eyes with mine. It wasn't easy—it was almost like she was looking through me now, like she didn't really see me, which just infuriated me more. Before I did something I might regret, I grabbed my gear and brushed by her.

Chapter Twenty-Four

The bus let me off about six blocks from the address on the flyer Shanti'd given me. Feeling hesitant about the fundraiser in general, I hadn't done a very good job of sharing the info with anyone. In fact, I'd had to actively *hide* the event the night after our last practice. I'd accidentally left the flyer out in the laundry room after cleaning my gear, and Vicki had asked about it. I just said someone at school was handing them out, and then threw it in the recycling bin. I'd had to fish it out later that night. I still wasn't sure what their response would be, and I didn't need any more complications or overly emotive expressions of worry or delight or disdain. I ended up telling them I was hanging out with Anna, my go-to excuse.

I'd thought about asking Fee and Caihong to come, but I wasn't sure I wanted to overlap worlds yet. I was still stoked about roller derby but was also feeling a little off-balance around the stuff with Kat and Shanti. After that messed-up interaction at the end of our first practice, Kat had continued to be super hard on me during our second practice. Shanti hadn't even been at the second practice. I'd just kept my head down and focused on skating and hitting, regardless of—or maybe because of—Kat's constant reprimands.

I hoped things would be simpler tonight—I didn't doubt it would be ridiculous and overwhelming, like Honey Hijinks had been, but I just didn't want to have to deal with any drama. And as much as Kat's comments rankled me, she wasn't wrong. Soft wasn't really my style and only led to hurt—the kind of hurt I'd spent so long pushing down. Things with Shanti had felt kind of nice, but also confusing and scary—it was only a matter of time before hurt entered the picture there, too.

With all these super-great feelings sitting in my chest, I arrived at the party. The address revealed itself to be a pretty run-down house. It looked to be two floors, although houses like this always seemed to have sketchy unfinished basements. Pale pink paint covered the outside in splotches. The porch steps looked caved in on one end, like they were slowly disappearing into the earth. Through a couple of open, smudged windows, live music pumped across the lawn.

I walked up the front steps, carefully avoiding the droopy side. When I opened the door after fiddling for, like, a good thirty seconds with the wobbly doorknob, the full force of the music exploded over me. An electric guitar, pounding drums, and what sounded like a synthesizer welcomed me inside.

A ratty roller skate sat on a table just inside the door with a sign that said, THE HONEY POT. A couple of bills poked out through the opening of the skate. Behind the table, one guy was straddling another guy, and they were making out. Unsure whether I was supposed to contribute, being a Honey myself and all, and not about to interrupt this serious tongue action, I added a five, just in case.

Four girls, one of whom was Sage, sprawled across the stairs leading to the second floor. They all looked over blurry-eyed as I walked in, and Sage gave me an exuberant wave when she saw me. A petite but ripped girl carrying a massive guy on her back galloped in front of me from the room on my right toward the music, which was blaring from somewhere to my left. Muffled but loud conversations emanated from every direction. I caught "dolly rocker," "rainbow bright," and "kiss my ass—it tastes like butterscotch."

As I'd predicted, this was going to be mayhem, just like the roller disco. But I was a little surprised to find I wasn't completely mortified by the thought of being here, despite my trepidation about Kat and Shanti. I guess I was getting acclimated to some of these roller folks—especially the other rookies. It was easier to spend so much time with people when it involved sweating and knocking each other around.

I followed the noise from the band and found myself in the living room, which had an enclosed porch off it. The band—three chicks dressed in varying degrees of Girl Scout clothing (but, like, a punk version) banged away on their instruments.

Their music missed most of the intended notes, but their facial expressions and sheer exuberance made up for their lack of skill. I paused in the entryway to the living room, hypnotized by the contorted faces and flailing hair.

"Bitches coming through!" was the last thing I heard before a force of arms and legs tackled me from behind and I landed face-first on the green shag rug covering most of the floor, hysterical laughter roaring into my ear and what felt like a two-hundred-pound flour sack on my back.

"Whoops!" the person on my back yelled, before rolling sideways off me and onto her back.

When I looked over, it was Lena—her delirious giggling interrupted every so often by a violent hiccup. Laughter rang out from around the room too.

Pushing myself up onto my elbows and twisting to look behind me, I could see Lena had her roller skates on and three other Honeys were crowded in the doorway to the living room with their skates on as well. Unsurprisingly, Potts was one of them and was rocking out in a private dance as the others stared at me on the ground.

"And that's what a roller derby conga line is all about, bitches!" Lena called out from beside me, stabbing the air above her with two index fingers. "Woooooooo!"

More laughter traveled around the room, and I joined in. Normally I might be pissed if someone rammed me from behind, even if it meant I got some bruising out of it, but I liked Lena. She was tough but easy to be around. And hilarious. It was hard not to laugh, and the laughter broke up a bit of the tension in my chest.

Lena finally looked over to see who she'd inadvertently tackled, and when she saw me, her eyes grew wide and she yelled, "Heeeyyyyyyy . . . fresh meat!" Then she rolled back on top of me and wiggled her body against mine, which was less funny. Not exactly the bodily contact I preferred.

"Okay, okay—Lena you fucking lush—get offa the rookie already." I gazed up to see Kat standing over us. This was definitely *not* how I wanted Kat to find me—lying flat on my face in her living room.

But here at a party with lots of my new teammates around, I decided to play it as cool as I was capable of playing it and just continued to laugh things off, hoping that "party Kat" might be less weird than "practice Kat" had been.

Kat helped me up (a good sign?) once Lena had finally— after a couple of tries—lifted her body off mine. She rolled back out the same entrance with the rest of her conga line, seemingly unfazed by the crash or her wild hiccups.

"Welcome to the madhouse!" Kat yelled over the music, and swung her heavy arm over my shoulders. Apparently we'd gone back to relatively friendly Kat, for now. I didn't fully let my guard down, though. The friendliness could just be the liquor she'd obviously already consumed, judging by her breath in my face. I hadn't forgotten the last time her face was in mine, or the words she'd uttered. Or how true they were.

"Yeah, I definitely felt that welcome," I shouted back,

rubbing my elbow, where a nice lump was forming.

"Bar's that way"—she pointed through another door lead-ing out of the living room—"four bucks a drink!"

"Thanks—this is your place, right?" I asked, trying to keep it friendly.

"Yup—the Pink Palace. Hive of the Honeys," Kat said, eyeing the room with pride. "Lots of opportunities to spend your money! Look around—you'll find 'em."

"Got it."

Before she withdrew her arm from my neck, she leaned in, and her face became serious. *Uh-oh.* She looked at me. I could tell she was trying to articulate her next words carefully. She managed to slur only a little. "Listen, Daya, this team's my family. You can be a part of it. But you can't go all soft." She rubbed her eyes and refocused them on me. "Soft. Gets. Hurt. Right?" She underscored each word with a finger to my chest. Her face was almost more intense as she said this than it had been when I'd seen her blazing around the track.

Put off-balance by her sudden switch but also feeling every single thing she said deep in my gut, I blundered through my own words. "Right, yeah, uh . . . okay." Her voice had betrayed that she knew exactly what she was talking about, which caused a brief ache in my chest for both of us.

I didn't have a chance to say anything else, though, because Kat thumped me on the shoulder—hard as ever—and contin-ued by me.

Now I needed a drink. I followed Kat's directions into the

next room, which turned out to be the kitchen. Three coolers filled with ice and beer sat against the kitchen island, and an assortment of liquor bottles was spread across the island's surface. The counter swam in spilled liquid.

I stuffed a few bills into the piggy bank on the counter and poured myself a shot of vodka, hauling that back before pulling out a bottle of beer from a cooler. Just something to chill me out a bit. I hoped that that was the most intense moment I'd experience tonight and tried to shake it loose from my body.

Squeezing the frosty, wet bottle in my left hand, I shuffled back into the living room to watch the band for a bit, having been abruptly sidetracked before. On the floor in front of them, I now noticed a jar with some cash in it and a sign taped to it that said, SUPPORT THE HONEYS, BITCHES. I guessed this was what Kat meant about opportunities to donate.

Leaning against the wall across from the three Girl Scouts, I scanned the space. A couple of happily buzzed dancers swayed on the carpet. A few other folks crisscrossed over each other on the couch, having one of those hilarious, intense drunk talks. Out on the enclosed porch, the mood seemed a little different—strings of lights set a cozy scene, and a few couples were taking advantage of the mood lighting to get their make-out on. I watched them a little too long before I realized I was being a creep.

Just as I was getting a little hot under the collar and beginning to wish for a hookup of my own—I was only human and it had been a while, after all—a person I didn't recognize appeared beside me with a sandwich board shaped like lips strung over their body. It read KISSES FOR A DOLLAR. TONGUE FOR TWO. They leaned in and bobbed their eyebrows at me. I couldn't help but smile. Tempted, but not really a public-display-of-affection kind of girl, I let them kiss me on the cheek and slipped a dollar into an opening between the painted lips, wondering where exactly it would land.

I kept myself moving, walking across the living room and back through to the foyer. I poked my head into the room across the hall, which was blurry with skunky smoke. An intense game of Pin the Tail on the Roller Girl seemed to be taking place, complete with a life-size cardboard cutout of Lena skating, butt out, primed for pinning. Though watching these folks try to stick a tail made of rainbow-colored synthetic hair to Lena's ass was entertaining, I moved on after a minute or so.

Following the hallway around behind the back of the staircase, I discovered an open door to the basement. The stairway was mostly dark, but I could see a dim red light at the bottom. Enticed by the mysterious red glow and hoping it was a sign of something improper, I started making my way down to it. The music from upstairs dulled a bit, a relief to my ears, which had begun to feel like someone had clapped their open palm against them repeatedly.

At the bottom of the stairs, the floor was cement with random bits of that rough-looking industrial carpet here and there.

Not completely unfinished, but close. The air set my skin into
goose bumps, and I was glad I'd kept my jacket on. To my right,
a long, shadowy hallway showed a couple of figures wrapped
around each other, the telltale sounds of heavy breathing and
low groans punctuating the faint sound of stringy music that
drifted out from a door behind me. Two more figures suddenly
crashed through the steamy hallway and lumbered toward me,
one of them screaming "Jojo's it! Run, you fuckers!" before
shoving me backward into the musical door.

Hearing more profanities and squeals following this stam-
pede, I turned and clumsily found the doorknob I was squashed
up against. I tumbled into the room behind the door, almost
crashing to my knees but managing to just falter a few feet
inside instead. Saved my beer, too.

From the futon right in front of me, Shanti looked up, a
book open and tucked into her crossed legs. Always a book.
Her hair was in a messy bun, and she wore an oversize sweater
and tights. Small speakers on the floor sent out the complicated guitar music I'd heard, and a few candles lay across the
ledge above the futon. The walls had maintained their origi-
nal wood paneling, which was amazing, and more industrial
carpet covered most of the floor. A single mattress lay snug
against the corner of the room to my left, the blankets neatly
folded in around it.

I stood, somewhat embarrassed, about three feet from
Shanti. "Hey," I said, unsure of what else I could possibly say
or how she was feeling after that shitty episode with Kat at

practice. And still feeling the residual effect of Kat's words, part of me was trying to lift concrete blocks into place too. Everything in this room kept shoving those blocks to the ground, though.

"Hey—I didn't expect to see you down here." She seemed surprised but not unpleasantly so. "Are you . . . looking for a palm reading?"

"Pardon?"

She pointed behind me and I followed her finger. The door had swung wide open against the wall with my forceful entry. On the side that had faced the outer hallway, a piece of paper with Sharpie on it read, *Palm readings: $2.*

I turned back toward her. "Oh, uh . . . I actually missed that. Kinda got sideswiped."

"You must've enjoyed that," she said, her face unreadable.

"Ha . . . yeah." A palm reading wasn't really what I'd been looking for—but she looked so quiet and still, and I'd already been taken out twice in the short time I'd been at this party. Usually that was my thing, but this seemed all right for a minute or two as well.

"Um . . ." I looked around the room. A weathered dresser leaned into one corner, a couple of sketchbooks stacked on top. The air felt warm, thanks to a buzzing space heater next to the futon. "I like your room," I said, glancing back at Shanti, who was still just sitting, staring at me with something like amusement on her face.

"Thanks." She threw her book to the floor. "So? Since

you're here and all . . ." She patted the space beside her on the futon. "Come on—it's the only way I know how to contribute to these fundraisers."

Right. Okay, you can do this. No big deal. "Uh . . . sure." I sat down so we were cross-legged and facing each other. I placed my beer on the floor and pulled two dollars from my pocket, but she pushed it away.

"Wait till we're done. Then you can decide if it's worth the two bucks."

"Why wouldn't it be?" I asked.

"Hey, sometimes people don't like what they hear."

"That's a bit doomy, isn't it?"

She shrugged and held out her hands, her eyes never leaving my face.

I gave her my right hand, both anticipating and apprehensive of her touch.

"Are you right-handed?"

"Yeah."

"Then give me your left."

"What? Why?" I didn't like the idea of letting anyone so close to my left palm.

"Because. That's just how it works."

My shoulders stiffened. *This sounds like bullshit.* Shanti had seen me slam my hand against the bike rack at the try-out. Had she noticed it was my left? Was this some kind of intervention? As I was getting more and more riled up trying to figure out her motives, she sneezed—three high-pitched squeaks that were so utterly absurd and adorable that my rising hostility and suspicion couldn't sustain themselves.

I laughed and, without fully realizing it, unfolded my left hand in front of me.

As she placed her right hand beneath mine and her left on top, she cocked her head and asked, "Are you laughing at me?"

My hand was cold from holding the beer, but hers were warm. And soft. "Maybe."

"Whatever. I suppose your sneezes are real rugged-sounding, huh?" The way she said "rugged-sounding" in what she thought was a rugged voice but was really just a semi-low voice made me laugh again.

But when her fingers grazed along the surface of my palm, creating a tingling so different from the sensation I was used to, my hand reflexively clenched into a fist and pulled away. Shanti held her hands palms out in front of her as though in defense and looked up at me, her face a mixture of surprise and question.

Don't be a freak, Daya. "Sorry. It tickled. I'm ticklish." Even though I wasn't.

"Oh. Sorry. I didn't want to add too much pressure—"

"You can add as much pressure as you want." *'Cause everything's cool. Nothing to see here. Nothing to worry about.*

"You sure?"

"Yup." I could feel my hackles rising again and tried to breathe through the tension.

She hesitated but then reached out and took my still-closed

hand, gently pressing open my fingers. This time, she held my hand in both of hers and began running her thumbs along each crease with a firmness that sent pricks of pain through my bruise.

Better than stupid fucking tingles.

"A line like this one"—she traced the crease traversing the middle of my palm—"tells me that you wish you were somewhere else."

She looked up at me like she expected me to say something, so I mumbled, "Uh, I guess—I mean, don't you?" *Doesn't everyone?*

Shanti nodded slowly. "Fair enough." She returned to my hand and stretched the skin outward with both her thumbs. "Your life line is a bit unusual. It's broken right here." She leaned over and peered into my hand for a few moments. Looking up, she asked, "Any ideas?"

Resisting the urge to pull my hand away again, I shrugged and left it at that.

She stared at me for a beat, then nodded again and looked back down. She ran her finger along the line just below my middle and ring fingers. Her touch was lighter again this time, and the damn tingle was back. My neck and shoulders instantly tensed up with my efforts to remain still.

"This is your heart line. It's well-defined. That's a good sign, Daya. Strong heart."

Right. My jaw clenched involuntarily. My heart didn't feel strong right now. It felt like it could crumble at any moment.

I remembered Kat's words and started to think this was what she meant by being soft. By being someone I'm not. *I shouldn't be here.*

She looked up again and smiled, but when she saw my face, her smile faded. "What's wrong?"

"Nothing."

She shuffled closer to me so our knees were almost touching. Even though the rest of my body wanted to retreat, my hand inexplicably remained in hers.

"We can stop. I wasn't trying to make you uncomfortable."

"I'm fine." I kept my face as neutral as possible. We were basically just holding hands now.

Another beat. Then: "Come on," she said, and rose from the futon. "Grab your beer."

"Where're we going?" Relief washed over me, but a small deposit of unwanted disappointment unfurled in my chest too.

"We're gonna find some fun." She pulled my hand into hers again, and against my better judgment, I let her.

We made our way down the dark hallway past a few engrossed bodies, through a laundry room, and up some stairs into the backyard. The air was chilly, but I realized I'd been sweating in Shanti's room and welcomed the coolness.

"Check this out."

A few strings of lights glowed over the patchy lawn. On that lawn, a circle defined by some rolled-up blankets surrounded two folks in padded dinosaur suits as they lumbered around each other, as if sizing each other up . . . until one suddenly charged at the other, stomach first, and bounced their opponent onto their back. Said opponent kind of flopped to the side due to their thick tail, then flapped their arms and legs around for a while. The same MC from the roller derby was on the side, yelling out play-by-plays. "And Jojo is down! Flail, Jojo, flail!" Watching Jojo struggle to get up was almost more entertaining than watching the two creatures fight. The small crowd around them seemed to think so too.

"So?" Shanti turned to me, hands in her back pockets.

I side-eyed her. "So what?"

"Don't tell me you're not dying to get out there."

"Shanti, I am literally *not* dying to get out there."

"Come on . . . you like getting physical, right? Bumping people around? Here's a perfect opportunity!"

Uh . . . yeah, except those suits won't allow for bruising of any kind. "Not really my thing."

She stepped in a little closer. A shiver crossed the back of my neck. My sweat must've been cooling, I told myself. "It'll be fun, I promise. And the team will love that you did it."

Ugh. The team. Right. And at least I'd be hiding behind a dinosaur suit, well away from the scary closeness in Shanti's room. I rubbed my face with my hands. "Okay. For the team, then."

She grinned and held out her hand. "Two bucks, please!"

"I have to *pay* to humiliate myself?"

"Yup. That's how we Honeys roll. Get used to it."

God. I handed her the money and asked, "Now what?"

After the current match finished in sensational fashion, with both wrestlers flopping to the ground out-of-bounds and languishing there for a few moments, it was my turn to suit up. Shanti gave my name to the MC and helped me get the suit on, which was tiring in and of itself.

My opponent was a very skinny, short dude whose hands barely reached out of the already short T-Rex arms of the suit. But man, was he ever bouncy. For the first several seconds, all I could do was watch him prance around the ring, his tiny, almost-hidden fists swinging around at his sides. The sight caused me to snicker, and at this, he rushed at me. I didn't even have time to react before I found myself lying on my side.

What the . . . ?

The crowd burst into cheers. "A surprise bump by Vinny stuns Daya! Will she be able to rise from her puddle of PVC?"

My surprise mixed in with embarrassment, and I quickly tried to turn over to get up. It was hard. Like, really hard. At first I started to get frustrated, but then I looked over at Shanti, who was covering her mouth, trying not to laugh, but her laughter was coming out in snorts, and even though I wanted to be mad about it, I couldn't help but laugh myself. Snort-laughs were funny, after all.

Finally in standing position, me and the guy squared off again. This time, I wasn't going to be lured in by his mesmerizing frolicking. I knew I could charge and smack him out of the ring no problem, but what would be the fun in that?

Instead I started to whirl around in a circle as fast as I could (it wasn't very fast), like a slo-mo tornado, and pummel the air with my fists. I could hear the crowd laughing, which was encouraging. The other guy took my cue and started doing the same thing until we finally connected in the middle of the ring and just kind of leaned into each other while continuing to twirl around—two dancing, green blobs, slapping at each other with our chubby arms.

After about ten seconds of this, we both collapsed to the grass in a mountainous PVC lump. My insides hurt from laughing, and I could feel sweat dripping into nooks and crannies no one needed to know about.

"Looks like our dino-wrestlers are too pooped to push anymore . . . It's a tie!" the MC announced.

Once Shanti had helped to peel the sticky suit from my disturbingly damp body, she said, poker-faced, "You ever thought of doing that professionally? You seem made for it."

"Ha-ha," I replied, wiping the sweat from my neck.

"It did seem like you were having fun, though." She handed the suit to a very excited, tall person.

"Yeah, it wasn't that bad." I was surprised by how true this felt.

"Thanks for being game. I can tell lots of this stuff isn't really your thing. Fair to say?"

I ruffled my shirt to cool myself off and collected my jacket from the ground. We started walking back toward the house. "Definitely fair."

"Well, then . . . it's cool you're doing it anyway."

I glanced sideways at her—she was looking at me again, a smile on her lips. I smiled too as she opened the door to the enclosed porch, where things had become exponentially more risqué. Shanti and I both paused for a moment, arms touching, staring at a particularly handsy threesome dancing slowly about a foot away from us. Kat was one of the three. She and two guys were getting pretty hot and heavy, but not in the usual girl-in-the-middle way. Instead Kat and one guy sandwiched the other dude. Definitely a new combo for me. The skater and boxer dudes I knew didn't typically hook up with each other . . . not in front of me, anyway.

I could sense Shanti grow uncomfortable beside me, but I'll admit, I was mesmerized by the scene.

The guy on the outside—the bread, I guess—was almost as tall as Kat and had a man bun and beard. The middle dude was a bit shorter than both Kat and Man Bun but built like a fucking superhero. Watching Kat and these two men let their hands rove over each other, their legs merging into each other's, I found myself a little turned on despite being both annoyed and shaken by my recent interactions with Kat, which also felt confusing. I didn't think I was so much attracted to Kat as just in awe of her. With Shanti, I wasn't sure what I felt either—just that it was entirely different.

Kat noticed me looking, and when she saw Shanti beside me, her face shifted into a mixture of irritation and exasperation.

In the next moment, she was in front of me, hands hanging

off both of my shoulders and her face too close to mine. "Daya! What the fuck! You gotta listen to me already." Her words toppled out like she didn't have full control of them. "Shanti's a lost cause. Trust me . . . I've tried to toughen her up, but she's not like us."

I looked over at Shanti, who'd backed away a couple of feet and was staring at the dance floor, her arms crossed.

"Us tough bitches gotta stick together, right? I can tell you get it—you don't let shit get to you. You don't let people shit *on* you either." She directed these last words toward Shanti, and even in the dim lighting, I could see Shanti's chin crumple. She didn't leave, though, which I thought must've taken something on her part.

I didn't really understand what Kat meant or why it was so upsetting to Shanti, but I didn't really care. Usually I thought crying was weak, but I really hated seeing Shanti so upset right now.

Keeping my voice firm and steady, I said, "You need to get your fucking hands off me, Kat." A few people were watching us now, though most were too drunk to notice what was happening.

She met my glare. Her eyes were unsteady, but I could see the surprise in them. "What'd you say?"

"This isn't cool." I gripped her hands and yanked them off my shoulders.

She swayed for a moment, but then got her bearings and raised herself up to her full height. Without her skates on, she didn't seem so intimidating, though. "Looks like you're not as tough as I thought, Daya. Too bad. Thought you had some real potential there for a minute. Guess you'll be riding the bench all season."

Fuck. That was not an option. "What the hell? What does this have to do with how I skate or hit?" I knew having this argument here with drinks in both of us wasn't helpful, but I couldn't stop myself. Panic at not being able to play piled itself on top of my anger, and my heart thumped hard and fast. "You know I'm as tough as you. You know I deserve to be out there."

"I thought I did. But it doesn't really look that way, does it? Shit doesn't stop once you're off the track—it comes at you from everywhere, and you gotta be ready for it."

Who was she to tell me about shit happening? "I know how to deal with my shit, thanks," I scoffed. As I said the words, I realized they might no longer be true, and fear joined the thumping in my chest. I tried not to let it show.

"Yeah? We'll see." She looked over at Shanti again and then back at me. The cocky expression was gone, replaced by something like disappointment. "But in my experience, opening yourself up just fucks you over. Don't say I didn't warn you." She turned and left the room, not even looking at Shanti as she passed by.

She didn't have to warn me. I already knew what she was talking about.

I glanced at Shanti, who was just staring into the space ahead of her, any remnants of enjoyment drained from her face.

I found myself wishing we were back outside in the cool air and laughing like before—and the thought settled my heartbeat a bit. I hadn't wanted to get into a fight with the most important person on this team or risk my playing time. But I had—all because I'd felt bad for Shanti. It was exactly what Kat was talking about. You risked losing things when you went soft. It was exactly what Thatha had taught me too.

And yet.

If I was being honest, all I really wanted to do right now was be with Shanti—even more than I wanted to go home and run through my ritual or worry about playing time. Because even though Shanti's thumbs pressing into my palm had felt dangerous, she'd also managed to smooth something out. To press past the pain and through to something deeper.

It hadn't felt comfortable. But it hadn't felt terrible, either.

The distance between me and her felt like miles right now, though. I could tell she was still crying and upset. I knew the right thing to do was to go over to her. To say something or do something. But I had no idea what to say in times like this. Silence was easier. I took a breath and went with the only thing I did know much about.

As I took a step toward her, she turned toward the wall, arms still folded and head tilted back, like she was trying to catch any remaining tears. I moved beside her and gave her a slight nudge, my arm to hers. Just a little body contact to let her know I was here.

She turned her head toward me, a question on her face.

I gave her another nudge and paired it with a half smile. She pushed back into my arm with enough pressure to make my feet have to shift over a little.

"Okay, I see how it is," I said, a little impressed.

Her smile grew for a moment and then fell again. She swallowed. "She's right, you know. You two are way more alike than you and I are."

I nodded. "Yeah. That's probably true."

Her eyes focused on my lips and grew sad. "I get it if you need to go or whatever—"

I did want to get out of here. I just wanted to do that with Shanti. Even if it meant pissing Kat off more. Even if it scared the shit out of me.

"So let's go."

Her eyes met mine. "What?"

"Let's get out of here. Can you drive?" *Holy shit. Okay. We're doing this.*

She took a few seconds to find her words. "Yeah—yes. I haven't had anything to drink."

"Cool. Lead the way."

Chapter Twenty-Five

Shanti had grabbed the keys to the van, and while she shoved a bunch of gear and stuff into the back seat, I buckled my seat belt and calmed my breathing. My heart was beating hard like it usually did when I got into a car, though I wasn't entirely sure it was because of the usual reasons. Shanti climbed into the driver's seat and started the engine. I watched her command this tank of a vehicle, operating the clunky stick shift without a second thought. I found it kind of sexy, which made me even more nervous.

Pulling away from the curb, she asked, "Where to?"

I shrugged. "I dunno. Maybe we could just drive for a bit?"

She nodded. We steered through the streets at an easy pace, both of us silent for a while.

I had so many questions I wanted to ask her, and even though I hated it when people asked me about personal stuff, part of me hated holding it all inside, too. And I was so tired of all Kat's bullshit. I thought Shanti must've been as well, so I forced myself to try.

"You okay?" I asked.

She stared out the front windshield for a few moments, then cleared her throat. "I just wish she wasn't always so disappointed in me." Her jaw tightened as she swallowed. I could tell she was holding back tears.

"Why is she? I mean—you're amazing." As I heard myself say this, my face got hot. "I mean, you—you're not disappointing. You're nice." *Ugh.* "Why's she so hard on you?" My words came out in a rush.

She lifted her hand to tuck a few strands of hair behind her ear. "She wants me to be stronger, so I won't get hurt."

That made sense to me, in principle. "But why's she such a jerk about it?"

"Because to her, 'stronger' means tough. Hard. It means aggression and fearlessness. And fists." She seemed to get lost for a moment, then added, "I'm not like that. As you know."

She glanced at me when she said this last part, and I instantly felt a bit guilty. I'd been expecting the same things from her as Kat did, I realized. I hadn't said it in the same way, but I'd shown it in others.

"I don't think being tough is the only way to deal with hurt," Shanti continued. "But my way can also open you *up* to hurt, I guess. Kat doesn't want to risk that. And she's mad that *I've* chosen to risk it. And scared, I think."

Kat, scared? It was hard for me to believe that, although I could understand why someone would be scared of being hurt. I understood that more than I was willing to admit.

"Is that what she meant when she said opening yourself up just fucks you over?" Saying the word "fuck" in this car, here, now, with Shanti, made me flinch a little, which was weird, since I said it all the time.

Shanti nodded ever so slightly. "Yeah. She's definitely been hurt by people she's cared about. Including me."

This was another thing I found hard to picture. "You?"

"Yup."

"I can't believe that's true."

She glanced over at me again, then back at the road. "It's true," she said, and leaned on the gas a little more.

Watching Shanti's side profile, I could tell she was thinking something through—the way she blinked and chewed on her lower lip.

I wanted to know what she meant, but I thought it best to let her think.

Several minutes of silence and driving later, I looked out the window to see us pull up to an apartment building with a meager little playground outside, illuminated by one flickering streetlamp.

Shanti turned off the engine and sighed back into her seat, staring out my window. She pointed at the building. "My mom lives there."

Uncertain how to respond, I said, "Okay . . ."

"I haven't lived with her for three years—since I was sixteen. She didn't really want us."

Damn. "She didn't?"

Shanti shook her head. "Our dad was never in the picture. He moved back to China after they got divorced—when we were little. And my mom's boyfriend's an asshole. Like, the kind that talks with his fists." She glanced at me, to check my reaction, I guessed. I just gave a slight nod. I didn't really know how to process this information. Shanti looked at her hands, still on the steering wheel, and continued. "They've been together since I was fourteen, Kat seventeen. Eventually, Kat would get into it with him, trying to defend Mom. And me. She was always so strong. I think she'd been secretly working out, too, trying to get stronger. But no matter what, Mom would always side with Rick."

Her voice cracked and she paused. I didn't want to mess anything up by saying something insensitive, so I just did what Dr. Hoang sometimes did—I repeated back what Shanti had said, hoping it would prompt her to say more. "She sided with *him*?"

Shanti nodded. "Yeah. Kat got so sick of both their crap, she saved up some money and one day she came home, slammed Rick up against the wall, told him and my mom they could pummel each other if they wanted, and practically lifted me off my feet to rush me out of there." She scratched at something dried and crusty on the steering wheel as her cheeks became wet.

"You never went back?"

"I did. Once. I was worried about my mom even after everything she'd put us through. This was months after we'd left, and our lives were just getting to some kind of normal, but I guess I thought—she's our mom. She must miss us, right? Kat didn't want me to go, but I begged her to come with me, to give Mom one more chance. Kat wasn't happy about it, but she didn't want me to go by myself, either. When we got there, though, my mom wouldn't even open the door. Just yelled at us from inside to fuck off. Literally. Those were her words. 'Just fuck off.' It broke my heart, but I think it broke more than that in Kat. She was so mad at me—"

"Mad at *you*?" I couldn't help but interrupt. "How could she be mad at *you*?"

"Because I made her go back. Just so we could get hurt again. And because I still can't bring myself to hate my mom. I don't think Kat has ever forgiven me for any of it. It's why I'm a 'lost cause' to her. Why I'm such a disappointment."

Shanti looked so sad. I wanted to comfort her but was just trying to wrap my head around all this. I got the part about needing to be strong, about wanting to protect yourself—I *really* got that part. But I hated the way it showed up between Shanti and Kat. Being strong shouldn't hurt the ones you love, should it?

Shanti wiped her face and started the engine. "You think I put up with too much from Kat, and maybe I do, but I know deep down she's just terrified. Of me getting hurt. Of getting hurt herself. How she shows that is messed up, I know. She's basically trying to bully me into doing things her way. Shitting on me herself because she thinks I let people shit on me too much. It's completely ass-backward." She shrugged. "It's complicated, I guess." Looking at me, she added, "But I do have my boundaries with her—I just don't bother when she's drunk like she was tonight. There's no point."

She put the car into first gear. "Sometimes her strength can be positive, too, you know? She'd do anything for the team."

I guessed that was one way Kat and I differed. I'd never had a team to fight for. I'd been listening to Shanti, partly confused by all the complications, but also experiencing moments of recognition—of seeing myself in Shanti's descriptions of Kat. Toughness to protect from hurt. Hurting to protect from hurt. The realization tightened my throat as we drove away.

I didn't want to just leave Shanti hanging, though, so I swallowed back the ache and offered, "Thanks for telling me."

"I just wanted you to know where all that was coming from. And that I'm not as weak as you may think. As you both may think."

I faced her. Her eyes were trained on the road ahead, but I could see in her set jaw and the lift of her chest how strong she really was. "I'm sorry—if I ever made you feel like Kat makes you feel."

Eyes still facing forward, she said, "Thanks."

We drove for a bit, lost in our thoughts. After a while, as we paused for a red light, Shanti reached over and flicked my thigh with her fingers. When she spoke, her voice had shifted from serious to shy. "Um—you can totally say no, but I really don't want to go back to my place. They'll be partying for hours, and I'm too exhausted to deal with an even drunker Kat. Could we . . . maybe . . . hang out at your place? I mean—if your parents wouldn't mind?"

So many things about her words made me instantly nervous and awkward, which made me say, way too abruptly, "My parents are dead. Car accident." I made it worse by adding, "They won't mind." *Fuck.*

"Jesus, Daya—I'm so sorry."

Her face held all the feelings I was so sick of seeing in the months after the accident. Pity. Concern. Uncertainty. Everything I saw in her threatened to bring up feelings I'd been working so hard to keep buried deep. Even after everything she'd shared, the realizations coming to me in her words, the thought of talking about my parents brought back a sudden urge to bring my left hand down against my knee.

"It was a while ago. Don't worry about it." I wanted to switch the subject. But I also wanted Shanti to come back to my place. The competing urges made me speechless and frustrated.

Instead of pushing me, Shanti continued driving. I didn't care where we were going. I was too busy gulping back my irritation with myself for bringing up my parents, and my frustration at not being able to say what I really wanted to say. Not to mention my fear around what I really wanted to say—

which was, *Yes, come back to my place with me. Please.*

As we drove through a desolate industrial section of town, my thoughts banged around in my head. What did I want right now? Definitely not to just go to bed. I couldn't sleep anyway. But it felt dangerous to be alone with Shanti, especially after she'd opened up about all these things. It felt like it did when Fee tried to nudge me into sharing with them. A pull and an ache all at once. Something about this danger attracted me—maybe something other than a physical pain was what I needed. Maybe the physical pain wasn't enough anymore. I found myself doing something even more dangerous.

"Turn right at the next light. My place is just up the road."

When we drove up to the house, I knew Priam and Vicki would be gone, because they'd mentioned some kind of event they had tonight, and I silently thanked the musical theater gods for whatever magic had swept them away.

I guided Shanti to my room, each step up the staircase punching a new tender spot into my brain as I contemplated what it was I was actually doing right now.

I'd left my room in a mess and quickly picked up a few clothes as soon as we walked in. My bedroom wasn't nearly as cozy as Shanti's, but I tried my best by turning on the lamp next to my bed and setting my laptop to play the only chill music I had—a mix that was literally called "Soft Shit." Shanti stood near the door, surveying the space. I did the same from my spot near my desk.

Needing something to do, I blurted, "I need some water. You need some water? I'm gonna go get us some water." Then I rushed by her and back down the stairs to get this all-important water from the kitchen. I gulped down an entire glass before refilling it and another and slowly making my way back up the stairs.

What exactly was meant to happen here? What did I expect? What did *Shanti* expect? Was I prepared to meet anyone's expectations at this point?

When I came back in, Shanti was leaning against my desk, facing the door. She looked up when I entered, adjusted her glasses, and smiled. All three actions together immediately soothed the rapid beat of my heart. I kicked the door closed behind me and handed over her glass of water. I leaned against the desk beside her. We sipped. Then sipped again.

Shanti's arm pushed into mine, gentle but firm. I pushed back, just a little. Soon she was standing in front of me, placing our waters on the desk and removing her glasses. Soon her lips were on mine, pressing not too softly. My mouth fell open with a breath and our tongues met. Something inside me swelled and my chest expanded to accommodate it. My hands gripped the edge of the desk—the bruise on my left hand pulsing—but when her body bent into mine, her chest meeting my own, her stomach pressed to me, all I wanted to do was bring her closer. So I did. My hands left the desk, found her waist, and pulled her in.

Soon she was whispering into my ear, "Can we lie down?" and I was already leading her to the bed.

Shanti leaned over me and ran a finger along my jawline. Her thumb found my lower lip and gently pressed downward, opening my lips so she could run her tongue slowly between them. The wetness of her tongue sent a surge of yearning deep into my chest and lower still. When she looked at me, I think she saw it. She kissed me again, more deeply this time, and let her hand follow the path of my longing, over my breast, along my stomach, undoing the button and zipper of my jeans.

At this, a breath in my chest caught—not because I'd never been in this position before, but because—why? Maybe because this didn't feel like any of those other times. Maybe because it felt . . . deeper, defenseless, unpredictable. She could sense this too. She paused. Her hand rested on my stomach for a moment.

"I'll only do what you want me to do."

I wanted her to do this. I took a deep breath and told her so. She removed her shirt. Helped me to remove mine. Kissed the bruises growing across my right shoulder. Found my rapidly rising and falling stomach and kissed the skin there too. Touched every aching part of me both inside and out until my body seemed to let loose the ache into her lips and fingers. Gentle and soft like I'd always thought being with a girl would be, but also strong and crushing and deep in ways I hadn't imagined.

Before my mum died, I hadn't been able to see all the ways she loved me. I'd been so caught up in proving how strong

I was that I could only see what I thought were her weak-
nesses. How little she understood about boxing and sports.
The way she gave in to Thatha. How she stayed quiet when
I wished she would speak. I should have seen how her real
strength was in the way she gently held space for both my dad
and me—how little she needed muscles and force and fists to
make us feel safe.

Now—too late—moments with her would come back to
me, appearing so differently through time and grief. Like the
time I'd grown so frustrated with my math homework that I'd
thrown my assignment aside and stomped down the hallway to
the kitchen, where my mum was sitting at the table, paying bills.

"Oh, hello," she'd said, looking up over the top of her
glasses.

"Hi." I'd opened the fridge door and plunged my head
into it. Dinner at our house wasn't until later. That's when
the brown folks ate. Unfortunately, my body needed food way
before that, especially with the amount of training I'd been
doing. I grabbed a dish of tapioca from the fridge and a banana
from the fruit bowl.

As I was getting a spoon, Amma had asked, "Shall we
have a cup of tea?"

I looked up at her, a bit surprised. Usually she'd just let
me go about my business without interrupting. "I have lots of
homework." Not that I wanted to do it, but I was also grumpy
as hell and didn't have time for tea. I banged the drawer shut
harder than I meant to.

"I can bring it to your room?" She'd taken off her glasses and rubbed her eyes as she asked. She looked tired.

"It's fine. Don't worry about it."

"I'm not worried about it."

She had the funniest smile on her face. I'd call it a smirk, but I couldn't imagine my mother smirking. She rose from the table and came over to me. "Sit down and eat your tapioca," she said, giving me a little push, which also surprised me.

Not really wanting to go back to my homework anyway, I plunked myself down at the table and started shoveling tapioca into my mouth. I watched as Amma got out the teapot and mugs. Set the kettle to boil. But she didn't go for the teabags like she usually did. Instead she dug around in the cupboard and pulled out a small tin canister with a sword-wielding lion on it.

When the water had boiled, Amma swirled some of it around in the pot and poured it out. I'd seen her do this before, to take the chill out of the pot first, but she usually only did it for company.

Then she scooped loose tea into the pot with a little plastic spoon that had been hiding in the tin, each scoop creating a *shushk* sound as she dug into the dried brown bits. When she looked up and saw me watching, she said, "This is the *real* Sri Lankan tea—it's *prac*-ti-cally medicine." I didn't often notice my parents' accents, but I noticed hers now, how her consonants cracked like strikes against a tiny cricket bat.

As the hot water streamed into the pot, it made a hissing,

bubbling sound. Amma placed the top on the pot and covered the whole thing with a knitted pink-and-white tea cozy that her mother had made and that she'd brought from Sri Lanka. As she waited for the tea to steep, she heated some milk in the microwave, warmed the mugs with more hot water, and then spooned sugar into each mug.

Watching her felt almost like meditation. I'd forgotten about my tapioca and was drawn in by her hands, golden bangles shining around what I'd always considered delicate wrists, carefully self-manicured nails so different from my roughly clipped ones. They moved around the pot and spoons and mugs as though performing a magic trick—only this time, nothing was disappearing. Instead she was conjuring up something. Something for me.

The look on her face was an unfamiliar mix of determination and calm. She seemed so perfectly at ease performing this particular ritual. Or maybe she was just at ease performing it for us.

I'd underestimated my mother. She'd always been stronger than I thought she was. She'd always loved me with a force I hadn't recognized. A force so gentle and consistent I hadn't even noticed it was there.

Chapter Twenty-Six

I hadn't meant to fall asleep. I'd *meant* to artfully and gently persuade Shanti to head out before my aunt and uncle got home. But when I awoke the next morning, it was to the sound of Shanti slipping back into my bedroom after using the bathroom down the hall.

When I saw her, excitement rose in my chest . . . until I realized where I was, what time it was, and where she'd just been.

"Morning," she whispered, sliding back into the sheets beside me and pecking me on the lips.

I pulled my head back and sat up, thankful I was wearing a T-shirt. Being naked right now would just feel too damn defenseless. "Did anyone see you?" I was sure my eyes and tone betrayed my panic.

She lifted herself on one elbow and considered me for a moment. "Um . . . yes—but it wasn't a big deal, I promise. I'm sorry, I really had to pee, and I tried to be super quiet, but—"

Fuckity fuck. "Who saw you? My uncle or my aunt?" I swung my legs over the side of the bed and pulled on some sweatpants.

"Your aunt. She was really friendly, though." Shanti's eyes formed a mixture of concern and assurance. I could tell she was searching my face to read my response.

I crossed my room and leaned against my desk, gripping it with my hands. My mind flashed to last night—our kiss, Shanti's soft waist—but I couldn't think about that right now. "What'd she say?" I asked.

Shanti climbed out of my bed again and put her glasses on. "She just said hello and asked if I was a friend of yours."

"And what'd you say?" I demanded. Some part of me felt like I might be overreacting, but in the glaring light of morning, everything seemed bare and immense—Shanti, our conversations last night, our time *not* talking—and I really didn't want to give Priam or Vicki any reason to poke into any of that. I'd never had anyone sleep over before, so regardless of what happened last night—whether they knew the truth or not—they'd ask me a thousand questions that I didn't have the answers to. I still wasn't ready to upset the defined boundaries I'd established with them. . . . This current boundary breaking was more than enough to get my head around, and at the moment, I wasn't doing a good job of it. Everything was happening too fast.

"I said yes, I was a friend of yours and just stayed over

because we were studying late. She asked me if I was Anna, but I said no. I hope that's okay. I didn't really know what else to say. Sorry."

Shanti stood on the other side of the bed, her shirt rumpled, the boxers she'd borrowed too big for her. One hand gripped her other arm, which hung prone by her side. Seeing her like this, I felt all my panic tumble into affection. I wiped my hand over my face to smooth out the worry and walked over to her to put my arms around her waist. This was completely alien territory to me—comforting others, feeling the need to comfort others—but the need was so strong right now I barely had to think about it.

"Shit. *I'm* sorry. I'm just freaking out a little. Things with my uncle and aunt are . . . weird. And generally frustrating. I don't know how to explain this to them. I don't really want to."

"You live with them now? After . . . ?" she asked, straightening out her glasses.

"Yeah . . ."

She nodded and left it alone, which I massively appreciated. "Well, I could try slipping out without them seeing me. Might make things less weird?"

I hated that my heart leaped at the suggestion, but I really didn't want to have to introduce Shanti to Priam and Vicki, or worse, navigate any kind of conversation between the four of us. "That might be the best plan right now, but"—I gave her waist a squeeze—"I liked . . . this." I meant it. Even though I was scared shitless to mean it.

Her face shifted into surprise and a shy smile. "Me too." She placed her hands over mine on her hips. "So . . . you're okay? With us . . . last night?"

Fuck if I knew what I was. But I knew that last night had felt way different from any other hookup I'd ever had, and that Shanti made me feel something I wasn't used to feeling— something like calm. Something like safe. But that didn't mean I knew how to express any of that in words. So I didn't.

"Are you?" I asked.

"Definitely." A wide grin spread across her face, which made me smile too.

Unfortunately, these pleasant moments quickly dissolved into a series of painful ones.

When I tried to guide Shanti down the stairs and out the front door without Priam and Vicki seeing or hearing us, I'd forgotten to tell her to avoid using the banister, which tended to creak when you pushed or pulled too hard on it.

As she pressed a hand onto it and the wood groaned, the next sounds we heard were, "Helllooooooooo!" from the kitchen and then a groan of my own.

Vicki and Priam appeared around the corner, both in their special weekend brunch aprons—custom-made to look like the torsos and legs of showgirls.

Fuck. Me.

"Daya! Daya's friend! Come, come—brunch is now being served!" Priam sang in an exaggerated baritone, followed by

Vicki's soprano solo of, "Avocado toast, poached eggs, fresh fruit, coffeeeeeee!"

Shanti's face would have made me laugh out loud if I didn't feel so close to disintegrating into embarrassment. Her lips had fallen ever-so-slightly open, and her raised eyebrows clearly conveyed her astonishment.

Priam and Vicki whooshed us into the kitchen like we were two dust bunnies and they were two especially obnoxious brooms.

"What's your name again, darling?" Vicki asked as she guided Shanti into a seat at the kitchen table.

"Shanti." Her face still hadn't changed, but she attempted a smile now.

"Lovely! I'm Daya's aunt Vicki and this is her uncle Priam. It's so exciting to see Daya having *friends* over. She *never* has friends over. Have you two been friends for long?" All this was said as Vicki and Priam flitted from the kitchen island to the table, bringing with them food and condiments each time.

I hadn't sat down yet. Part of me couldn't quite accept that this was happening. But when Shanti looked to me for help, I forced myself into my seat and jumped in. "We just met skateboarding."

Vicki paused mid-flit and Shanti shot me a look. *What'd I say?*

"Oh—I thought you were school friends. What were you studying for last night, then?"

Shit. That's right. Shanti told her we were studying late. "We were going over . . . tricks. For skateboarding. Shanti's new to it, so I . . . showed her some things." Not my best lie.

"Oh?" Priam said, and looked to Vicki. "Who knew skateboarding was so complicated!" He was smiling, but Vicki's pursed lips communicated that she wasn't buying it.

"You were up late, studying skateboarding?" she asked, placing the Dorothy and Toto salt and pepper shakers in front of me rather pointedly.

"Yeah . . . ," I replied, keeping my eyes on Toto. My gut was churning. I could feel my carefully constructed boundaries slowing falling apart, whether I wanted them to or not.

Both Shanti and I just sat there for a few moments, staring at the table. I could practically feel her blushing from her chair next to me. I suspected my own face conveyed all kinds of things I didn't want it to. My suspicions were confirmed in the next moment.

"Ohhhhhhhhh!" Both Priam and Vicki let loose this animated expression of their mutual recognition and I had to fight the urge to grab Shanti's hand and flee the scene. Glancing up, I could see them exchange a gleeful look as Vicki reached out and clutched Priam's arm. The next moment, they'd slid into their chairs and were both leaning their chins into their hands, beaming at me and Shanti.

Good God.

"Now, girls, I know I speak for Priam when I say this. You have nothing to be ashamed of—Priam and I have *oodles* of 'Friends of You-Know-Who'"—Vicki picked Dorothy up from the table by the head and swung her back and forth—"and we simply *adore* them!"

Friends of Dorothy? What the hell is she talking about?

"Yes, we do!" Priam followed. "They're some of our *favorite* people!"

Suddenly Vicki was back on her feet. "You know what? This calls for a capital *C* Celebration!" She disappeared into the living room, leaving Shanti and me speechless and Priam grinning from ear to ear at us, as though he knew exactly what Vicki was about to do, which I couldn't imagine he actually did.

And then music started playing from the living room—"Seasons of Love" from *Rent*. A minute later Vicki swept back into the kitchen with two small rainbow flags on sticks—because, obviously, she had a secret stash of tiny rainbow flags somewhere. She poked these into the middle of the avocado toasts sitting untouched on Shanti's and my plates. Then she joined Priam on the other side of the table, and they began to sing along with the song. They were serenading us. Celebrating our gayness.

This was way worse than having to dress up and perform a roller-skating routine in front of strangers. Shanti would never want to come back here. *I* never wanted to come back here.

But then I heard a fit of giggles from beside me and looked over. Shanti had picked up her flag and was waving it in time to the song, her face glowing with *actual* amazement and delight.

A hint of amusement passed through me, even as disbelief overtook my face. The encouragement from Shanti caused Priam to stand and invite Vicki into a waltz around the kitchen as they continued to sing. I tried to catch Shanti's eye to communicate my very real torment, but she just sat back in her chair, trained her eyes on the dancing duo, and kept waving the damn flag. Giving up on any hopes of making an early departure from this "celebration," I slumped back in my chair, folded my arms, and glared as hard as I could at Priam and Vicki, who were somehow incorporating at least four or five different dance styles into a number that—as far as I knew from the musical—was normally performed standing perfectly still.

But then, there was nothing normal about this. As I watched them flounce around the kitchen with Shanti's rainbow flag flicking every so often into my sight line, the past twelve hours seeped into my brain—the thorny situation with Kat, an amazing-but-still-mystifying night with Shanti, and now this. The only thing I'd set out to do—kill it on the track—had so far been complicated by confusing dynamics. And the kind of stuff I avoided like the plague—intimacy, my aunt and uncle, musicals—seemed to be invading me from all sides.

Just as these thoughts began to set panic alight in my chest once again, Priam and Vicki were reaching the climax of the song and trying to replicate the numerous voices emerging out of our stereo from the living room, including the one that goes super high at the end. As *both* of them tried to reach that note, Shanti reached over and seized my hand, finally turning her head my way to look at me with what could only be described as a combination of amusement, disbelief, and euphoria.

I'll admit, it was difficult for my displeasure and panic to sustain itself in the face of her surprising but equally endearing reaction. What surprised me even more was when she gripped the crap out of my hand in her excitement and what I felt—instead of the usual pain in my palm—was something else entirely in my chest.

After the showstopping number ended, Vicki and Priam took their bows—something they found a way to squeeze in at least six or seven times a day—and seated themselves back at the table. Still beaming at us through slightly heavier breaths, they began eating their breakfast. Shanti looked at me, shrugged, and let go of my hand to start eating as well.

Between bites, Vicki asked a series of annoying questions that neither Shanti nor I knew how to answer.

"How long have you two been . . . what do the kids call it these days?"

"If you were a musical duo, which one would you be, you think?"

"Who's your favorite *Glee* couple? You can't say Brittany and Santana!"

Shanti and I muddled our way through this overeager interrogation as best we could, but as soon as I'd inhaled my avocado toast and eggs (and stolen Shanti's last piece of fruit to speed things up), I pulled her out of her chair and told Priam and Vicki we had to go.

"Oh! Where are you off to?" Priam asked.

"We've got . . . skateboarding practice," I shouted as I practically bodychecked Shanti away from the table.

"Oh, Daya, couldn't you just take a break from all that thrashing about for once? We never get to see you and your friends!"

And you still haven't figured out that that's by design? "We won't be 'thrashing about.' We skate. On a board. And I like it." The edge creeping into my voice must have done the trick, because Priam jumped in.

"Oh, all right then—but maybe we can all go to a show together sometime or something! Do you like musicals, Shanti?"

Shanti made sure to look straight at me as she replied, "Absolutely!"

Jesus.

Once upstairs, I shut my bedroom door behind me and leaned against it. "Don't say a word."

Shanti stood in front of me and placed her hands on my hips, her lips leaning in toward my own. "Fine. I won't."

Chapter Twenty-Seven

Since I'd lied and said we had to go, I had to cut the kissing short to gather our things and escape the house. When I shut the passenger-side door of Shanti's van, she asked, "So? Where to?"

I thought about it as the van slowly clunked to life. Good question. The last place I wanted to go was Shanti and Kat's place, and I was pretty sure Shanti didn't want to go there either.

"I don't know. Someplace you can think of?" I asked, suddenly feeling a little worn out. From breakfast, yes, but also from lack of sleep and excessive emotional output.

She stared out the windshield for a few seconds, then smiled. "Yup."

We were quiet, which was fine by me. I was somewhere between completely discomfited by this new dynamic between me and Shanti and strangely anticipatory about it—like I couldn't wait to see what would happen but I was also terrified about what might happen. But not too terrified to stop me from going anywhere with her right now. This feeling of wanting to be around someone so much just led me back to being discomfited. And exhausted.

Fuck.

When she pulled up to what looked like a seniors' home, though, I started to rethink my need to be anywhere she was.

"Uhhh . . . ," I began, staring out my window at the beige-and-brick building to my right.

"Don't judge. This place is 'capital *R* Rad,'" Shanti said, mimicking Vicki's bubbly voice. "Come on." She hopped out of the van. I let out a burst of air and followed.

When the man at the reception desk looked up, all the wrinkles in his face stretched out in recognition and pleasure. "Shanti, ma belle! Quelle surprise! Comment vas-tu?"

Shanti leaned over the counter and they did that two-cheek kiss thing that I'd never done in my life. This all felt very French and hence, very foreign to me.

"Très bien. Oumar, c'est Daya. Daya, Oumar."

Apparently Shanti spoke French now? Pulling my questioning gaze (which she ignored) away from her, I reached out in a preemptive handshake—this guy looked like the type to two-cheek-kiss strangers even across a counter.

"A pleasure, mademoiselle, a pleasure."

"Oumar, we're here to get in on some Sunday Service."

My neck swiveled so quickly toward her I felt a twinge. "Beg yer pardon?" I said, before I could keep it to myself.

She annoyingly just placed a hand on my arm and ignored me again.

"Ah, bien sûr! Come with me, mesdemoiselles!" We followed Oumar at a painstaking pace toward a hallway at one end of the foyer.

Shanti seemed perfectly at home here, and that made me slightly less anxious.

"You've come on an especially remarkable day, mes coeurs! Ça grouille de monde ici ce matin!" He poked the air in front of him with his cane and translated, "Hopping!"

Cool. Yup. I can handle hopping "Sunday Service." Yup, I can.

He led us around a corner and down a longish hallway toward a door. I thought I could hear a mishmash of muffled sounds like cheers and beeps and crashes and even some colorful language coming from behind the door. Shanti tugged at my short ponytail and said, "Get ready" in a low voice.

For what? And why would Shanti bring me to something I had to 'get ready' for? Hadn't we had enough to deal with these past few days?

When Oumar opened the door with a flourish, what unfolded in front of us was, perhaps, best described as "elder games." Everything from shuffleboard to card games to pool to some kind of bowling game I'd never seen before to jumbo Jenga extended out in every direction, filling up every available inch of a recreation space. There were even two old-school arcade games in the corner—Pac-Man and Dig Dug—the sources of the beeping, I realized.

Oumar flung open his arms, almost belting an older woman to his right with his cane, and announced, "Sunday Service, mesdemoiselles!"

I turned to Shanti, who shrugged and said, "You think roller derby folks are competitive?" She nodded to a corner of the room, where a group of people were huddled around some kind of amusement. When I looked to Shanti again with a thousand questions on my face, she just laughed and took my hand. "I promise this is the kind of ridiculous you'll like. Trust me."

"Okay . . ." I took a breath and decided to believe her.

Dragging me over to the cluster of white-haired onlookers, she tapped on a couple of shoulders and was greeted by a number of familiar and enthusiastic "Shantis" and "My dears." The circle broke open a little to allow us in, and sitting at a card table at the nucleus of the gathering was Yolanda, serious as ever and arm-wrestling another woman who looked to be about her age. Bee stood behind Yolanda, barking all kinds of encouragements like a boxing coach.

The other woman wrestling Yolanda was twice as thick in every portion of her body than Yolanda, but somehow their entwined fists were perfectly poised midway, tensely vibrating with both women's efforts.

After a few seconds wherein my mouth drifted wide open and my eyes darted from each woman to their blue-veined fists to their plump little biceps, I couldn't help but let loose a "Woo!" I didn't even know was coming. Watching these two tough old ladies duke it out stirred up a kind of excitement in me that felt simple and easy. I didn't even care who won. I think we were all winning at the moment.

Shanti let out a "Woo" of her own, and when Bee caught sight of us, she followed with a howling "Gooooo Yoooooo!" which made me laugh.

The crowd of folks around us joined in with all kinds of hoots and hollers, and you could just see both Yolanda and her competition hunker down even further, their eyes brightening with the energy of those around them.

After what felt like several minutes, but might only have been about thirty seconds, the other woman seemed to tire, sweat dripping down her powdered face. She lost a half inch, then another inch, then another, and with each gain, Yolanda seemed to grow in stature until finally, in one last exertion, she pinned the other woman's clenched hand to the table in triumph.

Bee lost her shit. You'd think Yolanda had just won the World Gay Games or something. While Yolanda sat back and folded her arms in utter smugness and satisfaction, Bee thumped her walker in a tight circle around the two competitors—*thunk*, shimmy shimmy, *thunk*, shimmy shimmy—alternatingly wailing like an ambulance siren and then cackling hysterically. I noticed folks in the crowd gave her and her walker a wide berth.

This was madness. But it was the kind of madness I could get behind. Competition and a little shameless gloating. And also . . . fun?

Shanti tugged at my sleeve and indicated with a head nod to follow her forward. As Bee made a second victory loop, she swerved toward Shanti and me and paused her walker to spread her arms out wide, inviting a hug.

I followed Shanti's lead and leaned over the walker to gather Bee up in my arms. I didn't want to squeeze too hard, but she sure as hell squeezed the crap out of me. Kat must have gotten her muscle from Bee. I wondered if Bee had passed on anything to Shanti, or if Shanti's strength was all her own.

"Dollfaces! Did ya see that? Did ya see my girl whup some old-lady butt?" From the clapping and jeering going on around us, I suspected the crowd was used to Bee and Yolanda's antics.

"We saw it, Nana!" Shanti replied.

"That's sixteen wins in a row! How 'bout that, huh?" Bee said.

I looked at Shanti and said, "Amazing." She nodded and grinned.

Yolanda grabbed her cane and thumped over to us. She brandished her right bicep and, without a hint she was joking, said, "All-natural beef."

Shanti and I glanced at each other and stifled a laugh.

Bee brought us over to a card table with some pretzels and grapes on it. She plucked a grape from its stem and popped it into her mouth. Then she plucked another and popped it into Yolanda's mouth before Yolanda even knew what was happening, which was about the cutest thing ever. "So what brings you two gorgeous gals he-ya anyway?" Bee asked, cheek bulging with its grape.

Shanti shrugged. "I just knew you'd be here like every Sunday and thought it'd be fun to see you two. Daya made the Honeys, Nana! And she's been put through all kinds of shenanigans." She looked at me. "It's been tiring. But she's been an awesome sport about it all."

Come to think of it, I really *had* been a pretty good sport about everything. Considering how un-shenanigany I was.

"I thought some Bee and Yolanda time would be good for our souls," she continued.

"Well, ain't that sweet," Bee said. "So you made the team, then, did ya?"

"I did."

"Well, listen, if you made the cut, that means you must be a real gem. The Honeys only take the very best, ya know. Ain't that right, Yolanda!" She smacked Yolanda on the ass, causing a squawk to erupt from Yolanda's mouth.

"I'm not sure about the gem part, but I hope I can do the team proud." I really did. A pocket of dread opened up in my stomach as I remembered Kat's words last night, but I tried to stay focused on the moment at hand. I'd have to figure that other shit out later. And somehow, after last night and all this around me now, I felt like I'd be able to find a way.

"Aw, you will, you will," Bee piped up, and I decided she was responding to both my thoughts and my words, which made me feel a bit better. "Just keep puttin' all ya heart and sweat into it. You'll get there!"

"Now, who's up for a game of Ping-Pong? Two old babes against two young ones?" Yolanda asked, rubbing her bony hands together.

Shanti and I stared down at their walker and cane, then at each other.

We laughed. Yolanda almost smiled. And I realized how much I missed laughing.

> "Sudu haale, bath wele, sambole
> Rasa dunne, mulu lokema handunanne
> Lunu ha dehi api denna!"

"Dad!"

> "Api denna, ek weela, pana wage
> Lowe inne, heda penna, hina heela
> Sahayogen wede denne!"

"Amma—make him stop!"

The three of us were in the car, the baila on full blast, and Thatha was singing along with the windows down like he was giving his own solo concert to every other car on the road. I was sitting behind my dad and could see Amma trying to suppress a laugh in the passenger seat.

"Mum!" The synthesizer buzzed over the speakers.

She turned back to me, a downward smile escaping. "What do you want me to do, Daya?"

And then, as if to torment me further, she started singing along, head wobbling from side to side.

"Hemathena hemawita eka wage gelapena
Rata diva pinawana, rasa guna gena dena
Lunu dehi, lunu dehi!"

I sank lower into the back seat, but I wasn't really mad. Embarrassed as hell, but not mad. I loved seeing my parents like this—enjoying each other, letting loose. It didn't happen often, but it *did* happen. And it made me hope it happened when I wasn't around too.

The two of them managed to catch every frantic lyric and then sail into the famous "lunu dehis," followed by the quick, rolling *R*s of the singers' "rampapa rapams." I couldn't roll my *R*s like them, so I never sang that part, but the rest of the song was contagious, and if we hadn't been in public and I hadn't been a monumentally mortified teenager, I would've joined in.

For the moment, though, I just stifled my smirk and tried to keep my head lower than the window so no one outside could see me. But by the end of the song, I couldn't help but laugh along with them.

Chapter Twenty-Eight

Once we'd taken Yolanda and Bee home, and as we walked back to the van, Shanti laced her fingers through mine. I squeezed her hand and asked, "You don't need to answer this if you don't want to, but does Bee know about your mum and stuff? I mean, why didn't you and Kat just go live with them?" I'd been thinking about how amazing Yolanda and Bee were, how much Shanti and Kat adored them.

Shanti leaned against the front passenger door but didn't let go of my hand. She scratched her nose. I had the urge to kiss it but thought I should let her answer first. "Nana and Yolanda only moved here after we left my mom's. They moved here *because* we left. And they offered to take us both in. Nana felt terrible. She hadn't known how bad it was—because we hadn't told her. They lived so far away, and Kat didn't want to upset them. I've always wondered what might've happened if we'd told Nana sooner. If there'd have been less pain for everyone."

Shanti went quiet for a moment and I stood in front of her, awkward and still unsure about how to comfort her—*whether* to comfort her. I'd spent so long avoiding moments like this that I had no idea how to be *in* them. But when I thought about all the moments Shanti had been soft with me, even when I'd resisted, I realized how much I'd needed that from her. And I realized she probably needed the same from me now.

I fought past my discomfort and came in close to wrap my arms around her waist. She lifted her eyes to mine and half smiled. "How *did* they find out?" I asked.

"I called them. Kat was furious with me, but we needed help. Kat was working her ass off, and I'd started working too, but we barely made enough to live on our own. Kat tried to stop them from coming, but Nana insisted. When they got here, though, Kat refused to move in with them."

"Why didn't you just go on your own?"

Shanti shrugged and squished her lips over to one side. "She's my sister. She rescued me. I couldn't just leave her."

I stared at her lips as she said it. *Right. And now you feel like you owe her, even though she can be a jerk.*

She must have read my face. "You still think I put up with too much from her. I get it. But her love just looks a little different, Daya. You've seen it. Family—the team—it's everything to her because it's all she has. So if anyone else threatens that, she goes into fight mode. And sometimes I guess she feels like *I'm* a threat to myself because I'm not strong, like her. So she gets frustrated with me. It's not perfect and I don't always let her get away with it, but I know it comes from a place of love."

Does it? I tried to believe her and nodded, but something about this imperfect love felt too close to home. Like wanting someone to be strong because you loved them also justified being hard on them. Thatha's voice slipped through my mind. *If you show them weakness, Daya, they win. You must be better, stronger.*

She contemplated me for a moment. "What about you?"

"What about me what?"

"Some people might say you're in fight mode . . . once in a while." She tugged gently at my earlobe. "Where does that come from?"

Despite her annoyingly cute gesture, I felt my shoulders hitch up at what felt a little too much like a therapy question. "I don't know," I lied.

Her eyebrows rose.

"I don't." She could see right through me, but I didn't care. I didn't want to ruin this time with her by talking about my "issues," nor was I ready to look too closely at the answers to her question. I knew looking meant finding, and finding meant pulling up too many memories, too much hurt. That part was still too scary.

"Okay." She placed her hands on either side of my face. "I'm not going to force you to talk to me . . . right now. But I already have one important person in my life who refuses to talk about her feelings. I'd love it if you weren't the second, 'cause . . ." A hand slipped to my arm. She leaned in close, kissed me softly on the neck, then whispered into my ear, "I kinda dig you, ya know?"

It took only seconds for my shoulders to fall back into place.

"Daya!"

God. I'd just walked in the front door after spending the entire day with Shanti, and I was really hoping to just walk up to my room and collapse into bed. But of course, that was too much to ask. A racket of whistles, plucking, singing, and more came from the living room.

"Hi, Vicki."

"Daya, we had such a wonderful time with you and Shanti this morning. She's so . . . *sweet.*" She was carrying maracas.

Translation: *She's capital* N *Not what we expected for you at* all.

"Yes, so sweet! We'd really love to see her again." Priam rounded the corner from the living room with a mandolin in one hand. It must have been their "Jig and Jam Night"— a collection of their musical nerd friends dancing and jamming with instruments that, I was fairly sure, did not go together.

The jingles and drum thumps continued from the living room. I tried to remember where I'd put my earplugs.

"Um, thanks. Shanti's pretty cool." Truthfully, even though I was exhausted, just saying her name sent a small burst of excitement through my gut.

We'd spent the afternoon parked at the beach, making

out and talking and making out some more. We hadn't talked about my "fight mode" anymore—she'd given me some space from that and I'd been thankful—but I'd told her about Fee and how important they were to me, about skateboarding, and even that I'd boxed before—though I'd kept that conversation brief.

She'd told me about her classes and all the eccentric people she met at the bookstore where she worked. About her obsessions with the *Doctor Who* TV series and sci-fi books. About her favorite comic book characters. About how much she loved puzzles.

Every nerdy thing she said just made me want to kiss her. And every time I realized how much I wanted to kiss her, despite every nerdy thing she said (or maybe because of it), I had to take a deep breath to calm the panic in my chest that was telling me not to get too close—not to run the risk of letting someone in, of losing them. What if she saw the deepest parts of me and hated what she saw? But each breath kept me present, kept me in front of her instead of retreating, which was what a pesky part of my brain was telling me to do. I'd breathed my way into an entire day with Shanti, and thinking about that now gave me a little bump of energy.

"Have you eaten?" Priam asked.

I hadn't. Shanti and I had been too busy to eat. Traces of garlic and onions had been wafting in from the kitchen. I couldn't believe what I was about to say, but I said it anyway. "I'm starving."

Both their faces lit up. Vicki clasped her hands and practically squawked. "Well, you're in luck! We're just about to eat, and there's enough falafel to feed a marching band!"

When I finally did get to bed that night, I could barely sleep, despite my exhaustion. I couldn't stop thinking about Shanti, yes, but I had to admit I was trying to get my head around the evening with Priam and Vicki. I'd never paid much attention to their friends. In fact, I'd mostly avoided their gatherings. Echoes of my father's voice kept me from participating in their "nonsense."

But tonight, huddled to one end of the couch with my plate of falafel and tabbouleh in my lap, I'd been able to see a bit of what my mum must have seen. Priam and Vicki and their friends didn't seem to care less what they looked like, or how their absurd collection of instruments sounded together. They just tried whatever seemed right in the moment and laughed every chance they got.

More baffling to me, they seemed completely comfortable laughing at *themselves*. Like they expected to laugh at themselves. Like they were intentionally trying to *create* moments to laugh at themselves. It was so weird, but I'd almost choked on my food more than once laughing along with them.

And to their credit, Priam and Vicki never once tried to get me to join in the music making. The woman sitting next to me—decked out in a colorful parka and plastic crown for no apparent reason at all—leaned over and offered her tambourine to me at one point. But when I shook my head, mouth full of pita, she just nodded dreamily and kept swaying along to the music.

When I'd finished eating, I just continued to sit there, listening to the most confusing set list ever, wondering how anyone got to the point where they could be this at ease with themselves. When one guy started crooning some kind of love ballad to his boyfriend, my eyes started to droop and I excused myself, but now I just found myself lying in bed, staring at my bumpy ceiling. So much of the past twenty-four hours had pushed me way beyond what I was used to, and with my headboard just inches away from the top of my head, I realized I hadn't resorted to bruising once to manage the confusing mix of discomfort and exhilaration I was feeling.

After rolling around for an hour, I got up and putzed around—went to the bathroom, stretched, did some pushups, collected my dirty clothes. When I gathered a couple of wrinkled T-shirts from my desk, the notebook Dr. Hoang had given me appeared, still pristine as ever. I picked it up and opened to the first blank page.

Dr. Hoang had said to write stuff down that I wanted to say but couldn't. I wasn't sure what I wanted to say right now, though. I couldn't sleep because my mind was caught up in completely unfamiliar territory.

I pulled a pen out of the drawer of my desk anyway and sat back down on my bed. I stared at the first page, twirling the pen with my fingers.

I could just start writing all the thoughts burning through my brain, I guessed. But that seemed like a lot of writing. And the thoughts were coming too fast to catch them anyway, I told myself. I could write a list of to-dos. *Practice stops. Finish crappy English essay. Start crappy college apps.* Those weren't really the things on my mind, though. *Not quite the point,* I heard Dr. Hoang say in my head.

In the end, all I ended up writing was, *What the hell, Daya?* before stuffing both the notebook and the pen back in the drawer and lying awake for another two hours.

Chapter Twenty-Nine

"Daya, what the hell are you doing? You're prancing around like some kind of clown! Are you here to entertain or to win? This girl isn't anywhere near your level, but you're making her look ten times as good. What's happening?" Thatha's brow creased. His eyes glared in disbelief.

I swished the water around and swallowed, staring out across the ring at my opponent, who looked as tired as I was. Nothing had felt right since we left the house. For some reason, Amma had decided to come to my match that day, even though she hated watching me box.

"Why do you want to come now?" my dad had asked.

"I can support my daughter, can't I?" Amma had responded.

This was shortly after Amma's and my playful "fight" in the backyard. I guess at the time I thought she'd enjoyed it enough to want to see me in the ring.

"If you come, you can't distract her, okay?" my dad had

chastised as we walked to the car. "You know what boxing is, so don't expect anything else."

"Yes, Nihal, I know, I know."

The only one who'd spoken in the car had been my dad, running through everything he'd already told me when we'd trained the day before. I think having my mum there made him agitated, like he was on the defensive or something.

I felt something in between nervous and excited. I'd wanted my mum to see me box for so long, even though I doubted she'd be able to watch a whole match. I pictured her watching through her fingers, or maybe leaving after the first round.

But my dad's agitation was contagious, and by the time we got to the gym, I'd grown more nervous and less excited. I knew my mum would hate this. Why had she come? It would be torture for her and distracting for me.

My concerns for her had made me hesitant and shaky in the ring. I'd boxed a defensive bout instead of an offensive one, against my dad's coaching. Instead of going in for the attack, I spent most of the first three rounds avoiding my opponent's jabs, "prancing around" her hits instead of going in for my own.

"I think I'm just tired, Thatha."

"So? What do you want to do? Just play dead or something?"

"No, but—"

"But what? Daya, if you box soft, you lose, plain and

simple. So you might as well lie down and let that girl walk all over you, no?"

And that was basically what I'd done. Four rounds of being chased around the ring with my gloves up until the match ended. When the other girl was rightfully called the winner, Thatha couldn't even look at me.

Chapter Thirty

The rest of our roller derby practices turned out to be a bit complicated. Shanti and I talked about a lot of things after our visit to Yolanda and Bee, but we definitely hadn't been thinking about practice or our "status." We hadn't seen each other since Sunday either, though we'd exchanged dozens of texts ranging from perfectly mundane to obscenely cute. The feelings of uncertainty and unease around letting someone in hadn't left me, but I was trying to stay in the moment—and actively *avoiding* any thoughts about where this could all be going.

So when I showed up to practice on Tuesday night and saw her seated by the track, sketching something on a notepad with a tiny frown of concentration on her forehead, I experienced a surge of several states of being all at once: affection, trepidation, longing, uncertainty, and—when I saw Kat stretching nearby—a moment of intense anxiety.

What Shanti had shared with me about her and Kat's life had helped me to understand Kat's behavior a bit more, but that didn't mean I found her any less unsettling. I'd been so in awe of her strength and no-bullshit attitude—we seemed so alike in that way. But now I could see we had something else in common—how much that toughness could cause harm. We were both pushing away hurt and causing it at the same time. But I wasn't ready to let the hurt in. I wasn't sure if I'd ever be ready.

And despite my growing feelings for Shanti, I guess some part of me still felt like I needed roller derby—just in case. I wasn't under some delusion that my need to bruise myself had suddenly disappeared—the threatening ache inside me certainly hadn't. Having Kat on my side was key to being a part of this team and holding that ache down.

All these thoughts made me instantly act like a weirdo. Instead of saying hi to Shanti like a normal person, I beelined it to the other side of the track and geared up there without making eye contact with anyone.

But eventually, Shanti came over and stood by my little stretch of track. "Hey, Daya."

Okay. Be normal, Daya. I skated toward her. "Hey." I wiped the beginning beads of sweat from my forehead.

She sidled up to me and showed me her sketchbook. "Look." A felt-pen drawing of what looked like me ripping around the track filled the page, although she hadn't yet finished my left leg. Even legless, though, I looked fucking awesome. That fact and standing close to Shanti like this with her hand on my hip sent a little twinge through my chest.

"You drew this? It's amazing. What's it for?"

"We need flyers to promote our bouts, and I've been the one creating them for the past couple of seasons. I was thinking maybe we could use something like this for our next flyer."

I involuntarily glanced toward Kat. "Think that's a good idea?"

Shanti didn't skip a beat. "Why wouldn't it be?"

"Just—you know." I spoke carefully. "I'm new and stuff. Shouldn't you use someone everyone knows?"

"What better way to introduce rookies?" She looked at me like she really thought this was a good idea. She didn't seem bothered by the impending disaster of Kat's response to Shanti's hand on my hip. She must have seen the question-slash-worry on my face, though, because she removed her hand and added, "I won't use it if you don't want me to."

She looked a little disappointed, which hurt my heart a bit. "Maybe we can save it for later, like when I actually learn to look like that on the track?" I tried a smile.

Her disappointment fell away and she leaned in for a kiss, which I was not expecting and which automatically made me bend backward away from her and glance at Kat again. As soon as I did it, I knew it was a bad move, especially when hurt passed through Shanti's eyes.

"Sorry," I blurted. "I just wasn't sure we should . . . here . . . you know. Yet." *Was that even a complete sentence?* "But I want to.

I really, really want to. Just. You know." *I can't risk losing this team.*

She blinked and nodded. "Okay. I get it. But you know Kat shouldn't have a say in this, right?" She pointed between us.

"Let's figure it out later, okay?" I said, not really sure I was ready to figure anything out.

"Sure. No problem." She looked down at her drawing.

Damn. I wasn't used to this kind of thing. I didn't have to follow up with the guys I usually hooked up with or worry about hurt feelings. Casual had been the name of the game. "Hey." I tugged at her sleeve. "I mean it."

She looked up again and contemplated me for a moment. "Okay."

I breathed out in relief. "Okay."

"You should warm up."

"I guess I should. Any tips?"

"Yeah, stay off your ass," she said, and walked away.

For the entire practice, I did my best to just concentrate on what Alma had taught me—to focus on working with my teammates and supporting them when needed. Though I still brought ferocity to the track, I spent more energy than usual thinking through plays and creating room for the jammer using strategy more than out-and-out brute strength. I wasn't perfect—it was a new style of play for me, after all—but I thought I was doing okay.

You wouldn't be able to tell that by Kat's response, though. In fact, based on her feedback, you'd think I was a shit show.

"Daya, my nana hits harder than that!"

"If you protect your blockers that way, we might as well replace you with a pylon."

"Can someone please explain to Daya that we're not playing 'touch' roller derby?"

I tried to suck it up and stay focused, knowing she was just pissed about the other night and trying to get under my skin, but nothing I did seemed good enough. And the more frustrated I got, the more mistakes I made. The more I tried to make up for those mistakes, the more impatient and sloppy I got. This just led to further frustration, and I lost my drive. By the halfway point, I felt like a pinball being bounced around by the other skaters, proving everything Kat was saying to be true.

Shanti must have noticed, because at the water break, she came over to me and said, "Hey—you okay out there?"

I squirted some water into my mouth as angrily as someone can squirt water into their mouth. A perma-frown had taken up residence on my face. "I'm fine."

"You sure? Kat's being pretty hard on you. Want me to say something?"

"What? No! That'd just make it worse."

She put a hand on my shoulder. My immediate response was to shrug it off, but I didn't want to hurt her feelings again, so I bent over to adjust my laces instead, thinking that would do the trick. But Shanti just let her hand slide over my curved back and started rubbing it instead.

The next thing I heard was, "Oh, fuck. I knew it."

Kat.

I felt Shanti's hand leave my back, and when I stood up, Kat was in front of us, hands on hips in her endless Superwoman stance. Her mouth and jawline were all hostility, but her eyes and brow said something else. Something like worry. Or maybe: disappointment?

"I can't believe you chose soft, Daya."

"What?"

She came right up to my face, hands dropping to her sides. "I said, 'You chose soft.' Why the hell would you choose soft?"

After everything Shanti had told me, I knew where all this was coming from. I knew—in my head—Kat was reacting to something completely separate from me. But that knowing wasn't making it to my gut and my chest. Instead the familiar boiling and hotness were forming.

Daya, what the hell are you doing?

If you box soft, you lose, plain and simple.

The last time I'd chosen soft, I'd lost everything. Even with Shanti right beside me, even with images from the past few days with her still in my mind, I couldn't stop that sick, hot feeling from overcoming me. *I won't be soft. I can't be.*

"Kat—" Shanti's voice tried to force its way into the tension between her sister and me.

"Shanti, are you seriously going to screw this up for her?" Kat spat out. "You haven't learned your lesson?"

Shanti took a step forward. "Daya doesn't see it the same

way you do, Kat." She looked at me, expecting me to say something, I guess. But I couldn't. My chest felt like it was on fire.

"Oh yeah?" Kat said, her face still in mine. I could smell her coconut lip balm, she was so close. "How *do* you see it, Daya?"

Something in her face increased my heart rate. The expectation, the challenge, the disapproval. My jawline tightened to match hers. "No one here is soft."

A whistle blew from somewhere behind me, signaling the end of the water break. Neither Kat nor I moved.

"Daya—" Shanti tried, placing her hand on my shoulder.

Kat interrupted her. "Prove it."

Shrugging Shanti's hand off, I inched closer to Kat. My voice could barely get out through my locked jaw. "Fine."

Kat smirked, first at me, then at Shanti, who let out a breath of exasperation. I felt a twinge of guilt, but it was quickly overtaken by what felt like thick lava swelling throughout my body. There was only one way to push it back, and soft wasn't the way to go.

Kat clapped her hands over her head, gliding backward. "Hey, hey, everyone, we have a special challenge today. I've offered Daya a starting spot in our first bout if she can get past me."

Oh, game on.

Lena skated up beside her and plowed to a stop. "Say what now?" she asked, face contorted in confusion.

Kat ignored her. "Everyone line up on either side!"

Slowly, everyone—except for Lena and Shanti—lined up along one of the longer portions of the track.

"You have that length of the track to prove you haven't gone soft," Kat said, pointing as she rolled around me and then backward toward the starting line.

I skated over without looking at Shanti. If I did, I might lose my resolve, and I needed to do this. She'd understand. I hoped.

I faced Kat, who was about three feet in front of me. She lowered herself into a squat and held her arms out to her sides, then made a *come on* gesture with her hands. I tried to use her cocky expression as motivation and steeled myself, focusing on all the bruises I was about to get—how each one might give me the relief I needed.

Bending my knees, I started to skate forward. Kat adjusted to every move I made, her wheels stepping and pushing sideways, her body shifting its weight one direction and then the next.

I burst forward, aiming straight into her. I wasn't scared of her hits. I wanted them. I was going to absorb every single one. Her concrete arms slammed into mine and I slammed back into her. We zigzagged across the track while the team cheered and clapped. Her knee collided with mine, my shoulder crashed into her ribs. I didn't even want to get by her yet—I wanted to draw in as many bruises as I could. She knew it too. We were basically just smashing into each other, elbow pads and wrist guards clacking against one another's. Hips, shoulders, legs bouncing off, then colliding again.

"Come on, rook. That all you got? Yer running out of time, softie."

I stopped pushing for a split second—long enough to open up a bit of space between me and Kat. Kat must've thought I was getting tired, because a self-satisfied look came over her face and she straightened her legs ever so slightly. I used the opportunity and rammed my shoulder fully into hers, sending her flying backward onto her ass.

I didn't even bother skating to the end. Instead I stood over her. "I told you I wasn't soft."

Kat grinned from the ground, unfazed by my hit. "I knew it. You just needed a reminder." She rolled over and hopped back onto her skates. Encircling my neck with her arm, she announced to the rest of the Honeys, "Check out this bitch, y'all! That's how you do it!" The team cheered. Lena still looked confused, though, and Shanti . . . Shanti was nowhere to be seen.

Ice cubes clicked against the side of the bathtub as I turned off the faucet. Easing myself in, I ground my teeth against the frigid water, my legs first burning with pain, then numbing from the cold. I lowered myself farther until cubes floated around my chin and ears. An ice bath was the only way to recover from an intense practice or workout. Thatha taught me that. And I could appreciate the numbing sensation, the easing of my muscles, even if I had to accept the healing effects on my bruises.

No easing was taking place right now, though. My brain

needed to be frozen for that to happen. I wished I could sub-
merge my whole head and have the water immobilize all the
thoughts racing through it.

Practice had continued like normal after the impromptu
challenge. Lena cracked her verbal whip and had us gunning
around the track in no time. I noticed her and Kat having a
heated discussion while we were doing drills, though. I'm sure
Lena was pissed that Kat had promised me a spot on the starting lineup for my first bout. She was probably also wondering
who I was supposed to replace. I wondered that too, but only
momentarily, before I started thinking about how intense it
was going to be out on that track. How brutal.

Part of me had wanted to follow Shanti—I hadn't meant
to hurt her, but she must've understood I couldn't just let Kat
get away with challenging me. She might be able to put up
with that shit, but she knew who I was—what I was like. She
couldn't blame me for playing my part.

The bigger urge, though, was to get back to practice and
start hammering away. Kat's words had reached right into my
gut and pulled up something rotten. Something that made me
sick and angry at myself. That made me want to show everyone just how indestructible I could be.

Soft.

I wouldn't let that happen again.

Shanti texted me the next day while I was lying on my bed,
trying in vain to do my homework.

Hey. You free?

My first reaction was a small lift in my chest. But the rot invading my stomach quickly overcame any good feelings and dissolved them like acid.

Seeing Shanti right now would just get in the way of my resolve. I needed to keep focused on the goal at hand: stay strong, prove myself.

Not really. Homework. Ugh.

Oh. I'm outside. Sorry.

Shit. I shoved my textbook off my lap and peered out my window, which faced the alley behind the house. Shanti was sitting on her bike, just beyond the fence to the property. A light rain had started, and she'd only worn jeans and a hoodie. She'd be soaked in no time.

Priam and Vicki were downstairs, and there was no effing way I wanted a reprise of breakfast the other day, so I texted Shanti to meet me at the double garage doors.

A minute later she was guiding her bike in through the doors, carefully avoiding both Vicki and Priam's car and the rows of costumes and boxes. She held her bike beside her. I didn't offer any alternative. We were standing in the couple of feet of space between car and costumes. I watched her, a heavy pressure building in my chest, a tightness in my throat. I hadn't been in here since Priam tried to give me the boxing equipment. I didn't want to be in here now, either.

Water dripped off Shanti's helmet and onto her nose, her cheeks. Her eyes looked a little wet too. To avoid them, I focused on her chin.

"Little damp out," she said.

I knew she must be cold, that I should invite her in or give her a towel, but that wouldn't fit with my goal. That would just muddle everything up again.

Instead I replied, "Yeah," and waited for her to say something else. She came to me, after all, I justified to myself.

She looked down at her hands and squeezed them tight around the handlebars of her bike, then brought her eyes up to me again. "Listen, you probably have your reasons for letting Kat goad you yesterday."

My heart felt like it was banging against my rib cage. I didn't want to hear any of this.

"I just needed to let you know it didn't feel great. Especially after everything I told you about us, my mom . . ." She wiped her nose with her wet sleeve. "It felt like . . . like you were choosing Kat." She shrugged and aimed her gaze back at her hands.

Fuck. I had zero ability to handle this right now. I didn't want to talk to anyone about anything or think about all the ways I'd screwed up—all I wanted to do was get out on the track and back into my body. I needed to. I didn't have the energy to make Shanti understand that, though. Opening up all these places inside of me had left me too exposed already. Putting my body in the way of danger was the only way I knew how to continue protecting the deep down, inside pieces. But until I could do that on the track, I'd have to make do with my words.

I let my eyes rest on her hands as well and said what I

thought would make her go. "Yeah, maybe I was. Maybe we're just too different." I stuck my hands in my pockets. "This probably isn't gonna work."

She lifted her head sharply. "What? Daya—"

"It's fine, Shanti. It's not like we were dating or anything. Easier to quit while we're ahead." I shrugged like an asshole, hoping it would speed this conversation along.

She cleared her throat and I knew she was trying to keep her voice from cracking, but I steeled myself against the knowing. "I know what you're doing, because Kat does it too. But neither of you have to do it. I thought maybe you were starting to see that."

I shrugged again. *Just leave. Please.*

When I didn't reply, she added, "You know *this* doesn't make you strong, right?"

That was the last thing I needed to hear right now, and hearing it caused a surge of heat across my chest. The pressure, the thumping, the heat—it was too much. I needed to get out of here. I forced my eyes up to hers with a hard glare. "You think you get me? You think you know me so well just because you think you know Kat? You know *nothing* about me—"

She tipped her head to the side. "I don't?"

"No! You don't." *If you did, you'd leave me alone.*

"Well, I'm trying to. You could let me try." Her voice came out quiet, but clear.

Keeping my voice emotionless, I said, "I don't need you to try. I don't *want* you to. What I really want right now is for you to leave." I folded my arms across my chest. An added barrier.

After a beat, she said, "Shutting everybody out might feel like the easiest option, but from where I'm standing, it just looks really lonely. If you ever decide you want something different . . . let me know." Shanti heaved her bike up onto its rear wheel to turn it around, let the front wheel drop back to the ground, and retreated out the open garage door into the rain.

The relief I thought I'd feel at seeing her go never came.

Chapter Thirty-One

The season opener on the following Saturday was a double-header—two games, one after the other. Only four teams made up the league, so I'd get a good look at all the competition in one night. We'd be squaring off against the Skintastics, while the Hell Beasts and Hair Force Babes would compete before us.

We'd had one other practice after Kat's and my show-down. Shanti hadn't been there, and I was relieved. I couldn't think about her or where she was. I just focused on playing my game—hits and hurt. I took pity on no one—including Kat. *Especially* Kat. When she wasn't on my scrimmage team, I made sure to place her in my target zone and then blast myself at her with everything I had.

Instead of getting angry, though, she seemed smug. It kind of pissed me off, but I also got it. I was proving to her I could be just as hard as her. I planned to do the same thing at this first bout, especially now that I was starting.

"Last year, the Skintastics took the league title, but just barely," Charlotte explained as we suited up in a dismal changing room at the rink. "We were right on their asses the entire season and lost by only six points in the championship." She swung a thick arm around me and play-punched my chin. "We're gonna get 'em this year, rook. And you're gonna help us do that."

Charlotte's massive grin so close to my face revealed a row of determinedly crooked teeth that sent my mind backward. My mum had had an incisor that tilted a little forward, like it was competing for a spot near the front of her teeth.

I shook the image away. No time for that stuff. Eye on the prize.

A sock hit me in the shoulder, hesitated for a moment, then flopped to the ground.

"Smell it, rook! That's the smell of last season!" Lena yelled from across the room.

"Thanks, I'll pass." I kicked the slightly crusty item back toward her. I guess Kat had convinced Lena that it was a good idea to put me on the starting lineup. I'd be replacing another blocker, Saba, who was currently giving me stink-eye from her spot in the corner.

Oh well. Not my problem.

Despite the bleak lighting and musty smells of the changing room, the atmosphere tingled. All around me, my teammates were yanking at their skate laces, stretching our gold-and-black uniforms over their bodies (Lena had made me

use masking tape to add DAYA DOO WOP to the back of my
jersey for now, which made me want to crawl into a hole and
die), and crowding around the smudged mirror to get their
makeup on. Friendly smack-talk flew from one person to the
next, while others obsessed over the stickiness of the track and
which wheels they should use.

The energy was palpable, and the nerves gathering in my
stomach were no match for the fire in my chest. After so many
hours of watching and practicing, trying to prove myself, I was
dying to get out there and show just how hard I could be, how
much pain my body could absorb—how much trouble it could
create too. I was going to leave the track with bruises *and* dole
out a few as well. I felt sorry for whoever had to try and get by
me tonight.

As we warmed up on the track, it seemed most of the girls
from both teams knew one another. They joked and razzed
each other amicably as they rolled by or stretched. Even the
officials and refs chummed around with each other and the
teams. We rookies—Sage, Potts, Grace, and I—clustered
together for most of the warm-up, covertly glancing around
and taking everything in.

I hadn't planned on inviting anyone I knew to the match
tonight, but Fee had been bugging me about it ever since I
made the team, so I felt obligated to tell them at least. They'd
already texted me that they and Cai had found seats close to
the penalty box so we could all "have a nice visit periodically
during the match." Ha-ha.

I'd looked over and waved at them when I entered the rink. It made me a little more nervous to have them here, but my nerves quickly turned to embarrassment when they held up gold pom-poms and began shaking them back and forth over their heads. I rolled my eyes at them, which just caused both of them to thrash their arms about with considerably more vigor.

I wondered if Bee and Yolanda would be watching, cheering on their granddaughters. I couldn't ask either granddaughter, though. I hadn't seen Shanti yet, and I'd been trying not to think about her or about the irritating pangs in my chest. We hadn't spoken or texted since she'd left my garage three days ago. I didn't have any plans to reach out, either.

Kat was clearly "in the zone"—and the "zone" was something like beast mode. Watching her skate around the track during warm-up, I was reminded of how in awe I'd been of her that first derby I watched. Her muscles pulsed with a furious energy and the expression on her face was concentrated and stormy, as though lightning might lash out from her eyes at any moment. I told myself I'd match her energy and then some.

As the clock counted down, Lena and Kat called everyone in to our bench. We all had a nice sheen from our warm-up and looked flushed and ready to go.

"All right, honeybees! Time to taste that sweet, sweet nectar!" Lena began. "Blockers, look out for number eight—Huck Sin—she's fast and crafty, so watch her torso, not her feet, and keep low so you can react quickly. Kat and I'll call plays as we need to, so listen up for our cues."

Kat added, "The Skintastics are fierce, but we've got depth." She turned to Sage, Grace, and Potts and offered, "Rookies, we're gonna get you in tonight, don't worry. Just keep warm and be ready." Then she turned to me. "Shit's about to get real. You good?"

I nodded. "I'm good."

As we skated out to the starting line, a surge of adrenaline blasted through my chest. I swung my arms across my body to work out some of the excess energy.

A shout of "Killa Skillz" soared over the arena. I looked behind me. The crowd practically foamed—whooping and applause pierced by sometimes sharp, sometimes lengthy whistles, folks decorated in colors of all four teams: yellow and black, blue and green, black and red plaid, gray and pink. Placards waving back and forth, the announcer's fanatical excitement calling out our names and numbers.

Maybe it was because this was the season opener, maybe because my senses were heightened, but it felt like everything was in Technicolor and surround sound. More vivid, louder, right in my ear, and washing over me. A horn blasted. At first I thought it was the ref, but then I realized it was just a superfan with a giant kazoo. Who has a giant kazoo? Roller derby fans, that's who.

When the starting whistle did blow, there was a frenzy of pushing and shoving. Dom, me, and our third blocker, Jin, immediately managed to trap their jammer while Lena attached herself to their blockers to make way for Kat, allowing Kat to push through the Skintastics' blockers in seconds. Soon she was burning around the track, diving right back into the pack again even before their jammer had been able to get by us.

By the end of the first jam, we were up by four points, Kat managing to evade the other team's hits and push through the pack easily, thanks in part, of course, to her blockers. I'd played aggressively—shoving and pulling and bracing hard—and could feel the tenderness along my upper arms and my thighs already. After just two minutes of play.

Promising.

But, being my first time out there, I'd also been less sure of myself than I thought I'd be, so though my body was burning to explode around the track, I'd held back a bit, trying to gauge exactly where I should be and how much I could get away with when it came to hitting.

As we skated off so the next lineup could get out on the track, Lena slapped my shoulder. "Not bad, rook!" I appreciated this but found myself looking to Kat to see what she thought. After she finished squirting water into her mouth, she eyed me up. "Yeah, not bad at all. But now you sit for a bit. You're a rookie, after all."

What? Dammit. I didn't want to sit. Was this because I'd held back? "Really? But we just won that jam."

Kat swished some water around in her mouth for a good long while before replying. "And? You'll get in again. Just chill out." She turned away from me to talk to Dom.

Something happened on the track—Sage, Grace, and the others sitting on the bench rose up to their feet and cheered. Charlotte, also a jammer like Kat, had broken through the pack and taken the lead.

Still feeling the adrenaline from the last jam and jittery from wanting to be out there, I had to steady myself and regain focus by placing my hands on my hips and gazing hard at the ground in front of my skates, bringing my wheels to a still position. I pushed my fists into my hip bones, feeling the tenderness of one of the bruises Kat had given me.

Breathe, Daya, I heard Dr. Hoang again in my head.

Fuck breathing. I needed to get out on that effing track, fast. Standing around in all this madness was just making me antsy. Waiting for my time to come wasn't really my strength. And watching shit wasn't really my thing either.

But watch I did. The second jam finished. We were up by nine. Kat and the others went on for the next jam, except Saba was back on the line with them instead of me. I pressed harder into my hip.

Kat cleared the pack again and raced around the track. Her eyes blazed—there was something both savage and targeted in them. The way she leaned into her stride, it was like some force was acting against her, like she was battling some invisible team of blockers, expecting the worst and giving them her fiercest. The look was both scary and exciting.

And our blockers were killing it. I tried to zone in on them, even though I just wanted to be out there *with* them.

Lena, Dom, Jin, and Saba formed a virtual wall of muscle. Lena was an expert backward skater—so smooth and easy and solid. Dom homed in on the other team's skaters like a heat-seeking missile.

Watching them absorb the sideswipes and hip checks of the other team's blockers and jammer, I could practically feel bruises form on my own body. The anticipation became excruciating. After the past few days, the impulse to draw all my focus into my skin and muscle had resurged with a vengeance. I wasn't proud of it, but the familiarity gave me a kind of relief.

In my impatience, I rolled over to Charlotte, who was stretching at one end of our bench.

"Hey," I said, nudging her with my padded elbow. "What are the chances of me getting back on soon?"

She laughed, still following the pack with her eyes. "Raring to go. I like it!" She didn't say anything else for a few seconds. Then she side-eyed me and said, "Okay, once this jam is over, lemme ask Kat what's what. Not promising anything, though."

We won the third and fourth jams too, which made it easier for Kat to let me on with her for the fifth jam, when our lead had grown to twelve. But she made sure to grab me by the neckline of my shirt and tell me to "Block the shit out of the other team" for her and then added, "No soft shit out there, got it?" before skating out to the jammer's start line. The contact sent a jolt of fury through my stomach.

No soft shit?

No problem.

Now I was standing at the blockers' line with Dom, Lena, and Saba, feeling like a freaking Tasmanian devil—ready to whip into a tornado of destruction for the other team. No more holding back.

As soon as the whistle blew, the four of us found our designated positions and began pushing and jostling the other blockers. All three of their blockers instantly zeroed in on Dom and Lena, while their pivot—taller and wider than Lena or Dom—took on both me and Jin. This kinda pissed me off, but I stuck to the plan and started shoving her back to the outer edge of the track, creating some space for Jin to get past her and help the others.

I was skating backward and eyeing up Kat while simultaneously trying to shove back and ignore the chick in front of me. She'd pinned me for a rookie and had been smack-talking me the minute the bout started.

"'Sup, fresh meat? This baby steak's first bout? Ready to be ground up for dinner, rook?"

Jesus. Shut it already. More annoying than her trash talk, though, were her slappy-ass hands. Hitting with your hands was against the rules, but she kept smacking her palms against my arms and thighs so the refs wouldn't see and it was driving me nuts. Shoves and sharp elbows I could handle—even invite—but this shit wasn't going to get me any bruising. It was just fucking annoying. I started slapping her hands away, harder and harder.

"Uh-oh, fresh meat's getting pissy," she taunted. *Slap, slap.*
I swear to God . . .

"Can't take the heat, rook? Not tough enough?" *Slap, slap.*
Fuck. You.

"Whatcha' doin' out here, baby girl? Need your mommy?
Or maybe you're a daddy's girl?" *Slap, slap.*

My skates screeched to a halt and my forearms rammed
into her torso with every ounce of rage I had. As she flailed
backward into the middle of the track, my entire body slammed
into hers to help her to the ground.

In the next moment, several skaters toppled over us and I
heard a yell of pure agony. Flat on my stomach, I looked up to
see several sets of Skintastics skates crowded around me, making sure I stayed where I was. I ignored them and kept looking to see who'd cried out. Now I could hear them repeating,
"Shit, shit, shit!"

"OH! That's gonna be a problem for Daya Doo Wop, folks!
Definitely *nothing* legal about that hit. Looks like one of the
Honeys is hurt from the melee too."

Following the coarse language, my eyes finally found the
source. It was Lena. She was on her back several feet ahead of
me, holding her knee. Kat and Dom were at her side, asking
her questions and trying to keep her from sitting up. A medic
had already rushed out to check her over.

As I started to get up on my hands and knees to go over to
them, one of the Skintastics blocked me, which started a whole
other thing. By the time the refs had teased us all apart and

ejected Slappy Hands and me, Lena was being led out, rolling along on one skate, between Kat and Dom.

I hated not being on the track and not being able to check on Lena, but I also felt like I might do something even worse if I stayed out there. On my way to the bench, I got more than one "nudge" from the Skintastics players. When I looked over, I noticed Kat glaring at me from her place next to Lena.

She couldn't really be mad at me for thumping that girl, could she? Like she wouldn't have done the same thing?

I sat my ass on the hard bench. As furious as I was, I wished I'd hear Bee or Yolanda yelling some obscenities at me from the stands, but it didn't sound like they were here. I scanned the Crash Zone and spotted Shanti, though. Apparently she wasn't interested in what was happening on the track. She was too busy talking to some girl with one of those annoying haircuts that looked messy but you knew they'd spent forever making sure it looked like that.

I wanted to look away but kept watching her, hoping she'd look toward me. And then she did. And I immediately shifted my gaze to the track, like a fucking coward.

Kat didn't say a word to me for the rest of the bout, even though I could tell she had something to say.

My stupid penalty had turned the tide of the match. The team couldn't get its groove back, and without Lena, we were missing a key blocker and pivot. We ended up losing by fifteen. Sitting on the bench for the rest of the bout, everyone else's attention carefully directed away from me, I had plenty of time to replay the whole scene and relive each moment of my anger. Each time I did, I came to the same clear conclusion.

I'd fucked up. Whether I played it soft or hard, I always fucked up.

Chapter Thirty-Two

"I knew you shouldn't have come!" Thatha yelled as he unlocked the car.

"Nihal, calm down. It's just a boxing match, no? Everyone has a bad match now and again." Amma touched my shoulder as she said this.

I went to climb into the back of the car, shrugging her hand off.

I shut the door against their arguing. Usually Amma protested only once and then Dad would get his way. Tonight, though, it seemed Amma was more vocal than usual. Their muffled sounds filtered through the glass, and I shifted over to the far side of the car to get away from them.

The next moment Dad had pulled open the driver's-side door with force and landed violently in his seat. It took a few seconds for Amma to open her door and slip into the car in front of me. A fold of her sari fluttered into view to one side of the seat. Gold and burgundy silk.

She only wears saris for special occasions, I thought. But then I realized that I'd been anything but special tonight. More like a fucking disaster.

Thatha's baila music blasted from the stereo. He turned it up even further, as if to prove a point. He didn't sing along, though. There was no laughter today.

I stared out the window as he pulled out of the gym parking lot. I could see Amma's reflection in the window ahead, gazing out too. I thought that was the end of the argument. I thought we'd sit in silence, like we did so often, and tomorrow Thatha would push me that much harder—to make sure I never boxed soft again.

I thought wrong.

Chapter Thirty-Three

After the bout, the energy in the changing room had completely shifted from before. The room remained mostly quiet, except for the intermittent rasping sound of Velcro being torn apart. The smell of sweat hung hot and sticky around us. A friend had driven Lena to the hospital to get her knee checked out at the medic's suggestion. I couldn't help but feel everyone throwing glances my way, and I tried to keep my head down. One pair of eyes I noticed wasn't in the room was Shanti's.

The urge to slam my hand against the bench was so strong I thought I'd explode from resisting it.

A few minutes in, a different explosion occurred. Kat erupted into the changing room and stormed right over to me, commanding, "Stand up, rook."

I looked up at her. Was I scared of her? Definitely. Was I going to let her treat me like a little kid even if I felt like a complete fuckup right now? No effing way. I pushed down any feelings of remorse I had and mustered up a defiant shield.

"Pardon?"

"I said, get your ass up. You owe this whole fucking team an apology."

"What?"

She bent over at the waist and stared me straight in the eye. "Are. You. Listening."

I heard Charlotte say, "Kat . . ." but then stop.

I just glared back at her, every muscle in my body tensing into concrete.

"Your bullshit just cost us that bout and probably the rest of Lena's season. That calls for an apology, don't you think? To your team? You know . . . your *team*."

The sensation of wetness in my eyes made me furious. I didn't want Kat to see, so I leaned down to undo my laces. I *was* sorry. But I was also fucking mad. And disgusted with myself. And about to detonate.

"Are you serious right now?" Kat was practically on top of me, but I still refused to look at her. She wasn't going to see the weakness pooling in my eyes.

"Kat, let's all just take a breath." This was Charlotte. I could see her sweaty-socked feet beside Kat's skates.

"Charlotte, do not get in the middle of this—"

"Actually, I will, because I am, and because you're *too* in the middle of it."

Charlotte's feet inched closer. "This is not the right time for all of this. Let's just cool our jets and come back to it."

Kat's skates stayed put for a full five seconds and then skated away. I let go of a breath I'd been holding. Charlotte crouched so I couldn't avoid her face anymore, even though I still tried.

"Daya, shit happens on the track. Don't get in your head about it, okay?" She knocked my knee with her knuckles and went back to changing.

I swallowed back whatever was trying to vacate my chest.

Shit happens when you cause it.

After a bout, we were supposed to stick around and help take down the boards, benches, etc., but I doubted anyone would mind if I just got out of their way. If I were them, I sure as hell wouldn't want me around.

I checked my phone as I was leaving and saw that Fee had texted me.

Hey you. I'm sorry I can't stay—Cai must've eaten something shady. She feels like crap. No pun intended. :/ Tough bout, kid. Try not to get in your head about it. I'm around if you need me. Drop of a hat.

They were the second person to tell me not to get in my head. What did that even mean, anyway? Aren't we always in our heads, whether we like it or not? I'd love to get out of my head, and I was going to try as soon as I got out of here.

Leaving the locker room, I saw that most of the crowd had dispersed, but a few folks were still milling around in the Crash Zone. One of them was Shanti. When I came out, she looked over. We made eye contact. I looked away first. Again. But not before I could see that she was still talking to messy-haircut girl, which just added another layer of shit to an ever-growing pile.

Outside, the air was biting cold. I slumped over to the bus stand a couple of blocks away and threw my gear bag against the sidewalk. It felt like every molecule in my body was banging against one another, trying to get some relief. Without a second thought, I held the bus signpost with my right hand and slammed my left hand against it. Once, twice, three times—

A pair of hands caught mine. "Daya, stop!"

I tried to keep going, but Shanti's hands were strong. Stronger than mine.

"You don't need to do this," she said.

But I do. The tears and rot were bubbling up.

"We can talk."

I can't.

"Let me be here for you."

This last attempt struck a special chord. "Here? You sure? Don't you have someone back at the rink who's waiting for you?" I was in her face now. Practically spitting into it.

She retreated a few inches. "I wasn't—that's not—"

The rot in my chest escaped, shaped as hateful laughter. "Jesus. Why bother?" I wasn't sure if I was talking to her or to myself. "How are you not getting the message, Shanti? *I'm* not your problem. You have enough problems of your own. Go deal with them instead of being such a pain in my ass."

I turned from her, swept up my bag, and stalked away. The walk was miles, but I'd do anything right now to get away from here.

Chapter Thirty-Four

I couldn't even begin to explain what had gone wrong. But beneath my whirling mind, I knew. I could replay each and every moment after we left the gym parking lot.

My father's furious fumbling with his seat belt as he drove out. Amma glancing backward at me through the reflection of the window. My swift glance away. Lights glowing across the dashboard. Guitar and drums blasting through the stereo. The silent seconds hovering beneath the music. And then the eruption of their argument once again—Amma defending herself, for once. Thatha frustrated by my mother's surprising boldness. My dad's arms motioning in fits and starts as he drove, punctuating his anger. Their voices vaulting back and forth across the car. Thatha's eyes leaving the road over and over to cut the air between me and him, him and my mum. Each slow moment that carried the car too far left. The burst of time that propelled us into the air and then dropped us like lead to the ground. The night's blackness outside my window suddenly crashing into concrete. Shattering glass. Crunching metal.

And then my body being pulled out and facing the night sky. Gravel pushing into my scalp. The muffled sounds of someone's voice in my ears. Tears falling unbidden from the corners of my eyes. Trying to respond, to ask about my parents, but only heavy breaths coming out.

Amma's sari flipping back and forth from the open and smashed car door like a flag telling me where she was. Thatha invisible inside the wreckage.

Nothing I could do would remove those images. No morning ritual, no haphazard skate tricks, no amount of sideswiping on the track. They'd always been there just below the surface, like blood coursing beneath skin.

Chapter Thirty-Five

I'd walked home after the scene at the arena. It must have taken over an hour, but I didn't remember any of it. I found myself collapsed on my bed, sweaty uniform still on, too tired and too defeated to even think about taking refuge in my headboard and hand. Too helpless. All the bruising had kept those images at bay until now. Focusing on the pain, the layers of soft tissue made angry purple—it had kept me protected *and* reminded me of the ache I deserved, just like my seat belt had somehow saved me but left a deep welt of hurt across—and inside—my chest.

When I finally trudged across the hall to pee, praying I'd avoid Priam and Vicki at least until the morning, I'd stayed seated on the toilet way longer than needed—gazing into the musical notes scattered across the shower curtain like annoying little reminders to "perk up" and "look on the bright side." Staring at them just made my eyes water, though, so I flushed, washed my hands while carefully evading my own reflection in the mirror, and crept back across the hall again.

"Daya Doo Wop!"

Please, no.

"Your shirt says 'Daya Doo Wop'! I *love* it!"

My hand froze around the doorknob to my room and I reflexively squeezed tight before turning to face Priam.

He couldn't avoid my face like I just had, and it made the delight in his own expression slip away. Something in the concern that crept into his features—the frown that creased his brow, the compressed line of his lips—reminded me so much of Thatha that my chest broke open. My face contracted and sobs escaped from somewhere deep inside of me.

"Oh my Daya . . ."

When I felt his arms around me, I didn't resist.

My bed sagged beneath the weight of all three of us—Uncle Priam, me, and Vicki. They flanked me, Priam's fingers patting my shoulder in a tentative gesture of comfort, Vicki's hand rubbing my back with enough zeal that my body wagged back and forth with each rub.

Uncharacteristically, they'd remained mostly quiet since Priam had guided me into my room and called Vicki up. Besides a bewildered "Oh, darling" from Vicki and a "Can I get you some biscuits? Chocolate? Cheezies?" from Priam, their response had mostly consisted of patting and rubbing.

I'd been unable to stop blubbering, a continuous stream of

snot and tears emptying into my lap until Vicki finally ran to the bathroom for a box of tissues and began mopping up my face with several.

After I'd had enough face dabbing, I finally gathered myself and took the bundle of wet tissues from her to wipe my own face.

Once I was done, Vicki finally started, "We're here, Daya. If you feel ready to tell us what's going on."

"Yes, Daya—you can tell us anything," Priam added. Pat, pat.

"Anything at all." Rub, rub.

Could I, though? Tell them anything? And if I could, where was the beginning? Or the end?

I knew that the slow-motion moments from the accident told only part of the story, but what moments told the rest? My pathetic boxing match? The limp punches and distracted footwork? Maybe what really mattered was everything that happened before we got into the car, before the match. Each moment I believed my dad when he told me I was strong. That I needed to be stronger. When he taught me what it took to survive and protect myself. Or maybe the most important moments were when I let myself side with Thatha. When Amma's way seemed so weak and powerless. Or did the story exist in smaller moments? A baseball bat swinging into a golf stroke. Backyard boxing matches. Amma's careful, exact folding—way before everything else—the silk shaping mysteries and magic around her body. "Lunu Dehi" in the car and the hissing of dark leaves in hot water?

What really matters in the end?

Those moments swept through my mind, thin and tattered like cloth windblown across miles. Sitting there on my bed between Priam and Vicki, though, I couldn't get them to drift from my lips. When I tried, they became tangled in the present moment—the one where no matter what I did, I made a mess of everything.

I stared across my bedroom, feeling vacant. My eyes came to rest on the drawer with that damn journal in it.

Write down what it is you want to say but don't feel you can.

I had nothing to lose at this point. I dragged myself over to my desk, pulled out the journal and a pencil, and came back to sit between Vicki and Priam. I could sense them sharing glances across me as I snapped the book open to a random page in the middle. I stared at the bare space and gripped the pencil like I was trying to squeeze the lead onto the paper.

I finally dragged it across the page and wrote the words: *They died because of me.*

Once I'd written it, I slammed the journal shut, a fit of panic overtaking me. *What am I doing? They'll hate me. Everyone will hate me. No one can know.*

"Daya?" Vicki murmured. "Can we see?"

But they had to know. Then I'd get what I really deserved. I'd been trying to punish and protect myself by bruising—trying to dole out my own justice while pushing away all those moments. But what I hadn't realized was that the most fitting punishment would be to invite all those moments back. Let them wash over me. Let others see how I'd ruined everything.

I threw the journal onto her lap and then slipped down to the floor, stretching out my legs and letting my arms fall to my sides, opening up to what was bound to come.

Behind and above me, I heard the journal's spine creak open, the flipping of pages, and then two quick, sharp inhalations.

And then two bums slid down beside me.

"Daya, you have to know this isn't true," Priam said, his voice almost pleading. This wasn't his breakfast drama voice, though. It sound different. More serious. Almost like my dad.

"Why in the world would you think such a thing, Daya?" Vicki whispered, like she really couldn't believe it. "It was just an accident. A terrible, unfair accident."

She placed her arm around my shoulders, but I didn't deserve it. I leaned forward. Her hand remained on my back.

As though I was telling only the space between my knees, I forced the words out. "Thatha got distracted. They were fighting. Because of me. Because I wasn't strong enough. He was so mad and Amma was so upset. And I'd made them that way."

My tears had dried up and I was already too broken to fracture any further. I just waited for Vicki's hand to pull away. For them both to pull away. For my real punishment to come.

Instead I felt four arms reach around me and pull me in.

Chapter Thirty-Six

"Daya, my brother could be a real asshole. I know that, and you know that."

I couldn't believe Priam was saying this. We'd moved downstairs to the kitchen and were seated at the table, drinking tea. I was exhausted, but even in my exhaustion, I could feel defensiveness rise up.

"He put you through college," I said, staring into my mug.

"That's true. He did. And I've always been grateful for that. But it didn't give him the right to judge my choices."

Vicki jumped in. "We're not saying he was a bad person—"

"Just that he was an asshole," I snapped.

"Well—yes." She hesitated and side-eyed Priam. "What we mean is, he could be . . . hard. But he had his reasons. And he could be kind, too."

Kind? That wasn't a word I'd use to describe my dad. *Committed, sometimes goofy, tireless, strong. But not kind.* My face gave away my thoughts.

"He was!" Vicki insisted, smiling a little. "Priam, tell her, darling."

Priam toyed with Toto the pepper shaker. "It's true," he said, aiming his words at Toto and nodding. "I know it was hard to see, but do you know"—he looked up at me—"that he taught me to play the piano?"

What? "Dad played the piano?"

"Beautifully! He gave it up when he came here—like he gave up boxing—but those fingers of his could do a lot more than just punch at things, you know? In Sri Lanka he taught me everything he knew, and he was so patient with me—even as a teenager."

Mind blown.

"He grew a little less patient here," Priam continued. "He had a lot on his shoulders, after all."

"That's not an excuse, of course," Vicki piped up. "I know he could be harsh, and we didn't like it." She reached across the table and placed her hand over mine. I let her. "We should have said something, Daya. He was too hard on you, and we should have stepped in."

"He just wanted me to be strong," I said, more to myself.

"Sweetheart, there are so many ways to be strong."

"Yes," Priam agreed. "Nihal *was* strong in his own way. He never let up, kept working and working to keep us all safe and sound. But it was your mom who was the *really* strong one."

Okay, now I know you're full of it. "Amma was *caring*, but not strong. She always gave in to him."

"Do you know who got Nihal his first job here?" Priam asked.

"And who stage-managed *our* first play?" Vicki's pointer finger shot up beside her face. "Or got your dad to let you try softball?"

"Or who told your dad off when he made fun of me?"

"Wait—she never told Dad off. She'd just keep quiet," I argued.

"She'd never tell your dad off in front of *you*, my dear!" Priam practically shouted in triumph. "She could give him a better telling-off than even our mother used to give him!" In his excitement to tell me all these things, Priam had expanded in his chair.

"Well, she never defended me." My voice came out small. Priam's body sank slowly backward.

Vicki squeezed my hand. "She did, Daya. At least, she tried. But you and your dad were thick as thieves. It was hard to break into that bond you seemed to have."

I knew it was true as soon as she said it. I didn't argue. But it just made me feel worse.

"But she adored you, Daya. And she was so proud of you," Vicki added, probably just to make me feel better. All this information was surprising and mind-blowing, but it didn't change the fact that I'd caused the accident.

"I lost that boxing match."

"Which match?" Priam asked.

"The one we were coming home from. I'd fucked"—

Vicki's cheeks instantly blushed—"I'd messed up the match. Amma had come to watch, and it flustered me to have her there. I was distracted and didn't box the way Thatha taught me to. He was so mad at me. And at her." I let my hand slip from Vicki's and sat back in my chair. "That's why they were fighting."

"Oh, Daya." Vicki held her face with both hands.

"Can't you see that no one thing anyone did could cause that accident?" Priam asked. "If you want to take that route, you could blame Vicki and me for encouraging your mum to go watch you box—which we did, you know."

I looked up at him. "You did?"

"Of course! She was so uncertain about it—the violence and all. We were uncertain about it too. But we knew it would mean something to you. So maybe the accident is our fault. We didn't know how nervous it would make you." He looked at Vicki and shrugged as though he really wasn't sure. She smiled at him with reassurance and held his hand.

I knew he was just trying to make me see the error in my reasoning, but this new piece of information actually brought up a tiny ounce of anger in my chest. Maybe it *was* their fault. Then I felt like a jerk thinking that.

"I don't blame you," I said, the words barely audible.

Vicki leaned over the table. "And we don't blame *you*, Daya. *No one* blames you. It's not anyone's fault."

I wanted to believe them. But I'd told myself my own version for so long, I'd convinced myself it was true. Fact. I was starting to see that facts could blur and re-form into something different if you let them.

"Daya." Priam leaned forward and took my hand in his. "Where will it get you? This believing you caused such a terrible thing? Where has it gotten you so far?"

Nowhere good. That's for sure.

I needed a different story.

Chapter Thirty-Seven

"Hey, punk. Get your little brown butt in here." Fee's body filled the doorframe. By "here" I thought they meant inside the house, but when I climbed up the steps and they didn't move aside, I realized they meant into a hug. Fee's arms spread wide and pulled me in, smushing me against their chest. We'd never hugged before and I was a little thrown off, but I was too exhausted to resist. Truth be told, I didn't really want to resist anyway.

After talking to Vicki and Priam last night, I'd needed to lie down for a bit. My head ached, what with all the emoting and processing. But once I'd closed my eyes, I just became even more aware of the thump of my heartbeat, the mixture of pain and longing, confusion and gratitude moving through my chest. Talking about Amma and Thatha had brought up so many feelings—ones I'd tried to bury, like guilt and sadness, yes, but also waves of appreciation and love that I'd forgotten had been part of the package as well. Eventually, though, my exhaustion got the better of me and I'd drifted to sleep.

When my phone pinged the next morning, waking me up, a jolt of excitement surged through me, thinking—hoping—it was Shanti. I hadn't wanted anything to do with her or anyone just a few hours before, but now . . . I didn't know what I wanted. The way my heart jumped at the possibility of seeing her name on my screen told me whatever I did want included her, though.

I'd been disappointed when the message was from Fee, but when the text had said their mum "now needs her furniture moved around, apparently," and Fee had promised "the best brown mama lunch you've ever had as payment," a warmth crept into my chest and I'd texted back that I'd be there in an hour.

As I was leaving, Priam and Vicki had poked their heads out from the living room and asked how I was feeling. Instead of trying to articulate all the emotions I was experiencing, I just hugged them both, thanked them for the chat the night before, and promised them I'd be home before curfew. For once, they'd been speechless.

And now here I was, hugging yet another person in the span of an hour. What in the world was happening to me?

Once Fee finally let me go, they invited me into their mum's home, and Dotty appeared from nowhere to yank me into another embrace. Whereas Fee's hug had been tight and bone-crushing, Dotty's was cushiony and soothing. She smelled like oranges and cloves.

She held me at her short arm's length and considered my face closely. "You look tired, my girl," she said. "How will you move my furniture with those droopy eyelids?" She was smiling.

Smiling back down at her, I replied, "I'll manage, don't worry. I need some hard labor anyway."

"Wonderful"—except it sounded like *vunderful* and my heart twinged—"I'll get to making us some lunch. You've never had rotlis like my rotlis, Daya. You better work up your appetite!" Her bun wobbled back and forth as her head did the same, and I had an urge to hug her again.

Before I could, though, Fee put their arm around my shoulders and guided me away. "Come on, punk. Let's go earn our rotlis."

We worked quietly for a bit, lifting and adjusting some of the heaviest furniture known to humankind, and I wondered if Dotty really had needed this task completed today, or if Fee had devised it as a plan to get me out of my head. Either way, I was glad to be here, with them, sweating, and smelling brown food wafting down the hallway.

After we'd managed to guide a particularly unwieldy chest of drawers down a narrow staircase into the basement, Fee leaned against one end of it to catch their breath.

"Tired?" I said. "I feel great." I jumped up and down a couple of times to prove how not-tired I was.

They rolled their eyes. "Not tired from your blowup last night?" Their face held both teasing and warmth, and though the thought of the bout sent my stomach plunging, I knew I needed to talk about it. And that Fee was a good person to do that with.

I folded my arms on top of the chest of drawers and rested my chin against them. "That was a mess."

"What happened, you think?"

"I let that chick get to me. But I was already geared up to throw down with someone."

Fee raised themselves off the chest and reached backward to stretch their arms. "Why's that?"

I worked my jaw back and forth a bit. "It's a bit of a story. How long till those rotlis are ready?"

Fee's response to each piece of my story—from boxing to the accident to roller derby to Shanti (I wasn't ready to share with them about the bruising)—was another hug and more hard labor. No advice about how to fix anything—just a promise: "You know I got you, punk."

Once we'd moved what Dotty had wanted us to move, we sat down at her kitchen table, which was laden with dahl, saag paneer, chutney, and of course, the celebrated rotlis. Nothing was more satisfying to me than unleavened bread products made by brown people, and I tore into the meal like I hadn't eaten in days. Then I remembered I *hadn't* actually eaten since before the bout yesterday—I'd been too distraught to consume anything beyond the tea I'd shared with Priam and Vicki.

"You've got a good appetite, like this one." Dotty gestured to Fee and her eyes glimmered.

I smiled through my mouthful of dahl and nodded.

Fee added, "No one can resist your food, Ma. And it helps to move thousand-pound furniture around first." They leaned over and kissed Dotty on the cheek. She made that universal brown mama lip-smacking sound and playfully pushed Fee away.

As I watched them, my heart ached a little, but seeing Dotty so clearly accept everything about Fee—everything they were and weren't—made me realize I had people like that in my life too. Fee, for one. Priam and Vicki. Shanti. I hadn't seen it because I didn't want to. It had felt easier not to have to depend on anyone else. Losing something—or someone—that you don't depend on doesn't matter so much. Doesn't hurt.

The thought of losing Shanti hurt. I needed to do something about that.

Chapter Thirty-Eight

I rolled down the side streets around my house, swerving my skateboard back and forth—toward the curb, away, toward, away. The curving motion calmed my nerves as I waited for my phone to ding.

I'd texted Shanti after leaving Dotty's, belly full but in knots of anticipation and worry.

I'm so sorry. About everything. Can we talk?

I hadn't heard back by the time I got home, so I grabbed my skateboard, which I hadn't used in over a month, and went out to clear my head. For the first time in a long time, I didn't have the urge to bang myself up. Easing in and out of the bends and loops of the neighborhood, I let my breath fell into an even rhythm and my body loosened into a comfortable stance. When my phone did finally ding, I'd almost forgotten I was waiting for it to.

I don't know, Daya.

I stared at my screen for a few seconds, then wrote, I get it. I was a total dick. I was scared. Still am. But I'm more sorry than scared now. Can I tell you that in person?

Nothing. Then three damn dots taunting me for what seemed like forever. Then:

I work till 5. Guess you could meet me here if you want. Books Are Best. 4th and Commercial.

A few seconds later:

Don't be a dick when you get here.

A plush gray cat greeted me when I stepped into the bookstore, working its way in a graceful figure eight around my ankles.

"That's Woolf. She wants you to buy some books."

Shanti was walking up a narrow aisle toward me, two tall bookcases towering over her on either side. The store was long but small, and only one other person besides Shanti and me was inside that I could see.

As if on cue, Woolf meowed loudly and stared up at me.

Grateful to have something else to focus on, I crouched and started to scratch her around her collar. Without looking at Shanti, I said, "She's very persuasive."

Shanti's hand appeared close to mine and began petting Woolf's back. My heart beat uncontrollably in my chest, no matter how hard I tried to concentrate on breathing and my own hand.

"Okay, that's enough pampering for now, furry demon. If we're not careful, we'll be petting her forever," Shanti warned.

I finally managed to look up at her and found her face hesitant, but curious. We raised ourselves to standing and stared at the floor for a moment.

This was my move, and I knew it. I took a breath. "I know I hurt you," I said.

Shanti's head tipped to the side. "You did."

"I'm sorry. You didn't deserve any of that."

"What's changed?" she asked.

Everything. Nothing. "I don't really know. I guess . . . I realized I was wrong about some things." I forced myself to look her in the eye. Tried a tentative smile. "And right about others."

She seemed to consider my words carefully before saying, "That's good to hear. But I'm not going to put up with any more of that stuff from either of you. I'm tired of it, Daya."

Oh. My head dipped in a nod. My eyes found my feet. "Right. You shouldn't."

A beat.

"So?"

I glanced up. "So . . . ?"

"Will I have to put up with any more of that stuff from you?"

"Uh . . . no? No, I mean. Definitely not." I scrunched my nose at my clumsiness.

She studied my face. "Okay then." Stepping a little closer, she raised her arms out in front of her. "Can you handle all this softness, or not?"

No sense ending this streak I was on. I walked into her hug while Woolf meowed her indignation from the floor.

We made small talk until the one customer left the store.

"It's not too busy, if you want to keep talking here. Or we can talk after I'm done." Shanti had me stacking books alongside her for a display at the front of the store.

"Um . . ." Opening up to Priam and Vicki had felt like a breaking open, like muscle tearing to grow stronger. Raw and painful but also fortifying. With Fee, I'd relayed so much of my story in one fell swoop that it was like I'd been assembling the pieces to keep them all together. To lay them out and observe them as a whole. Matter-of-fact.

Here, with Shanti, I felt like I was both trying to fix something and start over. I wanted her to know why I'd acted as I had, that I was sorry for taking my anger out on her and shutting her out, but I also wished I could just wipe the slate and move on. Coming clean about my feelings was new to me, after all, and it still felt foreign, blundering. All I really wanted to do was kiss her and have everything be the way it was that first night we spent together.

But I knew I had to do more than that. I started with the truth.

"This is really hard for me. I'm sorry it's not going to be perfect."

"I don't care about perfect, Daya. I still wanted to kiss you after you wore a sweaty dinosaur suit, after all."

I couldn't stop one side of my mouth from curling upward. "True." I felt like I was on the verge of tipping over. I turned to face her, a book in my hands just to feel something solid. I took a deep breath and began.

"I was in the car too . . . when my parents died. For a long time, I've felt like the accident was my fault. It doesn't make sense, I know, but I was brought up to be strong and instead I was weak and they fought and the car crashed and they both died." My words rushed out and my voice faltered, but I kept going.

"I guess—I guess I got it into my head that I needed to be tougher—harder—after that. And the bruises . . ." I looked away for a moment. Admitting this part wasn't easy. "The bruises made me feel better and worse at the same time. They helped keep everything down . . . but also made me feel like shit afterward." I found her eyes again. "But then you made it so easy to be softer. And that felt so good, but also scary. And then Kat—it's not really her fault—it was just easier for me to go back to being hard. But that didn't work either. Nothing seemed to work."

My voice was shaking and my cheeks were wet. I remembered I was in a bookstore, where anyone could walk in at any moment, and wiped my eyes with my coat sleeve.

Shanti placed her hand on my hip. "Something must have worked. You're here, now, doing something that seems really hard for you." I felt her hand press lightly into my body. "But you're still doing it."

Placing the book I'd been holding onto the display table, all I could get out was a "Yeah."

"I'm glad you told me all that." She paused, tentative. "Have you . . . told anyone else about the bruising?"

I shook my head. I hadn't shared this part of things with Priam and Vicki or Fee. It might have been weird, but I was more ashamed of the way I'd been bruising myself than I had been about my part in the accident. I was at least starting to see that the accident hadn't been my fault entirely, but the bruising—I couldn't blame anyone else for that except myself.

"I'm not pressuring you to—but it might be something to think about? Maybe? I mean, what do you think?"

Her questioning tone and hesitations told me she really wasn't trying to pressure me, and I was grateful for that. I just didn't know if I was ready to tell anyone else. Telling Shanti seemed the easiest—even if it wasn't *easy*—since she'd already known about it. But telling Priam and Vicki . . . I couldn't imagine what their reaction would be.

I rubbed my face with my hands, probably a little too aggressively, because Shanti moved a little closer and said, "Sorry—I'm not trying to stress you out. I just . . . want you to be safe." Her hand was still on my hip, and now her other one moved to my cheek. She was so close.

"I know. It's okay. I just . . . It's a hard thing to admit. I hate that I do it." I looked down at my feet.

"It must be hard. All of it. But it sounds like you're doing the strongest possible thing about it."

I glanced up at her. At her lips. "What's that?"

"Talking about it."

I sighed. "Yes. Lots of talking. And yes, it's been great and all. But maybe . . . we could take a little break from it for a minute?" I kept looking at her lips. Played with my hoodie strings.

Shanti nodded ever so slightly as she took my hand and pulled me to a small enclave in the store housing Staff Recommendations. With hardcovers pressed into my back, we kept each other quiet for the next several minutes.

Shanti and I had been interrupted by a customer who clearly didn't realize that there was a heated make-out session happening among the books, and Shanti had to get back to work. We agreed we'd hang out after Shanti's shift was over in an hour, though, so I killed some time bumming around the neighborhood, and then we met up again.

"Where to?" Shanti asked.

Obviously, I really just wanted to make out with Shanti some more. But something else was really bothering me, and I knew I wouldn't be able to move on until I did something about it.

"Do you think Lena would hate seeing me right now?"

Shanti thought about it for a moment. "I'm not sure, but I think it's worth a try. You know she's at my place, though, right? And so is Kat?"

Right.

Chapter Thirty-Nine

Shanti and I entered from the back of the house, down through the basement to her room. I needed a couple of minutes to gather myself before running into Kat. Shanti had said Kat was still pissed about Lena's injury, the loss, and me and Shanti getting together.

I couldn't change the first two things and I didn't *want* to change the third, so I was going into this with very little to offer. All I could do was apologize. I just hoped Kat would give me a chance to.

"Listen," Shanti said, "I know she sometimes shows it in shitty ways, but try and remember that Kat just wants her team—her family—to be safe. She doesn't want you to get hurt either—that's why she was so tough on you. That's why she's so tough on me. I think we can all agree her approach is crap. But she's not as strong as you, Daya."

"Me?"

"Yes, you. How many people did you open up to in the past twenty-four hours? How easy was it for you? I *wish* Kat could do that. Who knows, maybe you'll be a good influence on her at some point." She kissed me.

I didn't feel that strong right now. What I'd give to just stay in this room and keep kissing Shanti all night instead of facing Kat.

A while later we made our way, heavy-footed, up the stairs to the kitchen.

When we got there, we found Lena and Kat bent over the kitchen island, beers gripped in their hands, an open bag of No Name chips in front of them. Lena's cheek lay flat against the laminate countertop. Her weight was all on her left leg, and her right knee was bundled up in a tensor bandage and ice pack. Two crutches rested against the kitchen table. Kat's head was tilted up toward the ceiling—exasperation showing in her closed eyes and the uncharacteristic slump of her shoulders.

When we walked through the doorway, both looked over, varying degrees of surprise on their faces.

"What the—" Kat began, but Lena interrupted her.

"Daya, you little shit—get over here!" Lena hopped over on her one good leg and gave me a huge bear hug.

Unexpected.

When she was done, she plunked herself down in a chair next to the table and said, "Guess you got me back for taking you out in the living room, huh?" She was grinning.

I was dazed.

I shook off my bewilderment and sat in a chair next to hers. "Sorry" wasn't something I was used to saying, but I'd already managed to get the words out to Shanti, and seeing Lena's knee bulging with ice, I forced them out again. "Lena, I am so, so sorry about this. I really messed everything up."

"You sure fucking did," Kat growled as she stomped away from the island and stood over us, hands—guess where?—on her hips.

My shoulders immediately tensed, and I had to fight back the urge to go nose to nose with her again. Instead I took a deep breath in my chair, then rose and met her gaze, but I kept my shoulders loose and my voice as calm as possible. "I know I let the team down." The admission sent a twinge through my chest. "I wasn't thinking of the team—not like you always do, Kat. I was too wrapped up in a whole other fight—mostly with myself." I kept my eyes on hers even though they were starting to sting. "I'm sorry for letting that get in the way of doing what was right for all of us."

A slight frown crinkled her brow. One hand slipped from her hip. She actually looked lost for words.

"Aw, rook," Lena jumped in, "I seriously hurt myself at least twice per season. Granted, this one's a bit worse than usual, but Kat once broke my wrist—she tell you that?"

Kat rolled her eyes and scoffed, "Way to bring up ancient history, asshole." She looked at me. Wet her lips. Sighed. "Look, Daya, I like having someone tough like you on the team, but there are good ways to be tough and bad ways to be tough. You just gotta—"

"Seriously?" Shanti and I blurted at the same time. We looked at each other, a moment of amusement passing between us. Then Shanti turned to Kat and added, "You're going to lecture us on how to be 'good tough'?"

"What's that supposed to mean?" Kat asked.

Shanti came over and placed her hand on Kat's arm. "Sis, you know I love you, but your kind of tough sucks too sometimes."

I had to struggle to keep the smile off my face. Lena looked like she was struggling too.

Kat was definitely not smiling.

"My kind of tough has kept you pretty fucking safe, wouldn't you say . . . *sis*?"

She was pissed, but I noticed she didn't shrug off Shanti's hand, and Shanti kept it right where it was. "It has. And I'll always be grateful for that. But . . . aren't you exhausted? We were both hurt, but I'm okay—we're both okay. You don't have to be tough for us anymore."

Kat looked from Shanti to me to Lena and back to Shanti. I knew the expression on her face well. The struggle between wanting to let your guard down so badly but not wanting to risk getting hurt.

Unfortunately, for now, Kat chose to keep her guard up. "What is this? 'Cause it feels like some kind of fucking intervention, and I'm not down for it."

She tried to brush past both me and Shanti, but as if by reflex, I caught her hand. We both stared down in surprise and I let go quickly. She stalked away and to her room.

Shanti looked at me and sighed. "That went well, don't you think?"

"Give her time," I said. "Cement walls don't fall so easily."

Her eyebrows rose.

"What?"

She shrugged and laced her fingers through mine. "I'm just impressed by you, is all."

Not used to compliments, I felt my cheeks get hot.

Lena pushed herself up from her chair. "Well, chili cheese fries, this has been an enlightening exchange, but all the sharing has tired me out. I'mma hobble upstairs and overload on shit TV until I pass out." She grabbed her crutches and stood. Facing me, she said, "Listen, chica. You think you can get yer head on straight before the next bout?"

Did I? "I'm trying." Shanti squeezed my hand.

"Good. 'Cause you know what you're doing out there, and if you can just tune out all the trash talk—both your own *and* the other team's—you're gonna blow up the track." She punched me in the arm and swung her way out of the kitchen.

At practice on Tuesday, I apologized to the whole team. To my relief, most of the Honeys just took a few good-natured digs at me and then Lena told me to "Shaddup already so we can practice." I could tell that Dom and a couple of other

Honeys weren't going to let me off so easy, which I understood. I wouldn't have let me off easy either.

Kat stood in the back, arms crossed, but I just tried to remind myself how long it had taken me to pull down the hard shell I'd put up. I'd just need to be patient, like others had been with me. Maybe she'd come around, maybe not. But I hoped she would. I had a feeling our mutual struggles might be a bond if we could manage to avoid letting them get in the way.

I tried to wipe my head clean of our last bout and focus on the basics that Alma and Joe had taught me. I dug in and readied myself for whatever Kat was going to throw at me. To my surprise, though, she treated me like any other player and even threw me a "Nice work" at one point. The change might be glacial, but maybe she'd come around after all.

Every single bruise I ended up with from our practice came from hard work. I won't lie—I still got some satisfaction from a hard hit. But I wasn't seeking them out anymore. I was too busy trying to show the others—and myself—that I could be trusted to put the team first.

Chapter Forty

Fee and Cai had brought the damn pom-poms again. Like some kind of nightmare, Priam and Vicki had *also* brought pom-poms, except they had augmented their pom-poms with actual cheerleading costumes from some musical they'd been in at one point. Fee had brought Dotty, who was wearing an oversize Killa Honeys T-shirt. Across the arena in their usual spot, Bee and Yolanda were shouting obscenities at the Hair Force Babes, who were our competition tonight. Even Joe and Alma were here as special guest commentators.

Shanti was watching from the bench, next to Lena, who was still on crutches but as lively as ever, coaching the shit out of everyone. Kat was storming around the track, game face ready, as usual.

And I was about to start my second-ever roller derby bout against a team who'd probably seen my last bout and was going to make sure to pay special attention to me.

And also, there seemed to be a billion people in the stands. And my shirt still said DAYA DOO WOP on it. I didn't have the heart to switch it after Priam saw it.

Was I nervous?

You could say that.

"There's that Daya Doo Wop again, meddling with the Hair Force Babes' jammer! How does a brick wall like that move so fast?"

"What's Mz. Biz doing over there on the Honeys bench, Joe? It looks like she's poking the referee in the bum with her crutches. I'm not sure that constitutes a penalty, but the crowd seems to be enjoying it!"

"The Honeys' wild-eyed jammer Killa Skillz finds a hole, thanks to her blockers Daya Doo Wop and Charlotte the Harlot! She's zooming around the track like lightning. The Honeys are in the lead!"

"Potty Mouth takes out a whole group of her own teammates! They're sure fulla surprises, aren't they, Alma?"

"Ooh! Daya Doo Wop is pushed out of bounds into a group of very happy fans. That was a hard hit by the Babes' blocker Split Endz. Could be trouble, Alma . . . but . . . Daya just brushes herself off and—ha!—blows a kiss to her fans!"

"Well, shit, rook—you may have redeemed yourself!" Lena shouted at me over the girl she was wrestling for some inexplicable reason by our bench.

I wasn't sure I'd completely redeemed myself—some of the Skintastics were still giving me the stink-eye as they took to the track after our bout was done. I'd have to swallow my pride and apologize to them at some point—especially the girl I'd slammed to the ground. I promised myself to do that by the end of the night.

But I *had* done some good things out on the track today—I think I'd made Joe and Alma proud, at least, and *I* was proud of the other rookies and how well we'd worked together when we were on the same line. All that extra practice had paid off. Though I'd definitely messed up a few plays and maybe let my elbows fly out a little too far once in a while, even Kat seemed to be relatively satisfied with my performance, judging by the fist bump she gave me afterward.

Shanti snapped a towel against my ass. "Hey, superstar. Lookin' almost, maybe, *possibly* not too bad out there."

"Shucks. Thanks a lot."

She stood in front of me and glanced over at Kat, then back at me. Uncertain.

"So, does 'not too bad' get a kiss, or just a towel snap?" I asked, hinting with the tilt of my head.

She smiled, wiped my face with the towel, and let me press my lips to hers, sweaty mess and all.

"Oooooooooh!" Fee and Cai appeared next to us, shaking their pom-poms violently. Dotty stood giggling beside them.

"Okay, okay," I said, and made sure to give them the sweatiest hugs possible. "Shanti, you remember Fee. And this is

their girlfriend, Caihong. Dotty, this is Shanti. Shanti, Dotty."
Shanti and I hadn't discussed our status yet, but in my head, I
knew what she was to me.

"Where are Priam and Vicki, dare I ask?" I prayed they
weren't doing a cheerleading routine somewhere in the building.

"They're performing cheers for the Hell Beasts and Skintastics," Fee said, pointing behind me and Shanti.

I refused to look.

After we'd chatted for a bit, I finally went to gather Priam
and Vicki, and we all went to the Crash Zone. I wanted to
see Alma and Joe before the next bout started. Unsurprisingly,
Priam and Vicki and Alma and Joe fell in love with each other
instantly. Not so secretly, I hoped this meant I'd see a lot more
of Alma and Joe.

Dotty found me and wrapped me in a hug. "We're off,
Daya sweetie. I have to get these two"—she pointed over her
shoulder at Fee and Cai—"home before they turn into pump-
kins!"

Her giggle killed me.

I heard a *thump-step-thump* approach me from behind. I
instinctively braced for an assault to my calves.

"There she is!"

"How ya doin', shuga?"

After more introductions, I left this astounding collection of humans—Bee, Yolanda, Priam, Vicki, Alma, and
Joe—to discover each other's magic. I could picture them all
playing charades in our living room, and the thought didn't

make me completely ill like I thought it would.

I looked around for Shanti and saw her talking to Kat. It seemed like the kind of conversation that needed to be left alone, but that didn't mean I couldn't watch from afar.

There was tension, for sure, but also closeness. A hug was what I was hoping for, and when Kat pulled Shanti in—maybe a little more aggressively than an average human being would expect, but with a look of relief on her face—a swell overcame my chest that I couldn't control. I didn't want to, anyway.

I found a spot close to where I'd seen that first bout and watched the Skintastics and Hell Beasts roar around the track. Eventually I felt an arm encircle my waist and we watched together.

My world was full.

Chapter Forty-One

Dr. Hoang sat in her chair, reading the couple of pages I'd managed to fill in the journal.

One page was everything I'd thought made me strong before. The other page was everything that made me strong now. It'd been Shanti's idea. I'd scoffed at first—I mean, I was starting to come around to all this *feelings* stuff, but journaling still felt too "froufy." So we'd just talked it out first. I'd been surprised by how much I had to say, especially about the things that made me strong now. I'd been equally surprised by how much lighter I felt afterward.

When I'd gone home that night, I'd lain on my bed and filled the two pages with my scratchy writing. Bruising, silence, and defiance plus everything that came along with those things on one page—talking, trusting, and caring on the other. And so many names. Fee, Shanti, Priam, Vicki, all the roller folks . . . Amma. Thatha.

I'd had to think about adding Thatha's name to the second page. But in the end, I realized he'd taught me a kind of resilience, even if it had tipped over into stubbornness and distance. I'd take the part that was good and leave the rest.

Dr. Hoang closed the journal and looked up at me. I appreciated that she didn't seem smug about me finally using it. I was growing and all, but that still would've pissed me off.

"Wow." She paused, and I wasn't sure if I should say anything. But then she continued, "Sorry—I'm just a little blown away by you right now. It's making me lose my words."

A "Ha!" erupted from my mouth, startling Dr. Hoang. Her face turned to amusement quickly, though. I immediately got embarrassed. "Sorry . . . just, you . . . speechless . . ." I couldn't help but laugh again.

She laughed too, and it lifted the embarrassment.

After a moment, she tilted her head and asked, "So? Are we doing this, then?"

I sank into my chair. *I guess we are.*

Chapter Forty-Two

The following weekend Priam and Vicki knocked on my bedroom door as I was trying to catch up on all the homework I'd been ignoring.

"Come in."

They poked their heads through a small opening, both faces hesitant.

"No, I mean come *in*," I said, waving them toward me. I think they were still a little unsure about how to be around me, but I'd never felt so sure about wanting to be around them. Something had shifted—I still hadn't told them about the bruising, but I'd agreed to see Dr. Hoang more frequently and was working through things with her first. And though Priam and Vicki were still mostly overwhelming and basically the opposite to my natural way of being, I could see how much they loved my parents and me. How they were my family—a way to be with my parents even though they were both gone.

I was seated on my bed, computer on my lap. Priam and Vicki sat on the end of the bed, shared a brief glance, then faced me.

Looks serious, I thought, and closed my laptop. "What's up?" I asked.

Vicki started. "Daya, we—Priam and I—were thinking of visiting your parents today. It's been a while, and we wanted to ask you if you'd like to come along."

"We'll understand if you don't feel up to it, though, of course," Priam added, his hand darting out toward me. His eyes flicked toward Vicki's, worried.

My heart sank into my stomach, heavy with a mixture of feelings. I hadn't been to my parents' graves yet, except for the funeral. And even then, I'd been there only in body, not really in mind or spirit. That old feeling of guilt crept up, alongside uncertainty about how it would feel to visit them now. But on top of those feelings was a deep yearning to see them and a warmth for these two people in front of me who knew how much I missed both my parents, because they missed them too.

"I think . . . I want to go."

Priam and Vicki had, apparently, formed a little ritual of their own when they visited my parents' graves. Priam would play the mandolin and they would both sing a few songs.

My first thought was that rolling over in his grave didn't even begin to cover what my dad was probably doing as they played, but then I remembered how much I hadn't known about both my mum and dad until Vicki and Priam told me, and I decided to believe that Thatha was singing along or playing the piano wherever he was.

Once they were done with their concert, they both touched my arm and left me to visit on my own. The ground was damp and cold, but I sat down anyway, just inches from the small headstone with both my parents' names on it. I closed my eyes and took a few long breaths, reaching back into my mind for all the moments that had stayed with me—all of them—the hard ones, the soft, the playful, the frustrating. By the time I opened my eyes, my hand had found its way to the carvings in the stone—palm flattened against the letters, the individual lines and spaces sending a kind of pulse into my skin, the muscle, the blood. Traveling like a heartbeat through my body and finding a place deep inside my chest. I knew I'd keep it there—safe, soft, strong.

ROLLER DERBY:
A VERY BRIEF OVERVIEW

Roller derby has a long history—starting in the 1930s as a race on wheels and reaching its height in the mid-1940s, when thousands of spectators sold out Madison Square Garden.

The modern era of roller derby began in the early 2000s in Austin, Texas. This new grassroots movement was led by women and focused on the athleticism and realism of this rough-and-tumble sport. The release of the roller derby movie *Whip It* in 2009—directed by and starring Drew Barrymore—helped spread the sport around the world. It is now played everywhere from Alaska to Dubai.

While there are many different rule sets and some leagues still play on the traditional wooden banked track, most modern roller derby is played on a flat track. Flat track roller derby essentially took the dimensions of the tilted banked track and flattened them, allowing teams to play on dry ice rinks, outdoor basketball courts, or in community centers on a taped-down oval track.

The most commonly played rule set is governed by WFTDA—the Women's Flat Track Derby Association. There are five players from each team on the track, and one player from each team has a star on their helmet. The skater with the star is called the "jammer" and they score the points. The other skaters are called "blockers" and they prevent the jammers from passing while simultaneously assisting their own jammers to score. Points are scored every time the jammer passes an opposing skater, so they have the opportunity to collect four points for every pass of the pack. The game is played in intervals called "jams," which last for up to two minutes, and then the players switch out for another ten skaters. The jammer who is able to get past the four opposing blockers first is awarded the status of "lead jammer," and they may end the jam at any time. A game consists of two thirty-minute periods with a fifteen-minute halftime.

Roller derby is a full-contact sport with contact rules similar to hockey. You may not grab an opposing skater, link arms with your teammates to impede an opposing skater, or trip a member of the opposing team. However, body checks, booty blocks, and hip checks are all fair game. A high-level game of roller derby often looks like rugby on roller skates—but with more bodies flying into the cheap seats!

Roller derby is unique in many ways—it is played on traditional roller skates (the quad-style skates, not Rollerblades), it is one of the only sports where you play offense and defense at the same time, and weirdly enough—there's no ball! But what makes it truly unique is that it is a full-contact sport that has been created, developed, promoted, operated, and led by women. Although there is a small roller derby community of men, the biggest stars in this sport are women. And the WFTDA promotes a policy of inclusion for individuals identifying as transgender, intersex, and gender-expansive.

The WFTDA's motto is Real, Strong, Athletic, Revolutionary. Roller derby is so much more than the sport; it is a community that strives to empower and revolutionize the way we see women and athleticism. If you attended a roller derby game, you'd see women of all shapes and sizes, from all walks of life, speeding around a track on roller skates and having the time of their lives.

Lucy Croysdill aka LuluDemon
Founder—Pivotstar Roller Derby Apparel
Co-Founder—Camp Elite Roller Derby Training
Co-Founder—Girls on Track Foundation
Co-Founder and Head Coach—Rolla Skate Club
Former President—Terminal City Rollergirls, Vancouver
Team Member 2011 & 2014—Team Canada Roller Derby

ACKNOWLEDGMENTS

I'm grateful to live and write on land belonging to the Musqueam, Squamish, and Tsleil-Waututh First Nations. I acknowledge that I benefit from historical and ongoing colonialism and understand that I'm responsible for working toward a more equitable and just future for Indigenous peoples on this land. I commit to doing so in the ways I teach, write, act, and listen.

I was lucky enough to write this book with the same dream team: my agent, Jim McCarthy, and my editor, Jennifer Ung. Jim, thank you for your constant support and willingness to answer all of my Type-A questions. This wasn't my debut book, but I'm still a rookie and I appreciate your patience, advice, and good humor. Jen, your focus on character so aligns with my own and I feel fortunate to have had someone like you at the beginning of my writing career to guide me. I've learned so much about writing fully formed human beings and about care in language. Thank you for making me a better writer from one book to the next!

To the rest of the team at Simon & Schuster both in Canada and the US—as with *Kings*, my experience has been smooth, collaborative, and joyful. Thank you to all those in marketing, publicity, and sales for being incredibly important pieces to this complicated puzzle. Special shout-outs to Chelsea Morgan and their eagle-eyed squad of editors for their careful attention to detail. To Sarah Creech for designing yet another beautiful cover and to Rik Lee, who brought my trifecta of powerful humans to life in his art. And special, special shout-out to my Canadian super-publicist, Mackenzie Croft. Mackenzie, I feel like we've been internet dating for the past year and a half and I couldn't have asked for a better long-distance, literary relationship! Thank you for your enthusiasm, love for both *Kings* and *Bruised*, and, of course, all those exclamation points . . . just! Like! Joe!

To my beta-readers—Joanne Darrell Herbert, Ly Hoang, Christy Dunsmore, Tammy Do, and Alannah Safnuk—thank you for your ongoing support of me and my writing. Thank you for your always thoughtful, honest comments. I cherish each of you for your feedback and for your friendship.

To my "roller derby" readers—Aldera "Dazzler" Chisholm, Diana "Fireweed" Savage, Nicola "Legal Chaos" Doughty, and Saoirse "Finn-Atomic" McDonald-Lepur—thank you for your generous feedback on the ins and outs of this incredible sport. Your suggestions and corrections were invaluable and I hope I've done roller derby justice! Thanks also to Christina "Kill a Blockingbird" King, Nicole Terry, and Christina

Nicole "Double Slammiato" Kendall for their added insight into this incredible sport.

Speaking of roller derby, huge thanks to the Rolla Skate Club in Vancouver, BC (rollaskateclub.com), whose goal it is to change the narrative around women, power, and sports and who are providing so many incredible ways to do that. They and Roller Girl (rollergirl.ca) served as constant inspirations throughout my writing process. Special thanks to Lucy Croysdill (aka LuluDemon) for providing such important context to modern roller derby for this book. Additional research materials for *Bruised* included *Rollergirl*, by Melissa "Melicious" Joulwan, *United Skates* (directed and written by Tina Brown and Dyana Winkler), and *Blood on the Flat Track: The Rise of the Rat City Rollergirls* (directed by Lainy Bagwell and Lacey Leavitt), plus numerous hilarious, scary, informative, and awe-inspiring YouTube videos. I'm way too big a baby to play roller derby, but it's an exceptional sport and demands some serious respect.

Writing about teenage experiences requires a special kind of care, and writing about death and self-harm even more so. I am blessed with some of the most skilled and committed counselors and educators in my life. Thank you to Joanne, Ly, and Nicola (again), and to Haley Jacobs for making sure I held Daya's grief, pain, and growth with thoughtfulness and accuracy.

Similarly, Rae Takei (aka Rose Butch), I am so grateful to you for holding me accountable to my representation of

Fee in this book. Thank you for your feedback and for your inspiration!

Anaheed, from my little brown heart to yours, thank you for reminding me about the power of the simple act of making tea or peeling an orange for a loved one (and for your general cheerleading and support).

Thank you to mes chères collègues, Myriam LeMay and Eileen Jensen, for making sure my French was impeccable.

Thanks to my family for always being excited and supportive about this whole, surreal experience, and especially to my sister, Karen, who keeps coming to my events even though I can't imagine they're that interesting after the third or fourth time. And to my Amma, for always making such good tea with that pink and white tea cozy and for letting me make it for you too.

Also: Teenagers. I adore you and respect you. Your brains, your sass, your courage. And all the tough bits too. Don't be afraid to share it all.

Thanks as always to readers everywhere. Books are best. Keep reading.

And as always, to my love, my Jennifer. Your excitement about all this book stuff sometimes exceeds even my own, and that makes me feel pretty darn special. Thanks for letting me write while you literally built a roof over our heads. You're amazing and I love you.